TRIALS OF A MOUNTAIN MAN

LOGAN MOUNTAIN MAN SERIES - BOOK 2

DONALD L. ROBERTSON

CM Publishing

COPYRIGHT

TRIALS OF A MOUNTAIN MAN

Copyright © 2020 Donald L. Robertson
CM Publishing

All rights reserved. No part of this publication may be reproduced, distributed or transmitted in any form or by any means, including photocopying, recording, or other electronic or mechanical methods, without the prior written permission of the publisher, except in the case of brief quotations embodied in critical reviews and certain other noncommercial uses permitted by copyright law.

Publisher's Note: This is a work of fiction. Names, characters, and incidents are a product of the author's imagination. Locales and public names are sometimes used for atmospheric purposes. Any resemblance to actual people, living or dead, or to businesses, companies, or events, is completely coincidental. For information contact:

Books@DonaldLRobertson.com

❦ Created with Vellum

LOGAN FAMILY GENEALOGY

Ethan William Logan, 1779
  Married
  Rose Isabel Tilman, 1780
  CHILDREN
  Matthew Christopher Logan, 1797
  Mark Adair Logan, 1798
  Nathaniel Grant Logan, 1803
  Owen Lewis Logan, 1803
  Jennifer (Jenny) Isabel Logan, 1812
  Floyd Horatio Logan, 1814
  Martha Ann Logan, 1816

Matthew Christopher Logan, 1797
  Married
  Rebecca (Becky) Nicole Doherty, 1810
  CHILDREN
  William Wallace Logan, 1834
  Callum Jeremiah Logan, 1836
  Joshua Matthew Logan, 1840
  Katherine (Kate) Logan, 1851
  Bret Hamilton Logan, 1852
  Colin Alexander Logan, 1854

1

June 2, 1833, A small stream in the Rocky Mountains

The mountains echoed with the giant silvertip grizzly's roar as it rose to an imposing height.

Floyd Logan, having only momentarily returned to the bank, had been enjoying the morning while creating new beaver sets in the clear, gurgling stream. He spun to his right, bringing the sights of his rifle to align on the huge bear's throat.

The massive animal stood no more than twenty feet from Floyd. Stretching to its full height, at least nine feet, it roared again, mouth wide, large head twisting from right to left.

Its head stopped swinging, and the beady little eyes focused on the mountain man.

Floyd waited. He didn't want to shoot if it wasn't necessary. The last thing he wanted to do was wound one of these monsters. During his three years in these mountains, he had seen men killed and maimed by the grizzlies. Though he felt a slight shudder at what might lie ahead, he stood resolute, waiting.

His mind registered the sudden silence. All that could be heard, besides the big animal's breathing, was the sound of aspen leaves rustling in the breeze and the musical tinkling of the creek as the water hurried on its way.

Floyd waited, his rifle sights steady on the throat of the bear. After what seemed to be an interminable time but in reality was only a few seconds, the bear dropped to the ground and, after a low menacing growl, turned and shuffled off, disappearing through the aspen.

A few more moments, with the rifle to his shoulder, passed. Floyd lowered it, released a long sigh of relief, watched where the bear had disappeared, and eased the hammer down. He waited, watching. His heart slowly returned to normal after feeling as if it would leap from his chest.

He shook his head and scanned the surrounding trees, nothing. The morning had started out well, much like most mornings now since Jeb Campbell, his partner, had felt the urge to go to St. Louis.

Floyd had risen before daylight, started a fire, had breakfast and coffee, and headed for the stream he explored the day before. There was plenty of beaver sign, and he hoped to add a few pelts to his supply.

He planned on going to the rendezvous this year and wanted enough furs to trade for short-term supplies to hold him over until Jeb returned. His friend had taken all of their winter and most of the early spring pelts with him, as they would bring a much better price in St. Louis than at the rendezvous.

Feeling relieved after his close call, Floyd bent over to pick up the traps and equipment he had dropped when the bear had roared.

Without warning, the massive grizzly crashed through the aspen saplings, having circled to get behind the mountain man. There was no roar, only the hard breathing as the bear charged.

Floyd felt his relief turn to dark resignation. He whipped around, hoping he had time to fire.

The bear's charge brought him within striking distance before

Floyd could get his rifle to his shoulder. A huge paw swung, striking Floyd a glancing blow across his left forearm, and the Ryland rifle sailed end over end—into the creek.

Two of the bear's five four-inch claws ripped across Floyd's arm, slicing through the elk hide jacket, deerskin shirt, and long johns, leaving wide bloody gashes to the bone in his forearm. But the bear didn't slow. It snapped at Floyd's head, missing except for a long canine tooth that scraped across the top of his head, ripping scalp, his head instantly red with pouring blood. Fortunately, the bruin's momentum carried it over and past Floyd, knocking the mountain man to the ground.

Roaring in anger, the bear spun like a cutting horse.

Floyd, the instant his rifle was knocked from his hands, and even as he was bowled over by the wide chest of the bear, was driving his right hand toward one of the pistols around his neck. He was thankful he had draped the belt around his neck while wading in the stream. His hand found it and ripped it from the holster. He had another brief thought of thankfulness he had not fastened the hammer thong.

As the bear was turning, Floyd was bringing the big-bore pistol up, taking aim on the bear's throat. He pulled the trigger and yanked the other pistol out with his injured arm while slamming the spent one back into the holster and reaching back with his right hand for his knife.

At the explosion of the pistol, the bear jerked back and roared in pain, but hesitated only for a moment. A moment was long enough for Floyd to aim the second pistol at the same spot in the bear's neck and pull the trigger. This time the grizzly rolled over on its back, all four feet ripping at its neck, trying to kill whatever was causing the excruciating pain. Then the bear seemed to forget the pain and rolled back to its feet. Standing on all fours, blood pumped from the wounds, pouring from its neck and mouth. At last finding Floyd, and spurred by the pain, the grizzly charged.

Floyd stood facing the bear, a pistol in his left hand and the knife his brother Nathan had had made for him in Nashville, in his right. He could feel the blood flowing from his head wound, but most of it was going down his neck and left side. What blood was making it to his left eye, he wiped clear with his sleeve.

Though he was resigned to what was coming, he remembered several other mountain men, including Hugh Glass, had survived grizzly attacks. He focused on the charging bear. The big animal slammed its jaw down toward the mountain man's head. Floyd was almost mesmerized by the sight of the gaping mouth and bloody saliva flying across him and the forest floor. The hot breath, deafening roar, and stench of the grizzly's mouth was almost overpowering.

At the last second, Floyd slammed the pistol past the teeth and inside the huge mouth. Immediately the jaws tried to close, but the pistol locked them open. The bear roared its frustration to the mountains. Spinning round and round, rolling on the ground, slapping at the invasive thing jammed between its jaws, the grizzly clamped tighter and tighter against the muzzle and the stock of the pistol, like a vise, locking it in place.

Floyd, blood streaming from his arm and head, drew his remaining pistol and, wasting no time, started reloading it. *One more hit,* he thought, *maybe that will do it.*

Blood, from the neck wounds, covered the ground around the grizzly, turning its fur red as it rolled. The big bear continued to fight the pistol with no success, but it was growing weaker. Blood still pumped from the two wounds as the bear continued to wrestle against the pistol lodged in its mouth. Finally the mortally wounded grizzly stood, big head hanging, swinging back and forth, as its eyes again found Floyd. Slowly the bear lumbered toward the mountain man, but this time the fierce energy was gone.

Floyd backed away from the beast. The bear stopped and lowered its head. Floyd finished loading his pistol and slowly moved, well out of range of the bear, to its right side. The grizzly tried to follow him, but was tiring and unable to move its massive head and neck. As its lifeblood continued to pump from the neck wounds, its head continued to droop, muzzle almost touching the grass.

Floyd had planned to fire a shot into the big grizzly's heart, but he now waited. He was in a good position, if the bear regained enough strength to turn and charge, to put the third ball in the heart. He waited.

The grizzly slowly lowered itself to the ground, its neck stretched forward, eyes cut toward Floyd, trying to watch him. He moved around where he could see both eyes of the bear.

He felt relief flood over him as he looked down at his arm. He was covered with blood and saliva, from his head, especially, to his feet. Yet his only wounds were the ones on his arm and scalp. He looked from his arm back to the bear.

This grizzly was a magnificent beast. Floyd watched the eyes slowly follow him. He squatted down a safe distance from the dying bear and, looking the grizzly in the eye, said, "What set you off, big fellow? We both would have had a much better day if you'd just gone your own way."

The bear's eyes blinked and the lids drooped.

"Last thing I wanted to do today was kill you. Course you should've killed me. Reckon someone's watching close over me."

He watched as the bear's chest heaved one last time. The big grizzly exhaled the remainder of air in its lungs and died.

Floyd slid the loaded pistol back into its holster and sat on the grass. His anticipated easy day of setting traps in this new area had certainly been anything but easy. He looked over at the creek, where his rifle now lay beneath the water, then down at his left forearm. It looked really nasty, the gaping slashes filled with saliva and detritus from the bear's mouth and already starting to swell. The rifle would have to wait. He needed to clean his arm and head, quickly.

The soft pad of unshod horses brought him back to reality. He looked over his shoulder to the right. Astride their horses sat eight Shoshone braves.

Oh no, Floyd thought, *just when I think things are getting better, they head in the opposite direction.* He stood slowly, turned, and greeted them.

"Howdy."

The Indians said nothing and rode their horses toward him until they had formed a semicircle around him and the bear. Finally, an older brave pointed his rifle barrel toward the bear. "You kill bear." It was no question.

Floyd wondered how long they had sat and watched. *I guess my experience might be looked at as great entertainment,* he thought.

He nodded. "I did."

"Why bear's mouth open?"

"I stuck something in it."

One of the Shoshones threw a leg over his horse and jumped down. Cautiously he walked to the bear and gently touched one of the bear's eyes with his rifle barrel. The grizzly didn't move. Still wary, the man, using his rifle muzzle again, shoved hard against the bear's head. The head rolled a little, but otherwise, no movement. Then he stalked up to the animal, bent down, and stared into its mouth. In awe he said, "Ahhhh."

The Shoshone who had been talking to Floyd fired a string of words Floyd did not understand. The Indian on the ground looked up and motioned his companions to him.

I've got to get this arm cleaned, Floyd thought, feeling light-headed.

The Indians leaped from their horses and headed for the grizzly's mouth. Floyd chose that moment to walk to the creek. Upon reaching it, he pulled his elk-hide jacket off and then his deerskin shirt. When he first moved toward the creek, the Indians stopped for a moment, watching him. After talking among themselves, they went back to looking in the bear's mouth, obviously discussing what they were seeing.

Floyd, using his right hand, unbuttoned his red long johns, pulled the top from his arms and his upper body, and tied the arms around his waist. By now, his arm felt like it was on fire. He stepped into the water and, leaning over, thrust the arm deep into the creek. The cold water was a shock to the open flesh. Excruciating pain slammed into it and raced up to his shoulder and neck, causing an excruciating headache. For a moment he thought he might pass out. This hurt more than when the Comanche arrow had been removed from his upper arm. It was like a cinch of fire around his forearm.

Each of the two gashes were almost an inch wide, and he could see bone shining through the water. Not good. There was no telling what kind of rotten filth had already slipped into his bloodstream from the bear's claws or his head from the jaws.

"That danged bear still might kill me," Floyd said to himself.

He was surprised when the Indian who had been speaking jumped into the water alongside him, reached into the water, grabbed his arm by the wrist, and pulled it out of the water. He stood there examining the gashes.

"Ver' bad. Need good cleaning. Wash head first. Then you come with us."

Floyd didn't know if it was an invitation or a command, but the way he was starting to feel, he didn't have much choice. He pointed downstream. "The bear knocked my rifle into the water."

"We get." The Indian turned to one of the younger braves, pointed to the water, and spoke in their language. The young man nodded, walked to the creek, and looked in. He quickly spotted the rifle in the clear water and jumped in. He thrust his arm deep into the creek and pulled the rifle from the bottom. He looked at it for a moment, held it up where they all could see the forearm, and shouted.

They all turned and looked. There were four deep gashes

across the forearm, and at the end toward the muzzle was a clearly visible scratch in the barrel.

While the Indians were looking at the rifle, Floyd washed and felt his head. The scalp lay loose at the edge of what felt like a four- or five-inch cut, but fortunately, that was the only tooth that found his head. He stepped out of the stream, thankful that the bleeding from his head wound was letting up, picked up his punctured hat, and slapped it on his head.

He pulled his long johns back up, rolled the left sleeve well above the elbow and, through the pain, slipped it on. Then he put his torn shirt back on, and as he started to slide his jacket on, for he was cold, the leader spoke again. "You leave coat and things. We bring. Must go now."

One of the other Indians had mounted and rode in the direction of where his horse was tied. Now he pulled up in front of Floyd and handed him the reins. Floyd took them and managed to show no pain when he grasped the reins with his left hand.

"My things," he said.

Impatiently, the leader said, "No time. We get." He said something to the other men.

Before Floyd could reach up to the saddle horn, two of the Indians grabbed his legs and lifted him into the saddle. He didn't much like being manhandled, but he felt relief he didn't have to pull himself up with his left arm. It was already at least half again larger than normal.

"Come," the leader said.

Floyd didn't remember much of the ride. He only knew they rode for miles. Their direction was northwest, deep into country he had never explored, strikingly beautiful with high snow-capped peaks, tall pines, and glistening aspen. They arrived at the Shoshone village midafternoon. He managed to swing his leg over the saddle and barely remained standing when his feet touched the ground. He held to the saddle with his right hand gripping the saddle horn.

"Come," the leader said, pointing toward a near teepee.

Floyd released his hold on the saddle horn and took a step. Each foot felt like it was covered with ten pounds of mud.

His arm pulsed with pain.

He took another step.

This time, the light of the afternoon faded abruptly into the dim light of evening, and he felt himself floating through the air.

He stopped floating when his face slammed into the pine-needle-covered ground.

2

He awoke later. A fly had found his upper lip and was strolling across it. With his right hand, he hit at it, brushing his nose. A sharp twinge of pain pierced through the fog of consciousness. He started to reach toward his nose with his left hand, and the intense pain radiating from his throbbing forearm stopped him.

He gave up and closed his eyes.

The next time he awoke, it was to the laughter of children. Irritated that his sister Martha and her friends were being noisy while he slept, he called, "Martha!"

Immediately someone entered the darkened room, allowing a shaft of light to play over him. He turned his head, and his eyes momentarily opened wide in astonishment. At least until he recognized the man standing inside his bedroom wasn't in his bedroom at all. He was in a teepee, and the man was the leader of the men who found him with the grizzly. Sluggishly, his mind made the long trip to reality.

Floyd rose on his right elbow. "I'm feeling much better. Thank you."

"It is good," the man said. He padded across the fur-covered floor of the teepee and sat cross-legged on Floyd's right.

"How long have I been here?"

"Many suns pass. You very sick. Had long red marks running up arm. Almost die. Nina, my wife, work long and hard on your arm."

Floyd looked at his forearm. It had a salve over the wounds. With his right hand, he gently prodded the flesh around the two gashes. There were large scabs over both. It still hurt, but not like the day he had ridden in. He flexed his hand. All of his fingers worked. He would always have scars there, probably sunken somewhat, but as long as the arm and hand worked, he was happy.

"Please tell her I am very grateful."

"You tell her. She come soon. What are you called?"

"My name is Floyd Logan. I am called Floyd."

The Shoshone nodded. "Flo-yd, I am called Pallaton."

"I am in your debt, Pallaton. If you hadn't come along, I could have died."

"Maybe. You strong man, fight bear hard. I think you fight to live, too. No die."

The flap of the teepee was pulled back. An attractive woman, who appeared to be in her early thirties, came in. When she saw Floyd awake, she spoke quickly to her husband. Though Floyd didn't speak Shoshone, he heard some common words he had learned over the past three years. She was asking Pallaton how Floyd was doing.

The chief responded to the woman. Floyd, using the sign language he had learned as a child from the Cherokee in Tennessee, and his past three years in the mountains, thanked her for healing him. He added she must have strong medicine.

At the last statement, she looked at Pallaton, then smiled at Floyd. She responded in rapid sign language. He watched her intently as she spoke, saying, "It was not me. The great spirit heals or does not heal. I only provide care for you."

He could see the pride on Pallaton's face when he said, "This woman my wife, Nina."

"Well, thank you anyway, Nina," Floyd said while signing his gratitude. "I am Floyd."

He raised the blanket to get up and realized he had not a stitch of clothing on his body. Looking around, he saw his clothes lying to his left. "Think I'll get dressed."

"Good," Pallaton said. He remained sitting on the floor while his wife stood near his side, her hand resting on his shoulder.

Resigned, Floyd pulled the long johns to him, unbuttoned them, and thrust them beneath his blanket covering. Still holding them, he guided them over his feet and pulled, standing at the same time.

This was the first time he had stood since passing out on his arrival. He wobbled slightly, and Pallaton was up and at his side. Floyd nodded to the man and buttoned his long johns, noticing the sleeve had been sewn. He held up his arm, pointed at the sewing, and said, "Thank you."

Once buttoned, he bent over to pick up his trousers, almost losing his balance. Pallaton caught him, holding his right arm. Floyd nodded his gratitude, picked up his last pair of wool trousers, and pulled them on. He had a quick thought strike him. Turning to Pallaton, he said, "My camp, horse and mule. I must go."

Pallaton shook his head. "No need. Everything here. Supplies, animals, and traps, all here."

Floyd let out a sigh of relief. "Again, thank you."

Pallaton gave one nod.

Floyd picked up his clean buckskin shirt and slowly held up both arms to slide it down and over his upper body. His stiff left arm didn't want to extend very far vertically, but with a little effort he forced it up. The shirt slid down over his arms and body. He looked around for his rifles and pistols, remembering that the bear had knocked one into the creek. Lying together, near the teepee entrance, were all of his weapons, including the rifle that went under water.

He walked stiffly to the weapons and picked up the superficially damaged Ryland. The scratch in the barrel and deep gashes in the forearm brought memories flooding back. He was fortunate he had survived. He examined the rifle. It had been cleaned and oiled. Testing the weight, he could tell the weapon was unloaded, the ball and soaked powder removed. He looked questioningly toward Pallaton.

"My son. He cleaned all guns. Fine guns."

"Thank him for me."

"You meet. You thank."

Floyd nodded, slipped his feet into his moccasins, and laying the rifle back down, said, "I'd like to go outside."

The man stepped to the flap. Opening it wide, he stood waiting for Floyd.

Floyd moved toward the light, with Nina close behind. He bent, stepping through the entrance, and straightened to his full height. He still felt weak, but not as much. It was good to stretch and see the high grass valley before him. He moved from the entrance and looked around the teepee-covered landscape.

There must be two hundred teepees, he thought. *I'm glad the Shoshone are friendly, or I'd probably already be dead, my scalp hanging on a brave's lance.*

Floyd had time to examine the man who saved him. The Indian was slightly shorter than Floyd, with wide shoulders. There were a few strands of gray in the man's long hair, now tied in a single braid down his back. His eyes were what caught Floyd. They were dark, like a leaf-stained pool, and intent, missing nothing.

People had gathered around Floyd and stared at him, some pointing to his sleeve where it was torn, and others to the wound in his head. With his concern for his arm, he hadn't noticed the head wound and now resisted the urge to reach up and feel it. There was no pain from the head wound. That was the important thing.

A little boy ran out of the gathering straight to him, stopping no more than a foot in front of him. The boy looked up at Floyd and spoke in his native tongue.

Pallaton said, "Boy asks are you the bear slayer?"

"What is your word for yes?" Floyd asked.

Pallaton told him.

Solemnly, Floyd looked down at the small boy, nodded his head, and in the boy's native tongue said, "Yes."

The crowd nodded, and there were a few smiles.

People are much alike, Floyd thought. *They appreciate when a stranger tries to use their language. I've got to learn Shoshone.*

The small boy turned around and raced to a woman standing in the crowd, pulled on her buckskin dress, looked up at her, and spoke quickly. She nodded and rested her hand on his little shoulder while holding Floyd's gaze.

Her high cheekbones and thin nose gave her a regal appearance. *Without the full lips, she would look severe,* Floyd thought, *but her lips soften her face, creating an almost Egyptian appearance, like the picture of Cleopatra in one of Ma's books.*

Pallaton spoke softly to Floyd. "She good woman. Her husband killed fighting Blackfoot. Her name Leotie. She help Nina with your injuries and your clothes." He made a motion of sewing. "She speak English good."

Breaking into Floyd's thoughts of the woman, a young man, of striking resemblance to the chief, stepped in front of them.

Pallaton said, "This is my son, Kajika. His name, in English, is Walks With No Sound. He speaks ver' good English."

While Pallaton was speaking, Floyd was examining the chief's son. The boy was taller than his father, almost as tall as Floyd. However, other than height, he could have been a younger twin of his father. He had the same intense dark eyes, broad shoulders, and black hair.

Floyd extended his right hand, and the young man reached past his, grasping his forearm. Floyd did the same and said, "I am glad to meet you, Kajika. Thank you for cleaning my rifles and pistols, especially the one that went into the creek. I'm sure you saved it."

Kajika gave a single, sharp bow of his head in thanks, and said, "You have very fine guns."

Floyd nodded. "Yes, I am fortunate."

Pallaton motioned for Kajika to join them, and walked toward a group of men who were preparing their horses for departure. They did not wear paint, so Floyd figured this was more of a hunting party than a war party.

Pallaton confirmed his idea by saying, "These men ride out to find buffalo. Here"—Pallaton raised his arm and moved it in an arc, indicating the valley they were in and the mountains surrounding it—"we are hidden and protected from Sioux and Blackfoot. They are ver' vicious."

Floyd nodded his understanding. He had yet to run into either tribe, but Jeb had told him to be extremely alert as he rode north, because of the Blackfoot. They had battled the white man from the beginning, though, like all of the tribes, they came to the rendezvous to trade. As far as most mountain men were concerned, they preferred to stay out of Blackfoot country. The Sioux? He had heard stories of them being friendly. He would have to be careful with Pallaton and the Shoshone. Floyd preferred to be on good terms with as many tribes as possible, and the way it normally went, if you were friendly with one tribe, their enemies were your enemies. He'd have to walk a thin line here if he didn't want the Sioux or Blackfoot as enemies.

There were fifteen men in the party. Some of the men carried old Northwest Trade Rifles in .60-caliber, while others their bows and lances. Pallaton spoke to the leader, who was a tall, strong-looking brave, obviously another chief. He nodded as Pallaton talked, fired a few responses back, and motioned for the men to mount.

Kajika spoke quickly to Pallaton. The chief shook his head as he responded. The younger man stared at his father only for a moment and then nodded, waved to the party's leader, and walked off.

The wives and children, all solemn, stood back as the men mounted and rode their horses down the creek, finally disappearing in the trees. Once they were gone, the women turned back to their work, and the children, those who were not older and helping their mothers, went back to playing.

Pallaton's eyes followed his son as he walked down the creek, toward a barely visible herd of horses grazing on the other side. "He good son, but impatient. He want to go on hunt, but we need him here to help protect the village. He will learn."

Floyd nodded, but his mind wasn't on Kajika. It was on sitting down before he fell down. The movement around the village had tired Floyd. He hated to admit it, but it felt like it would take more time to recuperate. He was impatient to get back to his trapping. He needed to have enough plews to sell at the rendezvous.

Without sufficient skins, he wouldn't have the necessary money to tide him over until Jeb got back, unless he dug into his savings. He certainly didn't want to tap what he had saved. His parents had taught him frugality. Then, a good friend and mentor, the man who had brought him west when he was only sixteen, Hugh Brennan, had further convinced him of the importance of saving his money. Hugh had showed him the importance of being prepared when opportunity came along.

Pallaton turned to Floyd to say something and stopped. He took his right arm and said, "Come, you tired. Time to rest. Bear take much from you. In fourteen suns, we have Bear Ceremony, give you back strength he took."

Willingly, Floyd went along. He saw Pallaton's wife, Nina,

talking to the woman with the child who had spoken to him. He thought for a moment and finally came up with her name, Leotie. Returning to the teepee, with Pallaton supporting him, he noticed the concern on the two women's faces.

The two men entered the teepee, and Floyd quickly moved to his bed and sat. "You are right, Chief Pallaton, I am tired, but I cannot just rest. I have a great desire to learn your language. Is it possible there is someone who could teach me while I am regaining my strength, so I might converse with you and your people?"

"It is good that you have—" Pallaton paused, his forehead wrinkled as his mind searched for the word.

"Desire," Floyd said.

"Yes, desire to learn our language. There is the one that speaks the English besides me, Leotie. She has helped with your healing and can teach you our language." He thought for another moment, gave a nod and said, "Good." He turned and left the tent.

TWO WEEKS HAD PASSED QUICKLY. He was learning the Shoshone language. He had taken to the language and also to Leotie. He had learned that her name meant dove, although she could be more demanding than what he would expect from someone with such a name. She was a stern taskmaster who took her assignment from the chief seriously.

Many of the pronunciations of the Shoshone were difficult for his English-trained tongue. Though he had learned Spanish while in Santa Fe four years ago, this was nothing like Spanish. Much of his work was strictly application and memorization.

In Spanish, corn is *maíz*, which was easy to remember, but in Shoshone corn is *ha'niibe*, which he found related to nothing except corn. Or the number two, which is *dos* in Spanish, but in

Shoshone it is *wahatehwe*. Often Floyd's pronunciations brought tinkling laughter from Mika, her son. His little tummy would shake as he tried to hold in his laughter.

Floyd became close to Mika. As he grew stronger, Mika would take him by the hand and lead him around the village. The little boy helped in Floyd's learning. While they walked, he would point at different things and say their names, *dabai* for sun, *muh* for moon, and *baa'* for water. With Mika's help and working with Leotie, he was learning the language quickly.

Throughout the day, the tribe was preparing for the Bear Ceremony, which would happen after dark. Floyd sat outside the teepee, cross-legged. He had tried to help, but Pallaton had brought him back, sat him outside, and told him he could not take part in the preparation. Now, he sat deep in thought. His mind drifted back to when he had first come west. His eyes grew heavy.

Floyd had met a Cheyenne maiden named Dawn Light, and lost his heart, so he thought at the time. His good friends, Jeb and Hugh, had convinced him of the folly of pursuing the young woman. Had he done so, it could have started a war with the Cheyenne, since she was betrothed to another Cheyenne chief, causing death and destruction for any white man, woman, or child.

Occasionally, she still came to his mind, bringing a twinge to his chest. Now, the time he had spent with Leotie and Mika was beginning to weaken those twinges.

He wasn't sure what he was feeling toward Leotie. He certainly liked her. When she didn't come around, he felt a longing that was hard to describe, a desire to be near her, to hear her voice, even when she scolded him in Shoshone so rapidly he couldn't understand.

Someone said something to him in Shoshone. He looked up to see twilight had taken over the glen. Kajika stood before him, looking impatient. "I said it is time for you to get dressed."

Floyd stood, his knees creaking after being seated for so long, and grinned at Kajika, responding in Shoshone, "I am ready."

With a quick move of his hand, Kajika motioned Floyd inside. Before stepping through the teepee door, Floyd looked around. The central fire had been built higher than normal. With the exception of the guards, who remained alert throughout the day and night, everyone, including the children, were inside their teepees, preparing for the night's festivities.

As Floyd walked in, Leotie was adjusting Nina's dress. The soft, light blond deerskin dress Nina wore hung straight from her shoulders. Fringe, trimmed and long, fell from the sleeves, the waist, and the hem of the dress. The upper part of the sleeves each had a line of beadwork, alternating red and blue elongated triangles that ran up and over the shoulders and circled the neckline. On each side of the upper part of the dress, front and back, was a beautiful beadwork red rose with striking bright green leaves. Lower on the dress were two smaller roses. Red, blue, and tan quills and beads hung to her ankles.

Floyd said to Nina in Shoshone, "Your dress is beautiful, as are you."

Pallaton beamed with pride at his wife.

She smiled at Floyd and, bowing her head slightly, said, "Thank you." Then she turned to Leotie. "Come, we must get you ready."

Mika was the first out of the tent, followed by Nina and then Leotie. As Leotie passed Floyd, she flashed him a brilliant smile. "I will see you soon," she said. "This night is for you."

3

Floyd felt Leotie's happiness for him and, from her, picked up the delicate, sweet scent of mountain iris. He had spent many hours with Leotie over the past two weeks and felt a deep contentment when with her.

But there were only a few weeks of trapping season left, and he needed to be working. He must leave soon. But he yearned to stay. With Dawn Light there was great excitement, but with Leotie, there was more. Excitement was there, but a serenity of mind also existed.

"Come, Flo-yd," Pallaton said. "It is time for you to dress. Take off your clothes and put these on. Leotie made them for you."

When entering the teepee, Floyd had been caught by the striking dress Nina was wearing, and then captured by Leotie's passing and his thoughts. He had not even glanced toward the chief. Now, when Pallaton spoke, Floyd looked at him and was struck with the power and authority this Shoshone chief evoked in his formal attire.

Pallaton, dressed in leggings, breechcloth, war shirt, and porcupine-quill vest, wore an eagle-feather headdress that fell almost to his waist. The eagle feathers were embedded in a red and white beaded band securing the long black and white feathers to his head. Fastened to the end of each feather was a strand of yellow horse hair. Floyd knew that the feathers weren't just for decoration, but each one represented a conflict where the chief had either killed an enemy or counted coup. Living with Nina and Pallaton in their teepee, Floyd had seen the many scars the older man's body carried. He had earned those eagle feathers with his blood.

Floyd stepped across the floor of the teepee to his bed. He quickly slipped off his clothing, slipped on and adjusted the breechcloth, and pulled on the leggings. The deerskin was as soft as a cotton shirt. He knew it wouldn't stay that way, for once it got wet, it would stiffen, but for now it was very comfortable. He slid the shirt on over his head. It fit perfectly and was decorated much like the leggings, with red and blue beads and porcupine quills. His buckskin leggings and shirt had been dyed a deeper brown, and in shadows would almost make him disappear. Lastly he pulled on the matching moccasins that had also been decorated in the same way.

Leaving his hat, he turned to Pallaton. "I am ready."

"Yes," the chief said, "we go." He stepped forward, followed by Kajika and then Floyd.

As the chief stepped from the teepee, several long chilling war cries split the quiet evening, followed by the rhythmic beat of drums. Immediately the men began dancing around the fire. It had grown darker outside, and even in the light of the blazing fire, millions of stars could be seen.

Floyd followed Pallaton and Kajika. When the men reached the fire, Kajika moved to his father's right side, and Pallaton motioned for Floyd to join him on his left. The three men sat at the head of a ring of warriors encircling the fire. Behind them were places for their family members. As soon as the chief sat, food was brought out, and they began to eat.

Nina brought food to Pallaton and her son. Floyd watched,

the smell of the roasted bison causing his mouth to start watering. He heard a soft shuffle to his left and looked up. It was Leotie. His eyes widened as he took in the lovely young woman standing in front of him.

She had changed into a long deerskin dress that was almost white. The sleeves, across the shoulders and bodice, and up to the neck were covered solid in a soft blue beading, with red quills outlining the blue. Long fringe hung from the sleeves, reaching to her knees. A two-inch band of the same blue encircled her at the hem, where additional fringe fell past her ankles. The fringe undulated with each stride of her long legs, occasionally exposing her trim ankles and dainty feet covered in soft white and blue moccasins.

Floyd's eyes took in the sight, finally reaching her eyes. Her pleased smile greeted his admiring look. When he realized she had been watching his reaction, he broke into a self-conscious grin and said in English, "You look mighty fine."

She dipped her head in a sign of gratitude, still holding her smile. "Thank you, Flo-yd. Are you hungry?"

"Starved," he returned.

"Then this is for you." She had brought a large wooden plate with roasted bison hump and tongue, and a bowl of corn soup with wild onions and cattails.

He devoured it quickly, accepting a second helping when she offered. Singing and dancing took place throughout the evening until Pallaton stood and raised his arms. The drums stopped, and the dancers moved to their places.

After everyone was seated, Pallaton said, "Tonight is a special night. All of you have met our good friend Flo-yd. Many of you have spoken with him and know of his great desire to come to our country and see the mighty mountains. You know of his great travels."

Mika had eased up and touched Floyd on the shoulder. The mountain man turned and saw the little boy. He smiled at him and motioned for him to sit in his lap. With a big grin, Mika moved around and sat on the big man's legs, where he could lean back on his thick chest for support.

Pallaton continued, "Each of you know of how, when Flo-yd was setting his traps, brother bear was upset for being disturbed. So brother bear attacks Flo-yd, opening his arm to the bone and tearing his scalp."

A small boy, sitting with his father, cried out, "Brother bear wanted Flo-yd's scalp."

This time a murmur of agreement, including laughter, ran around the fire.

"Yes," Pallaton said, "I too believe brother bear wanted Flo-yd's scalp." Now he looked around the fire, making contact with many of the youth. "And did he get it?"

"No," was shouted from all the youth.

"No, he did not," Pallaton said. "Our friend killed brother bear. I believe this was because the Great Spirit is with Flo-yd and did not want him to lose his scalp that day."

Everyone was nodding in agreement and looking at Floyd, who was wishing the ceremony, along with his embarrassment, would soon end. But Pallaton continued and it got worse. Pallaton said, "Flo-yd, come to me."

Oh my gosh, Floyd thought, *is this ever going to end?* He stood, picking up Mika as he stood, then set the boy in his mother's lap. Floyd moved over to stand in front of Pallaton.

The chief, facing him, placed his right hand on Floyd's left shoulder and continued to speak to the tribe. "Many of you may not know, but our brothers, the Comancia to the south, have met Flo-yd. They have given him a name that describes his attitude toward our enemies—Pawnee Killer."

At the mention of their enemy, many men leaped to their feet, brandishing their tomahawks, rifles, and bows, yelling and whooping.

Pallaton waited, giving the excitement time to wear off. "I

have a name for our friend, which, from now on, among the Shoshone, he will be known by. Igasho—man who wanders. Pallaton stepped back and turned Floyd so that they were side by side, and pointed at him. Everyone started shouting, "Igasho, Igasho, Igasho."

After the shouting had gone on for a time, Pallaton looked over at the medicine man and nodded. The medicine man, in turn, inclined his head toward the men at the drums. They began to beat them as the man began a slow dance. He held a long gourd rattle in one hand and, in the other, a two-foot length of elk antler wrapped in beaver pelt. Fastened at the end was the foot of an eagle with the talons extended. Over his head, the man wore the head and upper jaw of a grizzly, with a short cape draped over his back.

The men, women, and children watched the man as if they were in a trance. He danced toward Floyd and Pallaton. Pallaton stepped back as the medicine man began to circle Floyd, tossing white dust over him. Floyd stood solemnly as the man began a singsong chant while moving the talon-clawed staff above Floyd's injured arm and then the wound in his head.

The medicine man sang for what, to Floyd, seemed forever. Finally the volume of his voice crescendoed, and suddenly he brought the staff, which had been pointing at Floyd's head, slashing to the ground. His song cut off, the rattle stopped, and the drums ended. There was almost deafening silence.

The medicine man, much shorter and older than Floyd, spoke in a clear voice of authority that echoed through the glade. "Igasho, the bear forgives you and sends back your strength that he took from you."

Floyd nodded solemnly and said in Shoshone, "I feel my strength returning to me. Thank the bear for me." Then he thought to himself, *This is crazy, but I'm feeling better than I've felt since the attack.*

Pallaton stepped beside him as the medicine man turned and

walked away, and said in English, "It would be good if you could give him a *valuable* present. He has done a great thing for you."

Floyd nodded and waved Kajika to him. He leaned toward Kajika's ear and whispered, "Bring me the bearskin," then turned back to face his healer.

Shortly after Floyd had regained consciousness, Pallaton had presented him with the heavy skin of the grizzly. It had been beautifully tanned, and the long silver hair over the bear's shoulders accented the dark brown fur, making it a priceless possession. He had planned to give it to Pallaton, for all he had done, but the chief's pointed suggestion made up his mind for him.

Speaking as solemnly as the medicine man had, Floyd spoke, "The bear was kind to return my strength to me, but *we* all know" —he swung his arm dramatically to encompass all of the people watching—"it could not have happened without the sacred power of the great medicine man, Wahkan." Floyd turned to face the medicine man. "I could not live with myself if I did not present a gift to you, small though it might be, to show my deep gratitude for what has happened."

Kajika came running back, reverently carrying the massive bear's fur.

Floyd watched the medicine man's face as he saw the fur. Though the man maintained his stoicism, his eyes lit up at the sight.

Kajika stopped next to Floyd and carefully handed him the fur. Floyd nodded to his young friend and, with the fur in his arms, turned back to Wahkan. "I hope this will bring you good fortune, and the bear's spirit will keep you warm in the cold winters." He held the fur out to the Indian.

Wahkan had been a good medicine man for his tribe, learning his skills from his grandfather and then his father. But they had also taught him how to play to the crowd. Now his left hand began to pulse, causing the seeds in the gourd to rattle softly, clicking against the sides, barely audible to the tribe, but loud enough to build mystery. Then he passed the eagle-claw staff across the fur Floyd held. This went on for only a short time, and he stopped.

"The bear," Wahkan said, "is happy and will be content in my care. Igasho, I thank you and the bear thanks you." With his last statement, the medicine man took the bearskin, turned, and walked solemnly to his tent.

Pallaton raised his arms to his people and said, "It is done."

Abruptly, the celebration broke up, and the tribe members, speaking only in soft voices, made their way to their teepees.

Floyd saw Leotie and sleepy Mika move toward him, and leaned toward Pallaton, saying softly in English, "Thanks, that was an excellent suggestion."

"Yes," Pallaton said, "and Wahkan was pleased. You could not have given him a better gift." Then with an amused tone in his voice, he said in Shoshone, loud enough for the approaching Leotie to hear, "It is ver' late to be learning Shoshone language."

Nina, Pallaton's wife, threw him a stern look. "Come, it is our bedtime."

Pallaton chuckled as he allowed his wife to pull him away.

She glanced at her son, who had been standing at their side, enjoying his father's joke, and said sharply, "Come, Kajika."

Surprised, he looked at his father, who pointedly ignored him, shrugged and followed his parents.

Leotie had frowned at her chief's comment, but a smile slipped across her face, seeing Nina coming to her rescue. "Is it Shoshone you wish to learn, Flo-yd?" she asked, walking up close to the young mountain man and gazing up into his eyes.

Floyd grinned. "I'm up for learning every chance I get."

An audible yawn was followed by a petulant voice. "I'm sleepy."

The young woman looked down at her tired son and slowly ran her hand through his long hair. Nearing the end of the ceremony, she had unbraided the boy's hair, and it hung loose down his back.

She looked back up at Floyd. "I am sorry. It is long past the time of his sleeping." She reached out and lightly grasped Floyd's hand, their first physical contact. "I will see you tomorrow?"

At the feel of her warmth in the chill mountain air, Floyd felt his heart skip. "Sure, I'll be looking forward to it." He squeezed her hand in return.

The two young people stood for a moment longer, looking deeply into each other's eyes, the firelight flickering, causing them to twinkle. Mika jerked Leotie's free hand and pulled her toward their teepee. She smiled at Floyd, shrugged, and turned away.

Floyd stood in the fading reflections of the now dying fire, watching her move softly through the meadow. The deerskin dress did little to hide the sway of her body as she led her sleepy son back to their teepee.

Floyd looked around the village. Most of the people had already disappeared into their homes. He could see two of his new friends guarding the horses, and another slipping into the trees near the creek. They would be on watch for the next few hours. The village was protected. All would be safe another night.

FLOYD WAS JOLTED awake by first a long piercing yell, soon joined by others. He threw back his blanket, slapped his hat on his head, pulled his moccasins on, and grabbed his weapons. Though he was getting faster, his left arm still hampered him, and he was the third man from their tent, following Pallaton and Kajika.

A brave, who Floyd knew as Bidzil, his name, translated meant He Is Strong, ran up to Pallaton as Floyd straightened from exiting the tent.

By now the village was wide awake, and men were standing, with their fighting gear, listening to Bidzil report.

"The horses are gone."

This was a crushing report to Pallaton. Without horses, they would be crippled in the buffalo hunting and their defense.

The man continued. "I went to relieve the guards. They are dead, scalped, throats cut."

Immediately moans came from two families.

Nina rushed over to comfort the wives and small children whose fathers had died, and in their dying had failed to prevent the theft of the tribes horses.

"How many?" Pallaton asked Bidzil.

"Ten, no more. Blackfoot."

Angry murmurs traveled rapidly through the crowd.

Pallaton pointed at fifteen men, all strong and powerful. "We go. Travel light."

Floyd, at the side of Pallaton, said, "I'm going with you."

Pallaton shook his head. "You are too weak. We will travel quickly on foot. Go where horses cannot go. It will be very rough."

Floyd shook his head once. "I'm going." He had hoped to be able to make friends with the Blackfoot, but he could not sit back and allow his friends to be attacked and do nothing.

"There's more," Bidzil said.

Pallaton had turned back from speaking to Floyd.

"The woman Leotie must have taken her son to make water, for tracks from her teepee show she and boy go to trees and do not come back. We have searched. They are gone."

Floyd was not one to swear. His pa never did, and as a youngster, and even older, his ma would have washed his mouth out with lye soap if she heard him. But now, an oath escaped his lips.

Pallaton turned to him and said, "Get your things. We leave."

He turned back into the teepee ahead of Pallaton, ran to his possibles bag, made sure he had plenty of lead and caps, checked his powder horn, and grabbed a rifle. He had jerky and pemmican in his bag. There was plenty of water in the mountains. His knife and tomahawk were on his belt along with two of his pistols. He was ready.

Pallaton left his rifle in favor of his bow and arrows.

Kajika, knife on his elk hide belt, carried his bow and quiver across his back. "I would go, Father."

The chief looked at his son only for a moment and said, "Come."

Floyd stepped outside, leaving the two men with Nina, wife and mother. While they said their goodbyes, he thought of Leotie, and a fierce anger burned deep. *She had hurt no one,* he thought. *And what about little Mika. He's becoming like a son. If they are harmed . . .* He stood in the morning darkness, his face grim and hard. He failed to notice the chill of the mountains as the cold grip of fear, for Leotie and Mika, enclosed his heart. *I've got to find them.*

The men Pallaton had chosen, including Bidzil, gathered as Pallaton and Kajika stepped from the teepee.

4

"We will move quickly," Pallaton said, "but carefully. If the Blackfoot hold to their usual habits and try to race from this valley, across the mountains and into the plains, then we will have them. They will want to get to where the horses can travel fast. We will catch them in these mountains before they reach open country. We go."

Floyd fell in to the left of Pallaton, while Kajika was on his right. Bidzil, one of the best trackers in the tribe, led the group, with the rest of the men falling in behind the chief. There was no talking, no murmuring. They all knew time was critical. They had to catch the Blackfoot before the distance widened and their enemy disappeared with Leotie, Mika, and the horses.

They made it down Deep Creek from the village, stepping lightly around the tall lodgepole pines that grew within feet of each other. Floyd and the Shoshone moved quickly through the pines, breaking out into a narrow opening. Almost immediately they were into a thicket of aspen, but they never slowed.

Once through the aspen, still following the creek, they broke out into a wide meadow, open for hundreds of yards. The creek had been flowing east, but now it turned sharply south. In front of them was the wider Elk River.

Ahead, Bidzil was only a shadow as he moved across the meadow directly toward the river. He had paused only a moment when the tracks of the Blackfoot raiding party turned following Deep Creek toward the south and then southeast where it joined Elk River. There was an almost undetectable lightening of the sky.

Before long, Floyd thought, *it'll be full daylight. If the Blackfoot are too close, they'll see us, and we might never catch them.*

Even as fast as they were moving, there had been no stumbles, no noise from falls, only the soft whish of rapidly moving feet through grass and pine needles. In the wide open meadow, their speed picked up. The braves formed a skirmish line with Pallaton at the center. They raced, close behind Bidzil, toward the river, avenging specters floating through the high grass.

A herd of elk had bedded down near the river and were unaware of the Shoshones until the Indians and Floyd were in their midst. Floyd almost ran into one of the large animals, seeing him in the high grass at the last minute. Without thinking, he leaped high, his speed carrying him over the back of the shocked bull, which snorted and jumped to its feet.

Floyd was shocked by not only the bull rising, but that he had actually been able to vault over the animal. The thought raced through his mind, even as he raced across the meadow, *I'm glad he didn't do that two seconds earlier. I've never ridden a bull elk, and I sure don't want to start now.*

Reaching the river, Bidzil never slowed, leaping into the shallow river's flow. All did the same. The splashing was noisy, but it couldn't be helped. Hopefully, the Blackfoot were far enough away to hear nothing. Until the river, they had been running downhill from the village, but, after crossing, the terrain sloped up, gradually at first, then steepening.

Daylight was fast approaching. Leaving the meadow, the men

dropped back to single file, passing into a wide stand of ponderosa pine.

Trotting up the steepening mountains, Floyd could feel the strength in his legs, the muscles working to propel him up the grade. It felt good. Even having been laid up as long as he had, the fast pace had yet to bother him. *Maybe Wahkan, the medicine man, had something to do with it,* he thought. *But I imagine the racing with other braves, swimming in the creek, and the work I pitched in to do around the camp are probably the reason.*

The ground steepened more, and up ahead Bidzil had stopped. Pallaton brought the men to a halt upon reaching his scout. Pallaton and Bidzil sat, the remainder of the men following their example.

Bidzil said to Pallaton, "After the coming climb, we will descend the tall ridge to the river. We can drink there."

Pallaton nodded and turned to Floyd. "We will drink at what you mountain men call Mad Creek."

Floyd nodded. Though he didn't know the area well where the Shoshone camp was located, he had heard of Mad Creek from Jeb. There would be water in it, and it sounded like they would be in a canyon with the mountain Rocky Peak to the east. That also meant they had several tough hours of climbing and then descending before they had their next drink.

Pallaton looked around at his men, then said, "We go!"

Immediately they were up. There had been little talking among the men. They all wanted to hear what Bidzil and their chief had to say. Even as cold as it was, in the early morning light, each man's forehead showed the glisten of sweat.

Floyd wiped his forehead and then dried his hand on his buckskins. This was going to be a punishing climb, and he knew they had a long distance to go before this was over.

Bidzil took off in a jog, Pallaton and the other braves following. As they ascended the steep slopes, the sun peeked over the mountains, bringing what was usually welcome warmth, but not today. The men were already warm, and all the sun would do was pull precious fluid from their bodies. But it was more welcome than rain or snow, which would slow them down drastically.

~

Two strenuous hours had passed. They were descending toward Mad Creek visible in the distance. Floyd's calves and back were complaining. He was finding out the three weeks he had been sick from the bear slashes had cost him more muscle than he had first thought. But he was in the thick of it now and couldn't quit, nor did he want to. Leotie and Mika were out there somewhere, and he wanted, *no*, he had to find them.

Upon reaching Mad Creek, two men stood watch while the others drank. Then they were spelled to also drink. In the sand along the creek, with the walls of the canyon beginning, Pallaton drew a trail in the sand and looked up at the sweaty face of Floyd.

"We go north following the creek. It turns east through the canyon. When it turns north again, we continue east, down mountain to what you call Soda Creek. We reach Soda Creek, we will take a good rest. That will be halfway."

Floyd nodded. He was sweating profusely. His legs felt tight, his back hurt, and his breathing came in gasps. Thoughts of failure tormented him. *Not yet halfway? Have I asked to much of myself so soon after the bear attack? If I slow down, I'll slow everyone else and we'll lose the horses, Leotie, and Mika.* He fought the gasping, slowly regaining control, and took a deep breath. His moment of fear disappeared while grim determination flooded his body. *No*, he thought, *I'll die before I slow these men! Pa always said he never raised no quitters and I won't be the first.*

He turned back to the water and, kneeling, scooped water with his hands, drinking slowly as he maintained a sharp lookout. His three years in the west had turned him into a cautious and observant man. He was no longer the brash hothead who had traveled west from Tennessee with Hugh Brennan and Jeb Campbell. Before Jeb had left for the east, he had told Floyd he'd taught him everything he knew. The rest it would be up to him to learn on his own. Floyd grinned inwardly, took another deep breath, and thought, *I guess this is just more learning.*

Pallaton stood. Without a word, all the men jumped to their feet. They were anxious to get to the ambush point before the Blackfoot arrival. Floyd knew they were all thinking about the horses. Without them, many of the tribe would die. Years had passed since they had lived without horses, leading a hard life, often starving in the winter. None of them wanted to return to the past.

Pallaton nodded, and Bidzil started off at a trot, moving north along Mad Creek. As they turned north, the canyon walls steepened. Floyd, as he trotted behind Kajika, who was following his father, kept a close eye in front and up the sides of the canyon.

This was beautiful country, they had passed a number of beaver dams, and the green alpine meadows were covered with pink fairy slippers and shooting stars. The pink was offset with the blue and white of the Colorado columbine, the soft blue of the mountain iris, and the tall blue monkshood. Though there were many delicate yellow flowers, the showiest of all was the alpine sunflower. Its brilliant yellow covered many a meadow.

Floyd loved this country. He knew, as a boy, he had to go west. There was a pull and yearning he couldn't explain. He rationalized it as being the itchy foot his pa's and ma's folks had shown, as they opened what was then the west, Tennessee, Georgia, and Kentucky. Though he had explained it away, there was something else he could never put his finger on. What he was seeing, the tall lodgepole pines, the ponderosas and spruce, sprinkled with the loveliest of trees, the aspen, and all of the wildflowers were explanations.

He couldn't put it into words. He might travel to different parts of the country, back east to see his family, maybe farther west to see the ocean, but he knew he would always return to these mountains. This was his home.

The sun was high, and the canyon ran east and west, allowing the direct rays of the sun to bake the runners with its radiant heat. There wasn't a man who was not covered with sweat. It dripped from their noses. They wiped it from their foreheads with their hands and slung it to the side, but kept their ground-covering pace.

Coming to where Mad Creek turned north, Bidzil headed straight up the slope, leaving the creek. Running along the creek, the elevation rose gradually towards its headwaters. At the turn, they took to a draw that climbed over a thousand feet, but was less steep, allowing the men, though walking now, to climb without the assistance of rope. Nearing the top, Bidzil cut back to his left, where the angle trended down, still in tall ponderosa pine and spruce forests.

As they topped out and continued without stopping, Floyd noticed the small stream they were following was flowing east. Mad Creek had been flowing west. When he was trapping with Jeb, farther south, he had crossed this phenomenon several times. Lewis and Clark had called it the Continental Divide. Though short of breath, he exhaled a quick sigh of relief. At least now they were headed down.

They moved down the creek for a short distance. Pallaton stopped and waved Bidzil in. The two conversed only for a moment. Then the scout turned and started to the east again, leaving the creek. Pallaton waved the tired men forward, and to a one, they increased their pace to keep up with the chief.

A peak stood to their south, dirty snow remaining at its top. *If I'm figuring right,* Floyd thought, *that's Soda Peak. That means we've passed Soda Creek. Looks like no stop.* Like several of the others, Floyd's breath was coming in short gasps. The air at these altitudes was thin, and they had been either jogging or running for hours. What little walking they had done was because of the steeper slopes.

Floyd's mind was now concentrating solely on moving. Though he was still running with the other men, each step was agony. His lungs burned like he had a brush fire inside him, but he kept moving. *One more step,* he thought. *One more step.* And he kept up, never visibly faltering.

Finally, when Floyd felt he would be unable to take another step, in his dimming vision he saw again the wind-twisted firs that inhabited the lower reaches, and ahead the tall ponderosa pines waiting. They were coming back down to the tree line. They had covered a short distance into the pines, when they broke out on the shore of a crystal-clear lake. The men kept running at the same pace until reaching the water's edge. All were gasping, and these were hardy young Shoshone, with only a few exceptions. Again, two stood guard while the rest moved to the bank. Floyd resisted the temptation to throw himself into the water, knelt by the bank, and dipped water with his hands, as did the others.

Kajika and another of the younger braves took only two or three sips, then jumped up, motioning for the two men on guard duty to drink. Floyd continued to drink between gasps. His breathing gradually returned to normal. He glanced to the sun. It was two o'clock. They had been moving almost continuously up into the high country for almost ten hours, with only three stops. He was done in.

He had run in Tennessee for hours, but never at this high an elevation, and never up such tall, continuous mountains. Floyd looked around at the other men. Except for the guards, all were stretched out, some sleeping and others stretching their legs. He remembered Pa telling him about how horses could be chased and run down by men on foot. Never believing it before, he believed it now.

Even as he was thinking about the horrendous run they had

just made, his right leg spasmed, yanking his foot back against his butt. The pain was intense, and he started to try to stand. Kajika pushed him back and grabbed his right heel, slowly straightening the leg. Though the pain was extreme, Floyd neither grimaced nor said a word.

Kajika massaged the calf muscle until it released. Then he dropped Floyd's foot to the ground and extended his hand, pulling Floyd to his feet. "You must walk it out." As he was talking, one of the younger braves had the same thing happen, and someone grabbed his foot.

"On your feet!" Pallaton commanded.

Immediately everyone was up, walking, bending, and stretching. They also continued to drink. Floyd drank until he was feeling slightly bloated. Pallaton waved them around him. "We must be on our way. We will move straight down the Backbone of the World until we reach the place where we will kill the Blackfoot. It is growing late. We must get there before our enemy, or we will lose our horses and Leotie and Mika." He turned and spoke with Bidzil for a moment. Then Bidzil nodded and started off at a trot.

Floyd was feeling better. With the rest, and a few pieces of jerky he had in his possibles bag, much of his strength had returned. He had noticed all of the men pulling out either pemmican or jerky to eat while they were stopped.

They were constantly moving in and out of the trees. The lodgepole pines stood thick and serene, occasionally giving way to aspen, whose leaves glinted silver in the summer winds. However it was not all easy going. They were now on a narrow trail barely wide enough for one man, and in some places they had to place their feet toe to heel where the trail had given way.

A portion of it was made more difficult by a stream above them that had created a small but wide waterfall. Little water was flowing, but there was just enough to make a lengthy portion of the trail slick. It was the first obstacle that really slowed them.

Now they were having to ease along the slick portion, their fingers digging into the precipitous wall, to their right, for a fingerhold to maintain their balance.

Floyd had transferred his rifle to his left hand and was carefully watching his and the steps of the young brave ahead of him. To the left was open space for at least five hundred feet. He felt his foot start to slip and twisted his body as close to the wall of rock as he could, his right hand grasping for a hole, for anything his fingers could clinch into. Finally, there was a tiny piece of granite jutting out from the wall no more than an inch in length. He locked his little finger around the granite and held on for what seemed like an eternity. His foot stopped sliding, and he cautiously breathed a sigh of relief.

Then, in horror, he watched the young brave ahead of him tilt slightly outward, frantically attempting to swing his body back toward the wall while grasping at anything he could find—his hand finding nothing. Slowly, as if in a dream, the brave's upper body bent back into space. He turned slightly, enough for Floyd to see his face. Realization of death was written all over the brave's face, but his mouth remained closed, his eyes locked on Floyd.

It was like he was lying back into a feather bed, his arms outstretched from his sides. His body seemed to hesitate for a moment, perpendicular to the wall, eyes still watching Floyd, and he was gone. Floyd couldn't look down for fear of losing his balance. The brave never uttered a sound. The only thing heard was the dull thud of the young body striking the rocks below.

Floyd took a deep breath. There was nothing that could be done for the man, and they *must* rescue Leotie and Mika. Forcing his mind to focus, he watched his feet and took another step, then another, until he was clear of the narrow, wet path where fate had claimed its price.

It took twenty minutes for all of the men to make it past the precipice, time they must make up. When they had all made it clear, they again broke into a run, moving ever south toward what, no one knew.

Floyd couldn't take his mind from the captives. What was he feeling for this woman and her young child? Was it only compassion, or did it go deeper? Would they make it in time?

Floyd and the Shoshone party continued onward as the sun inexorably moved lower, pushing shadows across the towering land.

5

The desperate men reached the ambush point before the sun dropped below the mountains they had just crossed. All were running on adrenaline and were ready to take the scalps of every Blackfoot enemy who had stolen their families' survival. Bidzil had scouted the trail ahead, seeing no sign horses had passed.

Floyd's mind worked at double speed. *Would this be the trail the Blackfoot would take? Would they get the horses? Would Leotie and Mika be safe? Stop it!* he thought. *Quiet yourself.* Immediately he felt his training take over and calm return. Now was the time for rescue.

Moments later the sound of horses' hooves could be heard coming down the trail. The Blackfoot would be driving the horses ahead of them and driving them hard. He knew they would want to get out of this part of the country as quickly as possible. If the horses could have traveled straight over the mountains, that was the direction the Blackfoot would have taken. But they couldn't. So the Blackfoot had to take the closest useable trail, and this was it. Pallaton had figured correctly.

Pallaton had set the main ambush near the west end of the

trap. Floyd's job was to allow none of the horse thieves and kidnappers to escape. While the remainder of the braves would take the Blackfoot from the front, Floyd would close the back door. Though well hidden in cover, he was close to the trail. He had only one rifle with him, and he was thankful he hadn't tried to carry two over those mountains. But he did have two of his caplock pistols. He had previously checked his weapons. They were all capped and ready.

The horses thundered past with the first of the Blackfoot right behind them. He counted seven of them and waited. Unless they were farther behind, Leotie and Mika were not here. *Where are they?* Floyd thought.

But now he had work to do. He heard the high shouts of the attacking Shoshone. Almost immediately three Blackfoot came galloping back down the trail. Floyd threw his rifle to his shoulder, and when the sights aligned on the Indian's painted chest, he pulled the trigger. Immediately a red splotch appeared over the man's heart, and he started to fall from the saddle, but Floyd wasn't watching. Quick as a striking rattler, he pulled a pistol and lined up on another raider. He fired, knowing where the ball had hit, and turned his attention to the remaining Blackfoot charging toward him, lance aimed at Floyd's heart.

He had no time to pull the second pistol. He jumped to his left, grabbing the lance as the sharp head passed his chest, slicing through the buckskin covering his shoulder. Floyd pushed and twisted, driving the Blackfoot from his horse and slamming the big man to the ground, where he hit, rolled, and leaped up with his tomahawk.

Over the past years, under the tutelage of Jeb Campbell, his friend and trapping partner, he trained in the use of the tomahawk, and he liked it. With the right weight head, it was an excellent close-quarters weapon. Floyd reached back and pulled his own weapon from his belt. He felt good. Angry, at these men for stealing Leotie and Mika, and ready to exact justice.

The Blackfoot warrior dashed at him, tomahawk high above his head. The man brought the weapon down to drive the blade deep into Floyd's skull, but found his blade parried. Floyd deftly blocked the big man's blow, guiding the tomahawk blade to the outside. He threw a hard left jab into the man's nose, breaking it against his face. Blood spurted in all directions, and the Indian fell to Floyd's right, rolled, and again bounced to his feet.

He wiped his nose with his left forearm, glaring at Floyd, hate filling his eyes. Floyd suspected the man felt sure he would kill the white man with one blow of his tomahawk and be off. Wary now, his opponent circled, looking for an opening. The Indian was as tall as Floyd, a solid six feet. Wide shoulders, large biceps, and thick wrists went along with this man's confidence. It was obvious he had won many fights, where living was the prize.

Floyd feinted with his left fist, and the Blackfoot jumped to his right. Floyd grinned at him. The man didn't blink. His nose was still bleeding, and he reached up to it, grasped it with his left hand, and twisted it back into position. The blood on his hand, he wiped on each cheek, and tossed a malevolent grin back at Floyd. The Indian made a quick step to his left, and when Floyd started to move to his left to circle, the Indian stepped in and swung the blade low.

He caught Floyd off guard, but at the last moment, the mountain man jumped back, but the long run and sickness cost a fraction of his speed. The tomahawk blade sliced through his shirt like it wasn't even there, and left a long thin line of blood across his belly. The Blackfoot's grin grew bigger, and he said in English, "Now you die, white man."

"Bring it," Floyd said. "Why would I fear a stealer of women and children?"

The grin snapped from the Blackfoot brave's face like he had been slapped. His jaws clenched.

The two enemies continued their ballet of death, mashing

down the remaining yellow and orange blanket flowers that hadn't already been trampled by the racing horses.

The mountain man wanted this brave alive if possible.

The Blackfoot lunged as Floyd stepped to his left. The blade of the Indian's tomahawk whizzed past Floyd's face as he leaned back. The swing was from the Blackfoot's right to left, almost catching Floyd in the left side of his neck, but he saw the move coming, even before his opponent started swinging, and he was ready.

As the man's hand passed Floyd's face, he took a quick step back and slammed the flat back of his tomahawk onto the Blackfoot's wrist.

Paralyzed, the hand sprang open, fingers trembling, allowing the weapon to drop to the ground.

Still very much in the fight, the Indian's left hand struck forward, reaching for the tomahawk.

Unfortunately for him, his body had twisted into an awkward position, and Floyd made it worse when he threw a straight left jab into the Indian's right ear. The blow split the man's ear and threw him off balance, causing him to miss the tomahawk, stumble forward, and flail the air to keep is balance.

Floyd saw his opening. He dropped his tomahawk, grabbed the man's right hand at the wrist, and jerked the arm around and up, behind the Blackfoot's back. At the same time, his left forearm went around the Indian's throat in a chokehold.

He felt the Indian's left-hand stab across to pull his knife from his belt, at the same time pushing back and off the ground with both of his feet. The power in the man's legs drove Floyd back. He backpedaled unsuccessfully, attempting to maintain his balance.

This man was a strong and determined fighter, and Floyd had previously considered letting the man go, if possible, after getting information. But, in reality, this brave would never tell him or the Shoshone, no matter what they did to him, what he knew about Leotie and Mika.

Knowing he had to stop this fight now, for if his opponent reached his knife, though he was in Floyd's grip, he would stab backwards and very likely kill him.

Falling, Floyd summoned all of his strength and, with his forearm, tilted the man's head back as far as possible and released his right-handed grip on the wrist. Before they could hit the ground, and as the man was pulling the knife from his belt, Floyd twisted the Indian's head back. With his right hand, he delivered a powerful blow at the base of the man's skull.

The snap of the man's neck was audible to those watching Floyd from the ledge. They had come back to check on him and gathered to watch the fight.

The Blackfoot went limp in Floyd's arms, and the two men crashed to the forest floor.

Floyd lay still. He had landed on his back, and with the deadweight of the big Indian landing on top of him, all of the air exploded from his lungs. Finally he was able to gasp the cool mountain air into his deflated lungs. After several deep gasps, he pushed the Blackfoot from on top of his body and stood, looking down on the man who had just fought like a cornered catamount. The man's face had relaxed. There was neither grin nor grimace. In Shoshone, Floyd said, "Good fighter."

Kajika stood next to him. "Yes, Igasho. We see most of it. My father said you were foolish to drop your tomahawk. He could have killed you."

Pallaton gave Kajika a hard look. "What is said between father and son should remain between them. Go gather the horses." He pointed at two others. "Go with him."

Obviously feeling the rebuke, without another word, Kajika turned and marched away, followed by the other men.

Pallaton turned to Floyd. "I meant that comment to teach my son, Igasho. I did not mean it as an insult to you."

Floyd nodded. "You were right. I thought I saw a way to capture him and maybe find out about Leotie and Mika." He shook his head. "That *was* a big chance. I know better." He bent, picked up his tomahawk, and slid it back into the belt loop behind his right holster.

He stepped to where he had dropped the pistol and then his rifle, picking each up and reloading them. "Did you find out anything from the others?"

"No," Pallaton said. "They are all dead. Bidzil says there are three missing. They must have turned west, leaving these Blackfoot near the hot waters, before coming through the pass. That is all that makes sense. We will find their tracks on our return."

"Then we must leave now," Floyd said flatly, turning to go to the horses.

"No."

Floyd turned back to Pallaton. "No? They already have a big start on us." His face dark with anger, he continued. "We came the wrong way. We have no idea what is happening to Leotie and Mika."

Face calm and patient, Chief Pallaton said, "We came the right way. Horses most important to tribe. It is not the bear killer who speaks to me now, but a lovesick elk calf."

Floyd halted in his intended rush to the horses. He could hear the words of Lontac, the man of indeterminate age, but great skill in fighting, who had taught him much. He had been a boy of sixteen. His teacher's words came to him. "Anger is your enemy's best friend. When anger takes control, a man stops thinking."

Floyd stopped and took a deep breath. "You are right," he said to Pallaton. "I owe Leotie much. I could not speak the people's language if it was not for her teaching me. Thank you."

Pallaton nodded to his friend. "We must rest and eat. We have accomplished much. We have our tribe's horses back. Without them there would have been little food in the teepees. Many would have died. This is a good thing. Leotie is strong. She has taught her son well. They will survive what they must, or they will not. You cannot change that. You are good man, a strong man, Igasho, but you are young. Come, we will eat well tonight, rest up, and in the morning will take the horses to our people. Then we will find Leotie and her son."

The two men, and the others who had gathered, walked along the trail to where the main ambush had taken place. Unsuspecting Blackfoot braves lay dead, scattered among the tall ponderosa pines. There had been little chance for them. The ambush had been perfect in its surprise, allowing none to escape. Their corpses lay scalped in the shining mountains.

Death comes suddenly in this country, Floyd thought. *If Pallaton had not taken the chance to travel across the mountains in the most tortuous trip I have ever experienced, it would be the Blackfoot braves celebrating tonight, and not us.* His muscles still screamed in protest from the abuse he had put them through.

Evidently, the Blackfoot had unintentionally helped the Shoshone when they'd stopped to kill and butcher a cow elk. They'd tied the animal onto the back of one of the horses, and now their enemies would be feasting tonight and celebrating success.

The horses had been taken to water at a nearby stream and then hobbled on the lush grass of the meadow where they made their camp. A fire was started, and soon the elk was roasting over the low flame and coals.

The smell of the cooking flesh reminded Floyd how hungry he was. Floyd looked around at the men who were here. They each had pushed through with almost superhuman strength and won. Guards were posted, and he felt sure each man on guard would remain alert, though there was little chance of anyone coming along in this wilderness tonight.

Except for the light from the fire, there was total darkness. The stars, seen through the tops of the pines, were brilliant in their black background. There would be little moon to compete with them, and that would not be until early morning.

I wonder what Leotie and Mika will be eating this evening, Floyd thought. His mind searched as if in hope of reaching out and comforting the two captives. *Captives. How long will they be in the hands of the Blackfoot? Will we find them, and what condition will they be in when we do?*

Pallaton stood, and all eyes turned to him. He raised his arms to the heavens. "We must remember Enapay, for his bravery. Though he fell from the cliff, in his courage, he maintained silence to the ground. Enapay was a credit to his name, his family, a brave man. His was the sacrifice that allowed the Great Spirit to smile upon us and guide the Blackfoot into our trap.

"What would have been a great loss for our tribe has been turned into a great victory." He looked around the fire, making eye contact with each man. "Your run over the mountains, your slaying of the enemy, and your recovering the horses will be sung of forever in the Shoshone camps. You have saved our people because the Great Spirit gave you the strength to make it so."

The men sat, solemn and proud, before their chief. Finally, he said, "And today, Igasho remained with us all the way. He lived up to his name, Igasho, which we know is *man who travels far*, and then he killed three of our enemy. This has been a good day. Now eat!"

All the men jumped to their feet, brandishing their tomahawks and knives, yelling to the sky, and taking turns pounding each other and Floyd on the back. Then hunger overtook celebration, and they leaped to the elk, cutting big slices of the steaming hot venison.

Floyd felt the excitement, as had his cohorts, but, his stomach growling, he also felt hunger. Now he bit into the huge hunk of hot elk flesh he grasped in his hands, juices cutting tiny channels in the thick dirt on his face and down his fingers. Though his body was near exhaustion, he felt the high-quality protein strengthening him. He looked back on the day, thankful for making it all the way and still having enough energy remaining to fight.

As the men ate, Pallaton assigned each man a time to stand guard, Floyd being one of those assigned to the shift just before daylight. That was his favorite. He had always loved to greet the new day. Back home, in Tennessee, it was never necessary for his father to wake him. He was always ready.

After eating, he, like the others, gathered pine needles to make a softer bed. They had traveled light, and each would sleep cold tonight, with only their clothing for warmth. Yet Floyd knew there would be no one who failed to sleep tonight, for every man was near exhaustion.

He lay on the pine needles, staring at the stars. Leotie would see the same stars he was watching. Dawn Light, the Cheyenne maiden, drifted into his tired mind, but the thought was there momentarily, as his concern for Leotie replaced it. Sounds of soft snoring filled his ears, along with the reassuring soft munching of the grazing horses. The sounds of a shuffling porcupine could be heard not far away. He listened closely to the little animal, curious if it was moving closer or away. The steps stopped, began again, and faded away.

A warbler, still awake and near the small stream where they had watered the horses, filled the forest with its song. The stream gurgled while pouring around large rocks. Occasionally a soft splash could be heard from a trout taking an insect from its surface.

Floyd relaxed with the natural sounds of the forest. It would have been silent if any human was trying to slip up on them. Relaxed, his eyes drifted closed, and his steady breathing joined that of the others.

6

The sun was well over the mountains, its rays feeling good on Floyd's back. It had been a cold night. He had not awakened until a brave tapped him on the foot. His eyes had snapped awake, and he had moved quickly to his guard position. In the frigid air of morning, he greeted the new day.

Before sunrise, the other members rose and stoked the fire. Floyd made a point of not looking at it, though his body had yearned to be near the heat. It was necessary he retain his night vision, and looking at the fire would destroy it. People had died in this hard country by staring at their campfire. When danger came, their night vision was so hampered, they couldn't see their enemy until too late.

Now, well into the day, Bidzil rode ahead, watching for ambush, though they felt sure none would take place, and any signs of the party holding Leotie and Mika.

They had moved steadily west. Every man sat a horse, and Floyd was glad to be sitting on the back of Rusty, the horse given to him by Hugh Brennan when he had first ventured west almost three years ago. He was afraid he had lost not only Rusty, but his buckskin, Buck, and pack mule, Browny. Fortunately they had all been rescued and were glad to see him. It was a good thing the Blackfoot braves had killed the elk; otherwise Browny would have been roasted, for most Indians loved mule.

The trail followed through the same type terrain they had passed yesterday, only farther south. After dropping down from the pass, they had picked up the Yampa River, following it north. A while after it turned west, Slate Creek flowed into it, and they turned north, following the Slate until they could turn around the north side of Deer Mountain.

Nearing Elk River, Bidzil had pulled up, waiting for them. The tracker was on the ground, squatted next to tracks. Everyone dismounted. Floyd, Pallaton, and Kajika advanced while the others held back. Too many feet could erase the story of the tracks.

"Here is where they split," Bidzil said. "Four horses, three carrying men and one with Leotie and the boy."

Floyd could also see the different depths of the tracks. "I'll follow them from here."

"No," Pallaton said. "You must come with us. You can get the rest of your weapons and supplies."

Floyd started to argue, and Pallaton held up his hand. "Think, Igasho. You do not know when you will catch them. You will need your supplies to provide for the woman and boy. They may be hurt. We will give you medicines to take with you. You will need all of your lead and powder. You carried only a little over the mountains."

Floyd thought only for a moment. "You are right, Chief Pallaton. You again remind me to think. I am finding it difficult where those two are concerned."

The chief nodded. "Do not be concerned. I have seen you make good decisions. But when the heart is involved, good decisions become even more difficult. You must remember that. Do not be trapped or ambushed because you are being brash." Without waiting for a reply, he said, "Let us go, quickly."

The men mounted and galloped up Elk Creek toward the confluence of Deep Creek and on to the Shoshone camp.

∼

THERE HAD BEEN great celebration as the men and horses galloped into the village. The people were saved, and they knew it. But there was sadness also, for the loss of Leotie and Mika and Enapay. Nina was in front of her teepee, watching the celebrating. The returning braves leaped from their horses and ran to their wives or mothers. Each family hugged and congratulated the returning brave, with the exception of one.

Enapay's mother and father stood at the teepee entrance, watching the celebrants. When it became obvious their son was not in the group, the husband turned to his wife and wrapped her in his arms. A younger son stared at the horses and men.

Floyd watched Pallaton ride straight to the couple and dismount. He wasn't close enough to hear what Pallaton was saying, but he did not need to hear to know what the words were. He watched the father's posture straighten in pride. The chief continued to talk to the couple. When finished, he mounted and rode back to his teepee.

Floyd had greeted Nina and explained Leotie was not with the horse thieves, but had been held by three others who turned west near the Yampa river. He left her and immediately went inside and began gathering his things.

He saddled Rusty and fastened the pack frame on Browny. It took him no more than thirty minutes to load his furs and gear. With both of his Ryland Rifles in their scabbards and the two pistols in their horse holsters, and the two on his hips, he was ready.

Floyd had been concentrating on loading the animals, and though he was aware of the celebrating of the tribe, he was not paying much attention. With the last item, his saddlebags, tied on behind his saddle, he turned to look for Pallaton.

Chief Pallaton, Kajika, and Bidzil stood near the teepee, waiting. Floyd immediately saw that Kajika and Bidzil were holding saddled horses. Bags hung behind the saddles of both horses. He looked his question at the chief.

Pallaton spoke. "Did you think we would allow you to go by yourself to rescue members of our family?"

Floyd shook his head. "I hadn't thought of it one way or the other, but it is the buffalo season, time for your big hunt. Do you not need every man?"

"We have enough men for both. Kajika and Bidzil will go with you. Three is better than one."

Nina stepped forward. She had two deerskin bags in her hand. One was small, the other larger. She held the small one out first. "This is herbs and medicine for Leotie. Please give them to her when you find her." Holding out the second bag, she said, "Pemmican for you."

Floyd looked into her worried eyes and held up the two bags. "Thank you, Nina, and thank you for taking care of me in my sickness. I owe you much. I will give this to Leotie. We will return with her and Mika."

She stepped forward and grasped Floyd by the biceps, pulling his face down to hers, and lightly touched his cheek with the palm of her hand. "Be safe, Igasho, and return to us." She stepped back from Floyd.

Pallaton stood tall watching the mountain man. "I am glad we found you. It has been good for our village to have you here. You have become Shoshone. You will always be welcome." He thrust his hand to Floyd, and each man grasped the other's forearm.

"You and your people saved me, Chief Pallaton. I will be forever in your debt. Thank you."

They broke their clasp. Floyd stepped to Rusty and mounted. The village had quieted, and many of the people stood quietly watching the three men as they prepared to depart. Kajika gave his mother a hug and spoke with his father, while Bidzil told his wife and two children goodbye. Then they too mounted.

Floyd raised his hand, palm forward to the people, and said, in Shoshone, "Thank you." He held his hand steady for a few moments, then swung Rusty down Deer Creek and, followed by Kajika and Bidzil, rode from the village. *I shall miss these folks,* he thought. *They are like family to me.*

Floyd, leading Buck and Browny, led the search party into the aspen thicket and along the tinkling water of Deep Creek. His only mission now, fixed grimly in his mind, was to rescue Leotie.

Once they were well clear of the village, Floyd bumped Rusty in the flanks, and the husky red roan broke into a lope. In a short time they reached the Elk River and turned south to where the party with Leotie and Mika had turned west.

The sun was disappearing, throwing gold and purple shafts across the clouds when they pulled up where the Blackfoot raiding party separated. The braves with the horses had watered them here, just above where the Elk River joined the Yampa. The three pursuers swung down. Kajika led the horses to water while Bidzil and Floyd discussed the tracks.

"Where do you think they are going?" Floyd asked Bidzil.

The Shoshone tracker shook his head and then said, "West."

"But why?"

Bidzil stood, looking to the west. "Don't know. Blackfoot nation north. Quickest way is way the horses went. Nothing for them this way."

While the two men stood looking west, Kajika finished watering the animals and led them back.

"We still have some daylight," Floyd said. He took Rusty's bridle and the two lead ropes from Kajika and stepped into the saddle. Kajika and Bidzil followed suit. With a cluck to Rusty, the red roan stepped out toward the unknown. Three determined men rode west, their search for Leotie and Mika only beginning.

Two days had passed. The evening of the first day, the trail turned northwest, across rolling plains. Interspersed with deep chasms and high hills, the three stayed alert. Though this was the land of the Shoshone, there was always the possibility of running into Cheyenne, even Bannock from the west, Flathead from the north, or as had already been proven, Blackfoot from the far north.

This was still hunting time, and the buffalo were on the move. They had seen two big herds moving south, and where buffalo were found there was a good chance of finding Indians.

Floyd rode Buck at a fast walk, following the trail of the kidnappers. In front and to his left, he occasionally caught a glimpse of Kajika when he topped a rise. The dun Kajika rode blended well with the tall grasses turning brown in the mid-July heat. Bidzil was out in front, scouting, as usual.

Floyd pulled Buck to a halt and stood in the saddle. Far in the distance, he saw a thin trail of dust lift. Moments later, a larger line of dust lifted in the still air. He looked quickly to his left, to see Kajika had turned and was riding toward him. Not far ahead was a small creek, showing a narrow green break in the rolling hills. A few cottonwood trees lined its twisting path.

He bumped Buck into a lope. If a fight was brewing, the creek bed was about the best place he could see for a defense. Floyd reached the creek just before Kajika. He dismounted and led the animals into the creek bottom and tied them to several exposed roots. The banks were no more than five or six feet high, and though there was little more than a trickle of water flowing, the cut bank was about fifteen feet wide. *Wider than I'd like it,* Floyd thought, *but it'll have to do.*

He pulled both of his rifles from their boots, and also the pistols from their saddle holsters. After flipping the leather loops from the pistols he was wearing, he checked them both and slid them back in the holsters.

Kajika tied his horse and leaned his quiver against the bank with his bow. The lance he carried was placed next to the quiver. All they could do was wait. It wouldn't be long.

Another minute passed. Two shots were fired, and Bidzil burst over the rise, flogging his sweat-drenched bay toward them, leading three additional horses.

Shortly after Bidzil rode into view, a group of six Indians appeared over the rise, racing after him. But unfortunately for them, they were falling farther back, since they were distributed across the three remaining horses.

Floyd couldn't help himself. He shook his head and grinned. Their intrepid tracker must have been unable to resist the opportunity to relieve the other Indians of their horses. Floyd looked at Kajika.

The younger man had a wide grin on his face. "Bidzil no can refuse opportunity."

Floyd grimaced through his grin. "I wish he'd refused this one."

As the pursuers grew closer, Kajika said, "Blackfoot." He turned to Floyd and said, "I can shoot."

Floyd handed one of the Ryland rifles to Kajika. "I'll take the lead pair."

His friend nodded.

Floyd laid the forearm of his rifle across his possibles bag, took aim at the leading Indian, and fired. The leading Blackfoot brave sat straight for a moment, then tumbled from his mount. The man who had been sitting behind him stretched to reach the reins as the horse slowed. Floyd watched as the brave quickly gathered the reins and soon had his horse galloping after Bidzil.

Kajika had taken more time than Floyd, but finally the rifle fired. Another brave fell from his horse. That left four enemies.

Floyd rapidly reloaded the Ryland he was holding, adding a

double load of powder. Bidzil was only a short distance away, with the remaining Indians at least fifty yards behind him. Floyd slipped a cap on the nipple of his rifle, eared the hammer back and, now standing in the creek bed, threw the rifle to his shoulder and squeezed the trigger. The rifle roared, and the front rider of the closest double-mounted braves fell from the horse's back. The man who had been sitting behind him wavered momentarily, grabbed the reins, and dashed after his companions. The remaining warriors turned and sprinted away as Bidzil slowed, momentarily stopping above the creek bed. Then locating a game trail, he rode into the wash, leading the horses, letting them drink.

Floyd and Kajika watched the departing riders. One of the riders began swaying in the saddle, and just before he rode below their line of sight, he tumbled to the ground.

"The big boom?" Kajika asked.

"Yes," Floyd said, rubbing his shoulder. "I doubled the powder. That last shot went through the man in front and hit the one sitting behind him. Thought it might at least slow him down."

Kajika pulled his knife and ran up the trail out of the creek bed.

Bidzil called to him, "No time. Big party of Blackfoot. We must ride to the canyons. If they catch us here, we will die."

Kajika turned and dashed to the horses. Floyd untied his mounts and swung up. Bidzil rode over to Kajika and handed him the reins for one of his captured horses. With the leads of the other two, he galloped his horse due west, Floyd and Kajika close behind.

After two miles, Bidzil slowed his bay to a walk. Floyd and the younger man sidled in close to the tracker, and Kajika asked, "What happened?"

Bidzil looked puzzled. "Many Blackfoot follow buffalo into

Shoshone country. Big hunting party. I see small group, six men, stopped, so I slip through grass to horses. All Blackfoot were eating. No one guarded the horses. Not smart in Shoshone country. So I steal horses. They not notice until I am far away. When they see, they come fast." Here Bidzil's face wrinkled with a devilish grin. "But not fast enough. Two men on horse, very slow."

They continued to walk the horses west. No other words were spoken. Occasionally one of them would look back east. After the horses had rested, they picked up the pace to a lope.

Floyd glanced back to see a large dust cloud in the distant east. "Dust."

Bidzil pronounced, "Blackfoot."

Floyd knew a cloud of dust that large meant at least a hundred men. If they caught them out in this rolling prairie, no matter how many he shot, it wouldn't be enough. They had to find a place to hide. *I hope Bidzil has a place in mind,* he thought. He'd been in the west for over three years. *I'd sure like to make it to my twentieth birthday.* He smiled to himself. He could have stayed back east and would never have had this type of problem, but he couldn't see himself staring at the back end of a mule. *I'd rather be out here in the west than plowing a field over and over again. This is the life for me.*

Floyd glanced over his shoulder. The dust seemed to be nearer. To the west, he could see mountains rising ahead. He glanced at Bidzil and then Kajika. They both looked confident. They continued to ride toward the nearest mountain. It wasn't like the mountains they had left a few days earlier. It was just a much taller mound with a few trees near the top.

As they grew nearer, Bidzil started bearing toward the southern end, and the country got rougher. It was necessary to skirt several deep gorges, any of which Floyd thought might be good hiding places, but they continued. He was following Jeb and his pa's advice: See where you are. Don't just look, but commit it to memory. You never know when you might be along this way again.

He also turned in the saddle often, both left and right, looking at the land from a different direction. Landmarks look different after you pass them. It was smart to see and mark them from another view. Floyd looked back at the dust cloud again. It was definitely drawing closer. Now they were climbing, following the east side of a north-south ridgeline. The horses slowed to a walk. The animals were tired. At least, if they needed to make a run for it, they had extra horses, although he was worried about Browny, the mule. He had to carry his load all the time, but that was one tough mule.

They neared the top of the ridge and entered a cedar break. The tallest were no more than fifteen feet, but they blocked the view of their pursuers. For now that was good. If their view was blocked, so was their pursuers'. Bidzil led them over the top of the ridge, out of sight thanks to the cedars.

Floyd was surprised at the depth on this side of the ridge. They were dropping into a canyon. He could hear the sound of water below, but the view was blocked by the trees. They moved lower, dropping deeper into the canyon. It was impossible to see how far this canyon ran north and south, or how deep it was. *If we're trapped here, surrounded by angry Blackfoot warriors,* he thought, *we won't stand a chance. Maybe following a mule behind a plow wouldn't be so bad.*

7

The trail grew steeper, almost disappearing as it narrowed. They were now in single file, with Bidzil in the lead, then Kajika, and Floyd bringing up the rear. They dropped lower in the rocky canyon, the sound of the rushing water increasing. Bidzil led them around red boulders the size of houses.

The slope leveled out, and, of a sudden, they broke onto a flat, in a narrow basin. The trees were scattered but taller. Floyd looked back along their trail and could see almost to the top of the distant ridge they had descended, at least five miles to their south.

The Blackfoot had persisted in their chase and were crossing the ridge. He could see them as they passed between the scattered trees. Bidzil and Kajika were also looking back toward the rim.

"Change horses, now," Bidzil said.

In relief, Buck's back muscles quivered as Floyd switched his gear to Rusty. It took no more than three minutes, but the Blackfoot were getting closer.

They jumped back into their saddles.

"We cross river not far ahead. Water more shallow," Bidzil said.

They rode north, alongside the river, occasionally looking back, watching for the closing Blackfoot. Rounding a bend in the river, they were blocked from the view of their pursuers.

"Good," Bidzil said, "we cross now."

They turned the horses, riding to the edge of the shallow water, no more than one to two feet deep. Each side sloped gently into the rapids.

"We must hurry," Bidzil said. "Bad storm come."

The wind had increased, and Floyd looked up. Only a narrow strip of sky was visible from the canyon floor. For the first time, he noticed the faint red dust drifting in the wind, high above the canyon walls. They pushed the horses quickly across the shallows and, reaching the other side, again turned north. The shoreline was flat with scattered patches of bunch grass. He could feel the thick muscles of Rusty's back quiver now and again. The big horse's red head pulled against the reins.

They swung around another bend, and Bidzil led them through a rocky field, turning them up a side shoot off the main canyon. A small stream ran down the middle. Bidzil stayed in the stream as he headed away from the main canyon. They started climbing again.

The dust was growing thicker, biting at Floyd's cheeks in the swirling wind. He pulled his neckerchief up over his nose and continued to follow Kajika. They had traveled at least another mile, as visibility continued to drop in the slashing wind. What tracks they had left would be quickly obscured in this dust and wind.

Bidzil moved out of the stream to the right and angled behind a large boulder. He turned back, paralleling the flow of the stream, then cut behind another boulder that sat against the narrow canyon wall. Kajika followed. The two men and horses disappeared. Floyd, close behind Kajika, thought, *Where did they go? There's no room between that boulder and the cliff.* Yet he followed them, and when he got to the edge of the big rock, he could see there was just space for him to ride behind it and lead his animals.

He slipped around the boulder, through a narrow space with a low overhang, forcing him to bend down close to Rusty's neck. When he rose, he saw he had ridden into a hole in the canyon wall that widened into an open room, high enough for a man to sit a saddle. He swung down from Rusty, his hand cramping from the grip he had on Buck and Browny's lead ropes. There was plenty of space here for fifteen or twenty men and their horses, and it would never be seen from the stream or the river below.

"Come," Kajika said, "this will protect us from big storm. Blackfoot not so lucky."

Of a sudden, a bolt of lightning slammed into the cliff face just outside. The explosion echoed through the chamber. He talked to and patted the horses and mule, working to calm them, their eyes rolling in fear and confusion. For a moment, he thought they might dash for the opening, but at his calming voice, they began to relax. His compadres were doing the same with their mounts.

Bright blasts of lightning and deafening thunder crashed throughout the canyon. The fierce wind howled outside their sanctuary. The sound of the storm and wind, with lightning flashing, made it impossible to carry on a conversation. Initially, outside their cave, the dust and sand had been so bad it was almost impossible to breathe. But once the storm and rain hit, the dust was washed out of the sky, cleaning the air for all animals, including man.

The rain poured. There was no chance the Blackfoot would ever find them now. Of course, there was also no chance they would be able to track Leotie and Mika. They would have to figure out where their captors were taking them. It didn't take a huge amount of brain power to deduce that one. Not with more

Blackfoot braves this far south. Those who raided the Shoshone village were probably from this bunch, but that brought up another interesting thought. Where was the group with the horses going? *Maybe,* Floyd thought, *if they already had plenty of horses, they didn't want to be troubled with the extra animals during the buffalo hunt.* He nodded his head in agreement with his thoughts.

Once the lightning and thunder moved east, the men removed their gear from the horses. Floyd found some dry grass and started wiping down Rusty, Buck, and Browny. All three were extremely tired, especially his mule, Browny.

During the lightning storm, Browny had moved between Rusty and Buck. Mules were funny the way they liked being around horses. *But that makes sense,* Floyd thought, *when you figured most of them were raised by horses.* The animals had settled down, enjoying the attention from Floyd. He spoke softly to them as he worked. Once finished, he filled his hat from his water bag and gave each horse a hat full of water. They drank it greedily. "That'll have to do for now, boys. I'll give you some more later." He patted each one.

Once finished, he joined Bidzil and Kajika, where they sat near the remnants of an old fire, though there would be no fire tonight. None of them wanted to take the chance of the smell of smoke alerting a Blackfoot scout to their location.

Floyd, from his experience with the red men of the mountains, figured they could probably pull out in the morning. However, he also wanted Bidzil's opinion. In a low tone he asked, "How long do you think we'll need to stay here?"

Bidzil thought for a moment, as he was prone to do when asked a direct question, and said, "One night. Blackfoot have no shelter or food. They hunting when they chase us. They will be tired, miserable, and hungry. It rain, no thunder or lightning, they leave now. No tracks to follow, all gone. We leave in morning."

Bidzil had been staring at the wall. Now he turned to look at Floyd. "We are no longer able to track Leotie and Mika. They probably with large Blackfoot hunting party. They alert now. We no be able to get woman and boy back."

"We can try," Floyd said.

"You try, you die. Too many. They alert now. They will be watching for us."

"We can wait until they relax," Floyd responded.

"No try." Bidzil looked at Kajika. "We go back home. Search is over."

Kajika shook his head violently. "We stay, Bidzil. Leotie is expecting us to rescue her. Floyd will need help."

Bidzil's face was hard. He shook his head once and peered at Kajika with firm determination. "No. We stay, we die. It is important we go back to village and help with buffalo hunt. Tell chief about Blackfoot. If we are killed, they could be surprised by Blackfoot again. Then many die."

Kajika thought about what Bidzil had told him, then said, "You are right. They need to know. But that requires only one. You go and tell them. We will find Leotie."

Bidzil thought about what Kajika had proposed. He finally turned to the younger man. "You chief's son. You will be chief one day unless you are killed. You will be killed if you stay. You must go back with me."

Floyd's heart had sunk when Bidzil said they must return. Though he was good at tracking, Floyd knew he wasn't anywhere near as good as Bidzil. And what the scout had said made sense, but he was not going back. He wouldn't give up until he had found her, or knew she and Mika were dead.

Kajika stood, stared at Bidzil, and struck his chest once with his right fist. "I am Kajika. I am son of Chief Pallaton of the Shoshone. I will not abandon friend. If I must die, then I die. I am staying."

Floyd stood and said to Kajika, "I thank you, but Bidzil speaks wisdom. I appreciate you wanting to stay, but it would be better if you went back."

Kajika remained standing, his chest swelling. "No! I will not go back. I will go with you." He crossed his arms and stared at Bidzil. "It is settled."

Bidzil shrugged. "You will do as you will do." He turned to Floyd. "I will leave in the morning. Our people must be warned."

Floyd sat back down. "I understand, and I agree with you. Thank you for your help. Do you have any other thoughts as to Leotie?"

"Yes. The rendezvous is only three days' ride north. Maybe they take her and boy to rendezvous, sell her to trappers?"

Kajika sat as Floyd said, "Sell her?"

"Yes. Trappers trade for women often."

"Do they treat them well?"

"Depends on man. Like Indian, some good, some bad."

Floyd thought about Bidzil's statement. He was familiar with slavery, and like his folks, he would have nothing to do with it. He felt his skin crawl at the thought of what Leotie might be forced to do. He had to find her. Maybe her Blackfoot captors had ridden straight through to the rendezvous. It was on the Green River, where they were now, except over a hundred miles north.

He nodded to himself and said, "We leave in the morning for the rendezvous. I reckon we just need to follow the Green until we strike it."

Bidzil nodded his agreement. "Simple plan. With Blackfoot this far south, you must keep sharp lookout."

Floyd grinned and said, "You mean don't steal any horses from them?"

Bidzil pulled his head back and stared at Floyd. Then a faint grin broke across his face. "Yes, don't steal horses."

Darkness had fallen outside, which made the cave near pitch black except toward the cave opening. There, a small amount of intermittent light slipped in between the broken clouds scurrying by, allowing the new moon to shine through.

"Time to sleep," Bidzil said. "I guard first, then you"—he poked Kajika lightly on the upper arm—"and you," doing the same to Floyd.

The three men got up, felt their way to their supplies, and pulled out blankets. Bidzil threw the blanket around his jacketed shoulders to ward off the cold. After the rain, tonight would be a cold night, even though it was early July.

Floyd rolled out his bedroll, laid both pistols and rifles next to his bedroll, lay down, and pulled a blanket over him. He was asleep in moments.

∼

THE THREE WERE UP EARLY, saddled, horses watered at the stream in front of the cave, and ready as dawn broke over the canyon wall. They mounted, with Bidzil riding down the draw toward the Green. Floyd and Kajika rode up the draw. Both Bidzil and Kajika knew this country. The draw sloped gradually enough for horse travel to make it out of the canyon.

Bidzil had given Kajika one of the three horses he had captured. Both men now had an extra horse, if needed. Nearing the top of the canyon, they stopped, tied the horses and walked up to the edge, so they could peer over and search for the enemy. Floyd had pulled his small telescope from his saddlebags and now examined the countryside.

Easterners and city folks would call the land barren, Floyd thought. But this country was far from barren. The green patches of greasewood dotted the rolling slopes that were trending upward to the west. The silver-gray of tall sagebrush was scattered in between, with the shorter green rabbitbrush here and there. A small bunch of buffalo, no more than nine or ten, grazed in a shallow draw to the north, just their backs showing. *Probably feeding on salt grass, bluestem or fescue,* Floyd thought.

He continued to scan the surrounding area with the glass he had gotten in Santa Fe. That seemed so long ago, though it was only three years. *I've learned so much since coming west.* Floyd thought. *Even with all my trapping and everything I learned back home, there's still been so much to learn.*

Floyd completed his scan and handed the glass to Kajika. The young Shoshone had been watching Floyd, and properly placed the small end to his eye and immediately jerked it down, waving his hand in front of the lens. Eyes wide, he stared at the brass and glass instrument and, slowly, moved it back to his eye. This time, his forehead wrinkled as he looked at the buffalo and jerked the glass down again.

Kajika placed the glass to his eyes for the third time and examined the buffalo. He stayed on them for quite a while before starting to move it around. Slowly covering the sage- and greasewood-covered land, with awe, he gave the glass back to Floyd.

"Is it magic, Igasho?"

"No." Floyd searched for a word in his new Shoshone vocabulary, but could not find one. In English, he said, "It is science."

"Sci-ence?"

Falling back into Shoshone, Floyd said, "Yes. I will explain it tonight when we stop. But it is good, yes?"

Kajika nodded his head emphatically. "Yes, it is very good."

Agreeing neither saw anything threatening, the two men made their way back to the horses, mounted, and rode north.

They had crossed several ravines that, though drying, still had water standing from yesterday's storm. After crossing the third one, they stopped, dismounted, and stretched their legs, allowing the horses to drink. Occasionally, they were close enough to the canyon to see the river flowing at the bottom of the majestic pillars of rock.

Floyd's eyes devoured the beauty of the land. Pillars of rock stood hundreds of feet tall, silent, ancient sentinels, guarding, waiting. He hated that Leotie and Mika had been taken, but now he was seeing parts of the country he might have never seen. *How could a man ride through this country and not be humbled,* he thought. They continued north until reaching the first creek that flowed into the Green above the canyon country.

Kajika broke the silence. "We follow this creek. Buffalo and Blackfoot, maybe Sioux along big river. This will go around mountains and get close to big river farther north."

"White man calls it the Green River," Floyd said.

Kajika nodded and continued riding.

The two men stopped frequently, prior to coming out of each draw, to survey the countryside, always cautious, aware of the significant chance of running into hostile Indians. They rode slowly. Even though there had been heavy rain the evening before, a few hours of sun had dried the ground, and the least bit of dust might be spotted by someone who would love to have their hair on a lance.

As the sun drifted behind the hills to the west, Kajika said, pointing to some low willows ahead, "We stop. Good place there. Eat jerky. No fire tonight."

Floyd nodded, thinking, *You're danged right, no fire tonight.* They had seen several large dust clouds to the east, occasionally spotting the western edge of large buffalo herds. They sure didn't need any surprise visitors. Drawing closer, Rusty's head jerked up, as well as the other horses'. There was a light breeze from the north, coming straight at them from the spot they had planned on having a dry camp.

Both men pulled their horses up and spoke softly to them, hopefully preventing a whinny. They moved to the left where there was a buffalo wallow they could ride down into. Once in the wallow, Floyd placed the spyglass up to his eye. Since entering the open country, he'd kept it hanging around his neck on a leather string.

Examining the spot closely, he could make out two horses and a pack mule tied in the willows. They were well hidden to the naked eye, but the glass brought the area close enough where he could see the outlines through the willows.

He leaned over to Kajika. "I think it's a couple of trappers, like me, heading to rendezvous."

Kajika nodded. "Maybe. Maybe Sioux or Blackfoot kill trappers and have horses."

Floyd took off his hat and slipped the lanyard from his head, handing the glass to Kajika. The Shoshone took several minutes examining the flat, shook his head, and said, "All I see is same as you. Two horses and a mule." He handed the glass back to Floyd.

They sat in the wallow for another fifteen minutes, waiting to see if there was any movement around the camp. There was none.

Floyd turned to Kajika. "What do you think?"

The young Indian continued watching the trees and horses. He finally gave a small shake of his head, grasped his bow in his left hand, and said, "We can sit here until dark, but I don't think they are Blackfoot. We would already be running."

Floyd reached down and slipped the leather retainers from the hammers of his pistols on his saddle and did the same with the ones on each leg. Then he pulled a rifle from its boot and laid it across the saddle. "Well," he said, "reckon there's only one way to find out." He bumped Rusty in the flanks. With Floyd leading, they rode cautiously toward the camp.

8

Within hailing distance of the camp, Floyd and Kajika stopped.

Floyd called, "Hello, the camp."

"Well, it's about time you fellers made up yore mind. Come on in if'n yore friendly. Shoot, come on in if'n you ain't. We can take care of ornery cusses right quick."

Floyd continued in, riding in front of Kajika. No sense giving somebody a reason to get trigger-happy with an Indian riding in. He thought he recognized the voice. If so, they had two good companions to accompany them their last eighty miles to the rendezvous.

A man who looked like a walking anvil stepped from the willows, rifle in hand. The fellow couldn't be more than five and a half feet tall. In fact, his rifle looked half again as long as he was tall. His shoulders were disproportionately wide, suggesting he might tip over with every step. They were complemented with a barrel chest and massive arms.

His pardner stepped from the willows behind him, towering above the first man. The tall man looked to be near six and a half feet tall. Long arms ended in hands that dwarfed the lock of his rifle resting comfortably in the cradling hands.

Both men were clean shaven, and the tall one's dark brown hair hung to his shoulders. Floyd recognized the two of them immediately. He had met them at the rendezvous last year, at Pierre's Hole, with Jeb. It had been an eye-opening experience. Many of the mountain men he had met, either in the mountains or in Santa Fe, prior to his first rendezvous. In the mountains, the mountain man's life depended on him staying alert. If he was distracted or tipsy, it could mean the loss of his hair.

The rendezvous was completely different. There were several hundred trappers, adventurers, writers, painters, and of course, traders at the rendezvous, primarily men. It usually lasted for several weeks or until the liquor was gone. After the trappers had traded their beaver pelts, called plew, many never sobered up until the day they left.

Several fur trading companies attended the rendezvous, bringing trade goods the trapper was in need of, along with the fire water most everyone wanted, including the Indians.

About the time Floyd recognized them, the shorter of the two men hailed him. "Ho, Floyd. How ye be? Come on in here and sit a spell. Who's the Indian you've got with you? How you been doin'? Where you come from? Where's Jeb? Why ain't you got more beaver?" The questions didn't stop until Floyd, with Kajika, pulled up at the camp and climbed down. Finally the tall one said, "Shorty, how you expectin' Floyd to remember all those questions? Why don't you be quiet and let the man have a cup of coffee before you start yammerin' at him?"

Shorty whipped around to face his pardner. "Morg, don't you tell me what to do, you tall drink of water. I'll ask what I want, when I want. Nobody's gonna tell me what I can or cain't do. You got it?"

Morg shook his head and stepped forward to Floyd, extending his hand. "Been a while, Floyd. Who's yore friend?"

"Howdy, Morg, good to see you." Floyd shook his hand and turned to Kajika. "This here is Kajika. He's the son of Chief Pallaton of the Shoshones, south of here."

"Howdy," Morg said, extending his hand.

Kajika gave a single nod and shook Morg's hand in the white-man manner.

Floyd continued. "Kajika, this talkative feller is Shorty. He may talk a lot, but he's a stayer in a fight."

Kajika stepped forward and shook Shorty's hand in the same manner.

"Boys," Floyd said, "we need to take care of the horses first. They've had some heavy work over the past few days. Then we'll take you up on that coffee."

"Shoot, Floyd," Shorty said, "we'll give you a hand." He stepped forward and took the leads for Buck and Browny.

Morg started to do the same for Kajika, hesitated, and then grinned when Kajika handed him the lead rope and said proudly, "Blackfoot horse."

Morg nodded, taking the lead, and said, "Sounds like there's a story there. Maybe we can hear it after we get these animals some water."

Kajika nodded, and the four men, three mountain men and a Shoshone brave, led the horses to water. After the animals drank, they were led back near the other animals and quickly hobbled. The gear was stripped off and taken to where Shorty had dragged up some large stumps for sitting, and then the horses were given good rubdowns. When the men finished, they stepped back to the firepit and pulled up a stump.

Floyd said, "I could see your smoke at least two miles away."

"The heck you say," Shorty responded. He looked at the small fire and over to Morg. "What'd you do, get green wood? I told you dry birch or aspen." Before Morg could respond, Shorty turned to Floyd, shaking his head. "I'll tell you, Floyd. I ain't got the slightest idea what I'm gonna do with this beanpole. I cain't teach him nothing."

Floyd shook his head. "Shorty, one of these days that beanpole is going to string you up by your thumbs."

Shorty shot him a grin and handed a cup of coffee to Floyd and then Kajika. "Reckon you might be right." He stuck his hand out for Morg's cup, took it, filled it, and handed it back to the silent man. Then he stood and, with a stick, moved all of the bright embers together. The smoke was gone since all of the wood had burned, leaving only hot coals for cooking. He poured himself a cup, placing the pot at the edge of the coals, moved back to a stump and sat, taking a long sip of the hot black coffee.

The sun had completely disappeared behind the bluffs, and long shadows covered the majestic land. All four men sat quietly drinking their coffee, enjoying the sights and sounds of the evening. Somewhere to the west a pack of wolves were tuning up. Their smaller cousins, coyotes, competed from the south and much closer to the camp.

Floyd sipped his coffee and then said, "Those sound real to me. Everybody agree?"

Heads nodded, and Kajika said, "Those real sound, no Indian." He looked at Shorty. "Coffee good." He held out his cup.

Shorty took it and filled it again, nodding to Kajika.

Floyd had taken off his hat and laid it next to him. Even in the dim light, the others could see the scar running across his scalp on the left side of his head, from front to back.

"Boy," Shorty said, "looks like you come close to losing yore hair. What happened to you?"

Uncharacteristically, for an Indian, young Kajika spoke before Floyd could respond. "Grizzly attacked while trapping. He kill bear."

Both Shorty and Morg sat back in stunned silence as the remaining light faded into darkness, only red coals of the fire still glowing.

"Well, don't sit there like a lump on a log." Shorty said. "Tell us about it."

Floyd gave them a brief description of the grizzly incident and stopped.

The two mountain men looked at each other. Then Shorty spoke up again. "I asked you to tell us about it. We don't know much more than before you started. Tell us what happened."

Even as a boy, much like his pa, Floyd had never been one to brag on his accomplishments, and now he was embarrassed. He waited a moment too long, and Kajika, who had heard the story many times over from his father and the other braves who had been there, said, "I tell."

The young man then launched into a lengthy description of the bear, its size, and the fight. He went into vivid detail, embellishing the already embellished story. At one point, Floyd started to intervene, but then thought better of it. A young man like Kajika would be greatly insulted if he even suggested what the boy was saying was not fact. He sat painfully listening to the story. A few times a grin crossed his face at the great exaggerations that were being told as truth.

Later, Floyd thought, *when Kajika isn't around, I'll have to straighten out the story. He's making me sound greater than Hugh Glass, and that sure ain't true.*

After a long telling of the incident, Kajika fell silent. Floyd thought, *Finally.*

Morg leaned toward the Indian. "Were you there?"

"Shoshone watch," Kajika said, not answering the question directly. "Sat on hillside watching fight between Igasho and grizzly."

"Igasho?" Morg, a normally quiet man, again asked of Kajika.

Before he could speak, Floyd jumped in. He was tired and didn't want another long story about the trek across the mountains to intercept the Blackfoot. "Chief Pallaton, Kajika's father, gave me a name and made me a member of the tribe."

The two mountain men nodded, and Shorty threw a comment at Floyd. "Boy, I heard the Comanche down in New Mexico also gave you a name." He rubbed his chin, thinking, then abruptly held up a finger. "Oh yeah, it was Pawnee Killer. You keep it up, and you won't be able to remember all yore names."

"I doubt there'll be any more," Floyd said.

"Humph!" emanated from the short man. "We'll see.

"Looks like yore headed out for rendezvous, but you shore ain't got many plews. If that's all you ketched, it's gonna be a mighty bleak winter. You won't get more'n three months supplies for that."

"Jeb went to St. Louis with our furs. He can get a much better price for them back east. I just need enough supplies to keep me going until he gets back, or at least that was the plan. I need to tell you boys something."

It had been a long day for all. But at the change of tone from Floyd, the two mountain men perked up, both quiet and attentive.

Floyd said, "We are chasing Blackfoot."

Shorty popped off. "Well, you danged sure don't have far to chase. They're all over east of here. What with the buffler around."

"We're chasing a particular bunch. They raided Kajika's village, stole horses, and took a woman and her boy. They may have stopped with the Blackfoot east of here, but we think they are headed up to rendezvous to sell their prisoners."

Morg stretched his long legs, his moccasins almost touching the dying coals. His voice disgusted, he said, "There's those what will buy 'em too and treat 'em like dirt."

"Then they will die!" Kajika said.

No one doubted his determination.

Morg nodded. "They deserve it."

Floyd continued. "This is a good woman and a fine boy. She and Chief Pallaton's wife are the reason I'm still alive."

"From that little ole scratch on yore head?" Shorty asked.

Floyd shook his head, the movement hardly visible in the dark night. "No. The bear's claws got my arm, and it swelled up. I was out of it for almost two weeks. They nursed me through it, took care of me when I was mighty sick. I owe her."

Morg scratched his head. "Floyd, Shorty and me are headin' to rendezvous. How 'bout we ride along?"

"Thanks, boys," Floyd said. "We'd appreciate it. Make us a little stronger, should that big batch of Blackfoot spot us."

"Good," Shorty said. "The morning will be bringin' an early start. Reckon we oughta turn in."

"Sounds good," Floyd said. "How do you want to do the watch?"

Shorty stood. "How 'bout I take the first, then Morg, Kajika, and you? That'll make short watches for us all."

Floyd glanced at Kajika, who gave a single nod. "That'll be fine with us."

Without another word, the four men moved quietly to their bedrolls. Each man arranged his weapons alongside his bed before stretching out and covering with a blanket, preparing for a chilly night.

Floyd yawned as he stretched his long legs and pulled the woolen edge of his blanket up to his neck. The day had been long, and he was tired. A couple more such days would put them at the rendezvous. His mind slipped back to Leotie and Mika. *She has done so much for me. I owe her, and I just hope she is still at rendezvous. First, I'll try to buy her and Mika back, but Kajika was right. If they are the type of men who will buy another human, then they probably deserve to die.*

His thoughts drifted back to Tennessee. *Though we knew people who owned slaves, Ma and Pa never had any truck with slave-owners. They made it clear to all of us kids that every man deserved to be free.*

He remembered when it was made particularly clear to him,

his nine-year-old sister, Jenny, older by two years, and his younger sister, Martha. The family had just returned from town, and Pa had given a black man and his pregnant wife a ride in the wagon, with all of the kids. The two people had been very grateful, for it was a hot, steamy day. When they had dropped the couple at their shack, the family continued home.

Around the table that evening, Jenny turned to Pa. "Pa, what do I call a black man or woman?"

Pa had been eating. He stopped, looked down the table at Ma, who had laid her fork down, and turned to Jenny. "Why do you ask, Jenny?"

Everyone's head turned toward Jenny. He remembered his older brothers grinning, and Jenny uncomfortable with the attention. He could hear the toes of her shoes, for that was all that reached the floor from the tall bench they sat on, bumping on the floor. Anytime that was heard from Jenny, she was either nervous or mad, and at the time, Floyd knew for sure she wasn't mad, not at Pa.

"Well, Pa," she said in a low voice, still looking at her plate, "I've heard them called bad names."

Pa's voice grew hard. "Not from anyone in this house, I hope." At the same time he scanned everyone with his dark gray eyes that had turned hard and cold, points of red developing just above his cheeks.

Jenny shook her head vigorously, saying with a rush, "Oh no, Pa, I've never heard anyone in this family use those words."

"Good," Pa said. "I'll make it very easy for you three." Pa looked at Jenny, then me, and Martha. "If they're not grown, then you call 'em by their first name. If they're grown, you call 'em mister or missus, just like you do our friends. And for the adults, it is always sir, or ma'am. Does that make it easier, Jenny?"

She gave Pa her most brilliant smile and said, "Oh, yes, sir, Pa. That makes it truly easy. I talk to them just like I do to you and Ma."

Ma had smiled at her. "That's right, Jenny. They're God's creatures just like we are." She turned to me and Martha. "Do you two understand?"

Floyd remembered he and Martha, sitting beside each other, nodding briskly. Jenny's feet had stopped tapping, and Pa said, "Good. Now let's eat." Everyone dove in again.

Floyd let out a big sigh. Those had been good times. *I've got to be going back to see my folks,* he thought. *I was really lucky to have been born into that family.* His mind drifted back to Leotie. His eyelids grew heavy, and he drifted off to sleep.

9

The previous year Floyd had attended his first rendezvous with Jeb. It was there Jeb had become so angry. The low prices being paid by the fur companies to the trappers, coupled with the sky-high charges for supplies, caused him to refuse to sell the plews except for enough to make it through the winter. Those furs, plus their catch for the fall and early spring season that Floyd and Jeb caught, Jeb took to St. Louis. He invited Floyd, but with or without him, he was selling their fur back east. Floyd agreed with the decision, but elected to stay in the mountains. When the time came for him to go east, he planned on going all the way home to Tennessee.

At that rendezvous, Floyd had met William and Milton Sublette, Jim Bridger, Old Broken Hand, and Thomas Fitzpatrick, men he had read about in the papers back home, and heard more about from Jeb. It was overwhelming for his young mind, all these famous men in one place, until he got to know them.

The mountain men were mostly just regular folks who preferred the solitude of the mountains to the drudgery of the plow, or the rush of the city. They were hard, tough trappers who, when they gave their word, stood by it and expected others to do the same. For the most part, he found them to be opinionated, obstinate men of fierce pride. Floyd had looked around and decided he fit right in except for the heavy drinking.

His pa didn't hold with the use of spirits. He'd always said a man who drank to drunkenness was undependable and very likely an abuser of women and animals. In his short life, Floyd Logan had found much truth in that statement, although he knew several heavy drinkers whom he would depend on with his life when they were sober. Morg was one.

Floyd had no idea what Morg was like in a town or city, but at the rendezvous, the first thing he did after selling his fur and buying supplies for the next year was look for the saloon tent. Once there, he would drink until his money was gone, and ask Shorty for more. His good friend would never give him a dime to get drunk, although at the beginning of each binge, Shorty might join him in a drink or two.

Jeb had introduced Shorty and Morg to Floyd at the rendezvous. They and Floyd hit it right off. Both men were young, like him and Jeb, but like Jeb, this wasn't their first rendezvous. When Floyd met them, they had already been in the mountains for several years.

Morg had been raised on a farm, and when he was drunk, there was always one thing he talked about, having a farm of his own. Once Floyd learned more about Morg, he was surprised the tall young man would ever want to go back to a farm.

Morg's folks had died when he was still a baby, and he was taken in by an abusive uncle. He lived with the uncle and the man's wife until he was fourteen. During those growing years, his uncle beat him and his own kids, along with his wife. He also worked Morg harder than he worked his mules.

The abuse lasted until he was eight months past his fourteenth birthday. By this time, he towered over his uncle. When the thug took his whip to Morg, the six-foot fourteen-year-old took the whip away from the man and beat him near to death.

That was the day he packed what little he had and left the Missouri farm. His aunt begged him not to go until she realized there was no way to change his mind. From her ragged dresser, she then pulled out five dollars. She gave it to the lad, along with a loving hug, and sent him on his way.

That goes a long ways toward explaining why he drinks, Floyd thought, as he gazed across the valley where they were riding. It was dotted with several hundred teepees. They had continued to follow the Green, and had no trouble from Blackfoot warriors. He saw why, upon riding into the valley. The Blackfoot who weren't hunting were here, along with Flathead, Bannock, and Snake, the name the mountain men had given the Shoshone, because they first found them along the Snake River. He saw the first encampment of mountain men near a fur company's tents. Close by was a saloon tent. The teepees continued up the Green toward where Horse Creek flowed in. The four men guided their horses toward the tents.

Kajika pointed to the Shoshone tents. "My people. You go. I find out if my people have seen Leotie."

"Would they know her, Kajika?" Floyd said.

"They would know Shoshone woman and boy. I check and find you later."

Floyd nodded. "Don't take too long. I need to sell these pelts, but after that, we could need to leave anytime."

Kajika nodded. "If you need to leave before I find, you go. I'll catch up." Floyd watched his friend ride away, then turned back with Shorty and Morg.

"Morg," a voice shouted out from the opening of the saloon tent, "come on in here and wet yore whistle."

"I'll be seeing you later," he called back. "Got some plews to sell." He started, pulled up again, and called, "Who's givin' the best price?"

Several voices came rolling out of the tent. "Sublette and Campbell." Then the man who had first spoken said, "They've started a new fur company. They're the St. Louis Fur Company. But you'd better git over there quick. Rocky Mountain Fur and American Fur are here. I imagine they'll be puttin' their heads together soon, and prices will go down."

"Much obliged," Morg called.

While the two men were talking, Floyd pulled up and was taking in the scenery. Mountain ranges ran along the east and west side of the valley. Clear skies allowed the eye to see over a hundred miles. The rugged Grand Tetons could be seen in the distance, farther north. Beyond that was Colter's Hell, steaming hot water that spurted into the air. Floyd hadn't seen it yet, but he would. He looked back to the east, along another line of mountains, with peaks reaching forever to the sky. Jeb had warned him about Blackfoot country. The Blackfoot had yet to be peaceful toward the white man though occasionally they would attend a rendezvous.

This is gonna be interesting, Floyd thought. *Blackfoot are up north too. A man could lose his hair mighty easy up there, but Jeb said beaver are thick as deer flies on a hot day.*

While Morg was still talking, Floyd eased Rusty toward a larger tent. The sign over it read St. Louis Fur Company. Shorty and Morg came riding up. As soon as they pulled up, William Sublette stepped from the tent. His eyes quickly took in Floyd's small pack of fur, then switched to the large haul of Shorty and Morg.

"Howdy, boys. How are you? Looks like you and Morg did well, Shorty." His eyes switched back to Floyd's. "Too bad I can't say the same for you, young feller. Have a rough season?"

Floyd nodded. He didn't want to say anything about Jeb and only commented, "I'd say so."

"Yep, Sublette," Shorty said, climbing down from his horse. "I'd say we did mighty proud this season. What you paying?"

William Sublette rubbed his chin. "Depends on the condition of yore plews, boys."

"Top grade," Shorty replied. "You won't find a hole or nary a piece of tallow on these here furs. I'd venture to say on Floyd's neither."

Sublette turned to Floyd again, a puzzled look in his eyes, as if he was trying to remember. "Floyd." He thought a moment longer. Then his eyebrows rose in recognition. "Floyd Logan. You came up last year for the first time." He ran a finger along the left side of his face. "I remember you now."

Floyd was loosening the girth on Rusty. He turned and nodded. Most people had little trouble remembering him, what with his clean-shaven face and the long scar from the Pawnee knife fight when he first came west. The cut, though three years healed by now, was readily visible on his left cheek, from chin to cheekbone. It hadn't disfigured him, as one would think. Rather, it gave him a rugged look that women seemed to take to, and men mostly ignored.

"You were with Jeb Campbell." He looked around for Jeb. When he didn't see him, he said, "Is Jeb with you? I don't see him."

"No," Floyd said, "he ain't here."

"Split up, huh? That happens." He turned to Shorty and Morg, who had squatted to the ground, pulled grass stems, and were picking their teeth. "Just drop them furs, boys, and I'll get you your money."

Shorty looked up at the bigger man. "You ain't never told us what you were givin' for top-grade beaver. Heard there's a couple more company's here abuying."

Sublette stopped. "Why, boys, that hurts my feelings. You don't need to go anywhere else, I'll pay top price for top beaver."

"And that is?" Shorty said, eyeing the famous buyer.

"I'll be honest with you. Price is good this year, and I want your fur. No dickering, I'll give you six dollars a pound."

Shorty looked at Morg, who nodded. Then he looked over at

Floyd and back to the buyer. "Is that price good for our friend, here."

A small frown touched Sublette's lips, but for only a moment. "Sure it is. Now let's get you boys some money."

Floyd maintained a solemn face, even though he was ecstatic inside. Six dollars a pound was a great price. If they were paying those kind of prices out here, Jeb must have made a killing with the three hundred and fifty furs he had taken back east.

Sublette turned to Floyd. "How many plews do you have?"

Floyd pulled the short stack off Browny. "Twenty-two. Two of those are smaller."

The fur buyer nodded. "Could I see one?"

"Sure," Floyd said. He dug down in the stack, sliding one from out of the middle.

The pelt was folded in half. Since it had been folded so that the fur was inside, it was easy to check the quality. There was no sign of any dried flesh or fat on the fur and no nicks or cuts through the hide. The buyer looked up from the pelt, at Floyd.

"Did you do this?"

"I did."

"Where'd you learn to skin like this?"

"My pa taught me. I grew up trapping and hunting."

"Where?"

"Tennessee."

Sublette nodded. "How would you grade this pelt?"

"Top grade, scraped thoroughly, with no cuts."

"You've graded fur before?"

"Yes. I worked for Hugh Brennan in Santa Fe."

"You're that Floyd Logan?"

Floyd nodded. "I reckon I am. Mr. Brennan is a good man."

Sublette nodded in agreement. "He is." He stuck out his hand. "Glad to see you again.

"Come on in, boys, and get your money." He turned to three men who had come from the tent, and said, "Move those into the storage tent." With his last statement, he strode into the tent. Floyd and his two friends followed.

"So what's the total?" Shorty asked, leaning on the makeshift counter, a wagon tailgate laid across two barrels standing on end.

"For you boys, at six dollars a pound, and you have three hundred pounds, that comes to a total of eighteen hundred dollars. You splitting it even?"

"Yessiree," both men said together.

"Fine." He counted out two stacks of nine hundred dollars on the wagon tailgate.

Shorty and Morg picked up their money, and Morg said, "Let's go buy supplies." He took his eyes off the money and looked at Floyd. "You coming?"

"I'll be along, boys. You go ahead. I might be leaving fairly soon."

The two nodded and walked out with money stuffed in their coat pockets, Shorty telling Morg what he should do with it.

"Tell me again how many you have," Sublette said to Floyd.

"Twenty-two, but two of them are younguns."

"We'll just call that twenty-four at six dollars apiece. That'll be one hundred and thirty-two dollars."

"No, sir," Floyd said. "I know those two small ones are worth only three dollars each, at the most. I'll take one hundred and twenty-six dollars and be happy to get it."

Sublette smiled at Floyd. "Sometimes it's hard to deal with an honest man." He counted out the money.

Once Floyd had put it in his coat pocket, he said, "Have you seen three Blackfoot braves come into camp with a Shoshone woman and her boy?"

Sublette frowned and said, "Haven't seen 'em, but heard about them. I hope you don't have any thoughts of trouble with the Blackfoot. They're touchy enough, and rendezvous is neutral ground, as far as the Indians are concerned. I don't want anything started here."

Floyd gave the experienced mountain man a stern look. "If they're here, I'll leave with Leotie and Mika. Peaceable or not is up to them."

William Sublette straightened from looking at the furs on the table, his face hard. "Logan, I've heard about you. I know you for a good man, or Hugh Brennan wouldn't have hired you, and Jeb Campbell wouldn't have trapped with you. So why don't you tell me why you are tracking these Blackfoot warriors and this Shoshone woman."

"Woman and boy. Their names are Leotie and Mika. They were taken when the Blackfoot slipped into the Shoshone camp and made off with the tribe's horses."

"From the looks of you, they must have gotten the horses back."

"Yep. Killed all the Blackfoot who were with the horses."

Sublette contemplated the statement for a moment, then said, "Sounds like that's quite a story."

Floyd nodded. "Quite a story. Do you know what happened to Leotie and Mika?"

"I don't. All I heard was they rode into the Blackfoot camp. They might still be there, but if you go riding in, you could start a war. We've got Shoshone here too. It'll be an all-out battle, and I told you, I don't want that to happen."

Floyd took a deep breath, tamping down his quick temper and remembering his lessons with his mentor in Santa Fe. "Mr. Sublette, this woman and her son are important to the Shoshone village that saved my life. In fact, she helped nurse me back to good health. They want them back, and I owe her. If I find her with the Blackfoot, I'll try to buy her back, but if they won't sell her..."

The statement hung in the air, like a fuse to a keg of black powder.

Sublette's frown deepened. "Floyd, you have a right to want her returned to her family, but it's got to be done right. How about I assist? It's worth keeping peace in this camp if we could get them back peaceably. In fact, it is worth it to the St. Louis Fur Company. Let me go alone, and I'll see what I can do."

Floyd thought about it for a moment. "Reckon it's my job to get her back. I'll not be asking you to step in."

Sublette shook his head. "It's not for you, it's for every fur company in this valley. If we can keep the peace, we'll all profit. Let me try first. If I'm unable to secure her and her son's release, then I'll support you in whatever you decide to do."

Floyd extended his hand across the table to Sublette. "Much obliged. I'll wait here for their response."

Sublette gave a short nod, turned to one of his men, and said, "Get several hatchets, knives, and trade beads, plus four or five blankets. Load 'em up, and come with me."

Without a word, the man grabbed tow sacks and loaded the knives and hatchets in one and the blankets and beads in the other. Sublette reached out for the sack with the hatchets and said, "Let's go." He turned to Floyd. "Wait here. We'll be back shortly."

Floyd watched the man stride out of the tent and swing up on his gelding dun, careful of the edges in the sack. The man with him mounted, and they rode off with the gifts.

Floyd went back in and looked over the furs in the tent. The rendezvous had been going on for several days, and there were stacks of beaver pelts along the walls of the tent. There was also an assortment of other furs, including mink, marten, bobcat, badger, and muskrat. Off to one side were several grizzly hides.

Trading fur could be a moneymaking proposition, he thought. *But we're so far from the market, with no idea of the current prices, it's kinda chancy. A man can go from boom to bust pretty quick.*

He picked up a black marten hide. The hair was soft and luxuriant. They were pretty little animals, quick and curious. The feel of the fur carried him back to Tennessee. Part of his income, as a youth and then teenager, had come from trapping. He loved being out in the woods with the denizens of the forest. There was always something new to learn and see. Pa often spoke of how people could learn from the Indians. They had great respect for the animals they hunted and killed. Those animals provided food, warmth, and income. He was deep in thought, thinking about his pa, when the sound of horses' hooves pulled him back to the present.

He heard the men pull up outside Sublette's tents. The footsteps moved softly in the grass, and then Sublette was there.

"Well, Logan, they were here, but they pulled out yesterday."

"How many? Which way did they go? Are Leotie and Mika all right?"

10

Sublette held up his hand. "Now just wait. I'll answer all of your questions. When last seen, both were fine. The Blackfoot headed northwest, and it sounds like there were around twenty. I'm not positive, but it looks like they're headed back to their village, north of the Missouri River. That's a long ways and rough country. As I think you know, the Blackfoot can be mighty unfriendly."

"Thanks," Floyd said. He whipped around to exit the tent.

"Wait!" Sublette said.

Floyd turned back, his look questioning. "There's more?"

"There sure is. Leotie was sold to a trapper. The Indians kept the boy. He'll be with them up north. Likely, if he makes the trip all right, they'll adopt him. When they adopt a boy from another tribe, they treat him just like a son. He ought to be fine."

"First off, the boy's Shoshone, and I said I'd bring them both back, and I will. But what about the trapper? What's his name, and where is he?"

Sublette turned to a stack of fur sitting by itself. He pointed at it. "This is a stack of culls that I buy. They're not worth much, but I'll make a little from them. The trapper who bought Leotie contributed most of these. Either he was too drunk to skin and take care of them properly, or he just don't care. He's been in these mountains for several years and knows better."

He chucked a beaver pelt to Floyd, who didn't have to look long. He saw where the skin had been cut in several places, leaving, as it dried, gaping holes. Also there was enough meat remaining on the hide to have a meal.

Floyd tossed the damaged hide back to Sublette. "I get the point, he's sloppy and probably a drunk, but I need his name and where I can find him. This is a big valley."

"Man's name is Van McMillan. A big feller with a bad temper. He argued with me when I wouldn't give him full price for his fur. I offered him about one tenth of what it would've been if they'd been taken care of proper like."

Floyd thought for a moment, then nodded. "I remember him from when I was buying fur for Hugh Brennan. He brought in the same trash, and then he tried to bully me into paying him going rates."

Sublette watched Floyd closely. "Did you?"

Floyd grinned. "No, looking down the barrels of a 10 gauge changed his mind."

A smile flitted across Sublette's face. "Big-bore shotguns tend to have that effect on people no matter how tough they are. McMillan isn't tough. He's a blowhard looking to use his size to run folks over."

Sublette's brow wrinkled and his eyes tightened. "But his partners are all mean to the core, and they can back it up. Their names are Cleon Harris, Roscoe Bell, and Henry Page."

"I've met mean before."

"Understand, all four of these men are back-shooters. They won't give you a chance. If there's less than four of them standing in front of you, start looking around."

Floyd nodded. "Thanks, Mr. Sublette. You know where they're camped?"

"That's another thing. They pulled out right after they bought the girl. You can check farther up the Green about three miles. That's where they were camped. Someone around there will know exactly when they left."

Floyd started to turn toward the tent door again.

Sublette spoke up. "If you need any supplies before you leave, you can stock up at the tent next door."

"Thanks," Floyd said. He turned, stepped out, and moved quickly to the supply tent. He needed supplies, and though it pained him to wait, it would be a greater problem for him without sufficient supplies in the mountains. Plus, part of those supplies were powder, lead, and caps. Without those, he might find himself out of ammunition in the coming months. Jeb should be returning with supplies around the time he got back with Leotie and Mika, but he sure couldn't depend on that happening.

After stocking up with supplies and loading Browny, he moved to Rusty, checked all of his weapons, untied the reins, and stepped into the saddle. It was time, and he was ready. He should've killed McMillan back in Santa Fe. But he didn't, and now he'd probably have it to do.

Floyd stepped into the saddle, swung Rusty up the Green, and started north. Three miles, he'd cover that quickly. He clucked to the big roan, and the horse broke into a lope. The lead ropes tightened, bringing Buck and Browny along. Several men nodded and spoke as he passed. That was something else he liked, the camaraderie among the trappers. It was different out here, where your life might depend on a friend.

A horseman rode up next to him. He glanced over and saw it was Kajika. The Shoshone surprised him.

Floyd spoke to Kajika. "Leotie has been sold to trappers. I'm on my way to find them."

"I know. Uncle told me."

They both turned their heads forward and rode north. They were on a mission.

Reaching the area Sublette had described, they headed for a nearby tent. A mountain man, his wife, and three kids watched them approach. The sight brought to his mind last year and his first rendezvous. He had been surprised when he first saw such a group, and had communicated his feelings to Jeb.

Jeb had laughed. "They're just doing what comes natural, Floyd. There's plenty of trappers out here who brought their families with 'em. This way the wife and kids are close, and they're able to save money. Reckon it's no more dangerous for them than it was for the early pioneers back east. The French started it way back years ago. Course they was the first white trappers in this country."

Floyd stopped Rusty near the family and, after pulling up, said, "Howdy."

The man responded with a nod. "Sit and light a spell."

"Thanks, but I'm actually looking for some men. Mr. Sublette said that four trappers were camped around here." He looked around. Tents and camps were scattered up the Green.

"You talkin' about Cleon Harris and his bunch of no-goods?"

"That'd be them," Floyd said.

"They pulled stakes yesterday, and I'll tell you, I'm glad to see 'em go."

"Did they have an Indian girl with them?"

"They did, and she wasn't happy about it. Some Blackfoot came through with her and the boy. They stopped 'em and bought her." He shook his head. "A danged shame. She looked like a right nice Shoshone woman."

The man's wife spoke up. "She put up quite a fuss when they took her away from her son. She tried to stab one of those vermin. I think it was McMillan, him being the one who bought her, but he knocked her out with one of his big fists and then tied her up. My man was aimin' to do somethin' about it, but I stopped him. We need him, and if he goes and gets himself killed, what would we do?" She pulled the little girl closer to her. "It's hard enough out here when he's gone trapping, but if he was kilt..." She shook her head at the thought.

"Did either of you overhear where they might be headed?"

The man spoke up. "Me and the missus both heard 'em. Right after they got here, they was sittin' around their camp, drunker'n two sacks of skunks, and talkin' so loud I reckon anyone over them tall mountains could've heard 'em. Said they're headed not too far from here, along the Gros Ventre River 'bout where Crystal Creek runs in. Seemed to think they was gonna score a mint on beaver."

The man stopped for a moment and shook his head. "Beaver ain't what it used to be, and that part of the country's been pretty well trapped out. It'll take years for beaver to come back in there. I'd be surprised if the four of 'em will get much more'n a hundert pounds, if that much."

Floyd turned to Kajika. "You know that country?"

"I know."

Floyd touched his hat to the woman and, looking at the man, said, "Thank you. We'll be on our way."

He was turning Rusty when the man said, "You fellers be careful. That trash is mighty mean. Why, that Henry Page got into it with another trapper. Don't know what the fight was about, but Page pulled out his big toad stabber and ripped the other feller from beginning to end. Then he just went back to drinkin'."

"Much obliged," Floyd said as he again started to turn Rusty.

The man's wife spoke suddenly. "You ain't told him about the wolf."

Floyd pulled Rusty to a halt.

"Oh, yeah, the wolf. Seems this wolf, and there may be more'n one, come through camp almost two weeks ago. He come right down the valley, through all these camps, just like he owned this place. He attacked several folks. Bit 'em and all. I ain't never seen a healthy wolf come near a camp if'n he's alone."

Floyd looked over at Kajika, who was listening intently.

"So this here wolf come close by here. Lucky for us the kids were in the tent. He went on toward Cleon Harris and his bunch, who as usual were already drunk, stretched out on the grass. Fore they knew it, he'd bit two of 'em. I'm thinkin' it was Cleon Harris and Roscoe Bell." The man took his hat off and shook his head. "I think that there wolf was mad, you know, hydrophoby. If'n that be true, it could take a week or more to take effect. When it does, they'll go crazy, not be able to go near water, and they'll bite and scratch whoever gets close. Just a word to the wise, mister."

Floyd waited to see if the man had anything else to say. When it was obvious the trapper was finished, he nodded again and bumped Rusty in the flanks. "Thank you, folks." He raised his hand and rode north, Kajika by his side.

It took some time to pass through the rendezvous. They saw two other fur companies, the American Fur Company and the Rocky Mountain Fur Company. The rendezvous was nearing its end for this year, and from here on beaver pelt prices would be in a decline. The hat market, primarily in England and Europe, was switching to silk from beaver. It was less expensive and did not depend on seasons or trapping.

Difficult as it was for him to imagine that beaver prices would decline, he had heard other trappers and buyers, more knowledgeable than he, saying the heyday of the beaver was coming to an end. He also heard the beaver population was in decline. On the one hand, that was hard to believe, this country was so big, but on the other, in his short time here, he had seen streams become barren of the big industrious rodent. Often he would think, *I came out a few years too late.* But he was glad he was here now.

Finally, passing out of the rendezvous, Kajika pointed northwest, away from the Green River, and toward a saddle in the foothills of the mountains. "We no have far to go. Their camp only two, maybe three day, if they on the Clear Creek." He stopped speaking in English and switched to Shoshone. "What are your plans?"

Floyd answered in Kajika's language. "Simple. I plan on rescuing Leotie, and if any harm has come to her, I plan on killing the men."

"You're going to have to kill them. Otherwise, they will pursue you and shoot you when you are unknowing. I found out about them in the meeting with my family. They are men with no character. They lie and cheat. They are not men who can be trusted."

"Yes," Floyd said, "I have met one of them. The one who bought Leotie. I should have killed him when I had the opportunity, but I didn't." He thought back to the time he had met McMillan.

It had been in Santa Fe when he was working for Hugh Brennan. He had been left in charge of the fur house while Hugh had been out running errands. McMillan and his partner had come in with a load of furs. The man's partner's furs rated top dollar, but McMillan showed his disdain for doing a job correctly. The hides were heavily damaged from his careless skinning methods. The worst part was he had tried to slip in several rotten furs, and when he was called on it, McMillan had threatened him and had even started around the counter to get to him.

Hugh kept a 10-gauge double-barreled shotgun under the counter for just such circumstances. When the man passed the end of the counter and started toward Floyd, he pulled the shotgun. Staring at the business end of a 10-gauge shotgun caused McMillan to have a sudden change of heart. The man turned and left, muttering threats. His partner warned him to be careful. He said McMillan held a grudge and was dangerous, especially when a man's back was turned.

Floyd had wondered at the time, as threatening as the man was, should he have shot him because of the altercation? At the time he felt he had done right, allowing the man to live. Although Hugh told him, when he returned to the office, he would have dropped McMillan without a second thought. Now, as Floyd thought back on it, he wished he had. *Maybe,* he thought, *if I had killed him then, we wouldn't be dealing with this now. Is Leotie better off with McMillan than the Blackfoot warriors?* He didn't think so, especially with two of them bitten by a rabid wolf.

They reached the saddle and rode through. Kajika pointed to the ground. Sure enough, there were the tracks of the four men, their captive, and their packhorses. The tracks were old, but at least the trappers were headed in the direction they had talked about.

Still speaking Shoshone, Kajika glanced at the sun drifting lower in the west, and said, "Another ten miles, there is a good place to stop."

"We have a good idea where they're going, and you know the place. Maybe we should ride on. No telling what they are doing to Leotie."

"We will stop, Igasho. This is rough country. The horses need rest, feed, and water. Our rushing on will not change her fate. She is a strong woman. Unless they kill her, she will survive. She would want us to be patient and sure of our success."

Floyd knew his friend was right. He nodded, turned to look at their back trail, and saw dust rising, coming closer. "We've got a couple of fellows coming up fast on our trail. Why don't we wait here and find out what they want." He checked his weapons, just in case, and the two men waited.

Before long, they were able to make out the riders. It was Shorty and Morg. Soon, out of breath, the two riders pulled up.

Shorty grinned at Floyd. "You and Kajika, here, planning on making this party all your own?"

Floyd laughed and looked at Morg. "I just figured you boys would be pretty busy for a while in the saloons. Morg looked like he had worked up a mighty thirst."

"I did, and this here runt drug me out after two swallows. Doesn't leave me in a very good humor."

"Don't listen to him," Shorty said. "He's the one what heard you two were leavin', and rushed me to chase after you."

"Well," Morg said, a faint grin on his face, "I figgered you two might need the help of a real man."

Shorty nodded. "Yep, he did. That's the reason he brung me along."

Floyd shook his head. "I'm obliged to both of you for coming along. Let's ride, and I'll tell you what I've found out."

The four men, still heading northwest, picked up Muddy Creek, riding along it through Coyote Gulch. Once past the gulch, and as they turned northeast through the pine trees, Kajika led them over a low ridge to a grassy area near the creek.

Speaking English again, Kajika said, "Here is good. Out of sight from trail. We camp. Only small fire." He swung down from his mount.

"Looks good to me," Shorty said. "I'm needin' me some coffee."

Floyd pulled up Rusty and stepped to the ground. He looked the area over. There was good grass near the water. "Why don't we stake the horses out on the grass near the water. That'll allow them to eat and drink any time they like."

"Good," Kajika said.

Shorty stayed behind to get the fire and coffee going while the other three men unloaded their animals, brushed them down, and led them to water. It had been a while since they'd had a drink, and they were all thirsty.

After the horses and mules were watered and staked on the rich grass, the men walked back to the fire. Shorty had the water boiling for the coffee. Floyd walked over to one of his packs and pulled out a slab of bacon. He cut it in half, repacked one half, and tossed the remaining half to Shorty. "This'll make that jerky we have a little more tasty." Morg and Shorty looked at each other. Then Morg walked to their packs, opened one, reached in, and lifted a big slab of buffalo hump. When he brought it back, Shorty was sharing the story.

"These fellers, back at camp, killed a buffler. They was runnin' short of drinkin' money, and we sorely wanted some tasty hump. They gave us this"—he held the buffalo hump up—"and we bought 'em a bottle of john barleycorn. From the looks of that whiskey, I'm thinkin' we were the winners in that trade."

He started cutting steaks. "While I'm gettin' this cookin', why don't you fellers tell us about who we're chasing, and why."

Floyd and Kajika filled the other two trappers in about Leotie and her captors, describing MacMillan slugging her, and also about Cleon and Roscoe being bitten by the rabid wolf.

Morg shook his head, and his body shuddered. "When I was a youngster and my uncle had beat me, for whatever reason, he would make me sleep on the porch, and just before he'd go back in the house, he would tell me to watch for mad skunks. Every night he did that, I never went to sleep." Morg shuddered again. "I've been deathly scared of hydrophoby my whole life. I wouldn't wish that on even the baddest man."

"Nor I," Floyd said, "but I wanted you two aware that there are two men in that camp who could be coming down with it anytime. So don't take any chances."

11

The steaks were ready. Bacon had been cooked first, and the men had their share of bacon while waiting for the steaks. Shorty cooked them in the big skillet, leaving the bacon grease in the pan.

Though they'd had the bacon to ward off hunger, Floyd's mouth was watering at the smell of the meat. Each man had a plate except for Kajika, and Floyd gave him one from his pack. Now they began to fill their plates with meat. Juices leaked from the steak onto Floyd's plate as he easily sliced through the meat with the razor-sharp knife given to him by his brother Nathan. He stabbed a slice from his plate. The buffalo meat was hot, tender, and delicious buffalo with the salty taste of bacon. He glanced at Kajika. His Shoshone friend gave a sharp nod while chewing a large slice he had just shoved into his mouth.

Silence reigned as the mountain men ate. Floyd finished first. He looked over at Shorty. "That was mighty good, my friend. Where'd you learn to cook like that?"

Morg groaned. "Oh no, Floyd. Haven't you known Shorty long enough to know you never ask him a question that can't be answered with nothin' more than a yes or no? We'll be sittin' here all night listening to him fill our heads with how he was taught by some French chef—"

"Now there ain't no reason for you to be so ornery," Shorty cut in.

Morg rolled his eyes, and Shorty continued. "What he's tellin' you is right, about the French chef. When I was back in St. Louis . . ." Shorty began.

Fifteen minutes later, and with Shorty showing no indication of stopping, Kajika rose and said he had to check the horses. The sun had disappeared much earlier, and now, before the moonrise, it was almost pitch black. The animals had moved as close to the fire as their ropes would allow, and, though close, in the thick darkness were only visible as shadows. The young Shoshone stood and, without another word, stalked off to the horses. He took his time and moved the stock closer. They'd water them again in the morning before leaving. His timing was suspect to Floyd, since he finished with the horses and returned to camp about the time Shorty ended his story.

Floyd quickly said, before Shorty could get started again, "Well, boys, I'm thinking we've got a long day ahead of us. So we'd best get ourselves in bed. The morning's coming quick. I'll take the first watch, and, Shorty, if you'll take the second, Morg the third, and Kajika last, that should take care of it."

There were affirmative replies from everyone, and Floyd went to his pack, dropped the clean plate in, and walked back to his saddle and bedding. He had laid out additional weapons so they would be ready. Now he flipped out his bedding so that it would be ready when he finished his watch, and eased out into the forest.

∽

BEFORE DAYLIGHT, Floyd awoke, listened, and, hearing only the sounds of the forest, arose. He picked up a rifle and softly walked around the camp, nodding at Kajika when he reached the Shoshone's hiding spot. He continued moving, checking his horses, then his gear. The morning was cold, near freezing. Summer in these northern mountains was different than down in Santa Fe. July in the city would be warm during the day, sometimes even hot. *Winter up here,* he thought, *must really be a bear. If it's this cold in July, I don't even want to think what January will be like.*

He had slept long and well. Though they were quiet, he awoke with the changing guard each time. He would listen for a moment, then immediately fall back to sleep. He stopped at the fire, picked up the coffee pot, took it to the stream, well above the animals, and filled it. After raking up the remaining coals, he set the pot on them. Then he went back to his mounts.

Pulling fresh grass, he wiped the light dew from the horses' backs. After saddling Buck, he slipped the bridle on and let the reins fall, ground hitching the animal. He was confident, with the grass, water, and company, neither his horses nor mule would wander off. By the time he had returned from his animals, the camp was alive. Shorty and Morg were already at it. He ignored their argument, intent on not becoming involved.

While he was working, the other men had been busy. When he was done, everyone else was also ready. Shorty had finished brewing the coffee, after tossing a handful of cold water into the pot to settle the grounds. Each man was chewing on jerky as they stood and sipped their coffee. No time was wasted.

The coffee pot was emptied over the sizzling coals and packed. The four friends, all business now, settled in the saddle for a long day. Kajika led off, followed by Floyd, then Morg, and finally Shorty.

They rode alongside Muddy Creek until it joined the Hoback River, then followed the Hoback west. The day was passing quickly, but the men pushed on. They rode close to the high bluffs on the north side. Eyes wide and minds alert to the slightest movement or sound, heads swiveled constantly, watching for any sign of hostiles. Kajika turned them north, through a saddle, with a ridge to the west that blocked their view of the Snake River, as they paralleled it.

Kajika dropped back alongside Floyd. Their travel had been slower than expected, for they halted many times before riding into open areas so they could scan each bush and tree, looking always for hostiles. Softly, almost in a whisper, Kajika said, "No reach their camp today. Tomorrow, yes. Today, no."

Floyd nodded. He knew there was no sense in rushing. If he pushed them, he could be responsible for all of them dying. "We'll make it a cold camp tonight."

"Good. No fire."

Floyd dropped back to tell Shorty, followed by Shorty informing Morg. All faces were alert and solemn. This was dangerous country, and they were on a deadly mission.

~

A GENTLE KICK on Floyd's foot awakened him. It was Shorty. His finger was to his lips, and then he motioned to the trees where the horses were staked. Floyd slid his two pistols into their holsters and picked up a rifle, leaving one on the ground next to where he had been sleeping.

Once standing, he saw Kajika, knife ready, watching the line of trees. Morg leaned close to Floyd's ear, and though so close, his words were barely audible. "Injuns slipping around. Don't know how many, but at least five or six, maybe more. Heard 'em coming up from the creek."

Floyd nodded and, just as softly, said, "Probably after the horses. We'll try not to kill any if we don't have to, but we can't afford to lose those animals."

Morg nodded, and the four men disappeared into the forest.

Thick, Floyd thought. *Good protection, but also hard for us to move around quietly.*

The thought had only momentarily formed when he felt, more than saw, a shadow leap at him from beside a dark pine. Floyd caught the glint of a blade in the faint moonlight. He swung his rifle up and to his right, firing point-blank. At the blast, the night was rent with yells and screams. Several weapons fired.

It sounded as if the attacking Indians were all around them. Dropping his rifle, he whipped out two pistols. Concerned for his companions, he tried to look around, but another brave charged him. Floyd's shot struck the man in the forehead above his left eye. Collapsing, his momentum carried him into Floyd. Trying to push the man away, from the corner of his eyes he saw Morg draw his pistol and fire. Flame leaped from the barrel, lighting the faltering Indian's charge.

Floyd didn't see either Shorty or Kajika, but he still had problems of his own. Another Indian leaped from the shadowy pines. As he brought his remaining pistol up, his head exploded to complete darkness.

∽

FLOYD AWOKE with the worst headache he could ever remember. It wasn't helped much by his position. His hands and legs had been tied, and he was riding horseback, belly down, with his arms hanging on one side and his legs on the other. To make matters worse, ropes had been tied around his biceps and his legs, under the horse's belly, and pulled so tight he didn't know whether his hips or his knees would pop out of joint first. He had no idea how long he'd been like this, but the pain in his legs and back competed with the pain from his head.

His face was turned forward, pulled tight against the horse's side. From this awkward and painful position, he didn't recognize the animal. Finally, his need to know overcame his pain, and he tried to move his head. Looking forward, there were two braves riding in front of him, and none of his friends were in sight. He had to know if they were captured or dead. To look behind him, he had to lift his head, pulling it back away from the horse's body. The first slight movement to hoist and turn his head brought a lightning stab of pain to the back of his head and neck. It was all he could do to keep from gasping. He relaxed his body against the big horse's side and took a couple of deep breaths. The stabbing pain gradually subsided, and he was left with a terrible headache and the pain in his extremities.

After lying still for several minutes more, as the horses climbed through the timbered mountains, jerking him with each step, he took another deep breath and tried again. Slowly he was able to lift his head high enough to get it turned around. When he did, he was staring into a pair of jet-black eyes. They were the hardest and most unforgiving eyes he had ever looked into. It was all he could do to keep from looking away, but he held the stare for a few moments. Then he relaxed his head against the horse.

The Indian called something to one of the braves ahead of him, and they pulled up. He heard someone walking up to the horse and stopping on the opposite side. He could feel pulling as the man must be untying him. *Don't drop me on my head,* Floyd thought. *As bad as my neck hurts, I don't know if I can ta—*

He felt the tension of the rope between his arms and legs release, and his feet were thrown over the back of the horse. He dropped straight to the ground, striking on the top of his head. He tried to tighten his neck before he slammed into the hard ground, but had no idea if it did any good. All one hundred and eighty pounds concentrated on his already painful neck. His mind shouted through the pain, *You can't cry out! Don't utter a sound.*

Previously, he had thought his head and neck were hurting, but now the pain more than doubled.

The Indians were moving past him, to a horse behind him. In

a moment, he heard someone or something heavy also crash to the ground. Floyd waited, hoping against hope he wouldn't hear another similar crash. No other falling body was heard. There was the sound of a moccasined foot slamming into flesh and a sudden burst of air. Indians laughed, and again, behind him, a foot struck flesh, followed by a grunt.

The pain in Floyd's neck was subsiding, giving way to the horrible burning in his back and legs. He tried to move, to see what was happening, and searing bolts of pain shot up both legs and into his back, but he continued to push through the pain. He managed to turn over on his side, and could see the Indians standing around Morg. They were laughing and pointing at his friend, as the man tried to regain his breath. One had an arrow in his hand and was poking Morg with the point. There was blood soaking through his shirt where the Blackfoot had stabbed him.

Floyd had moved, and figured out the pain he was experiencing wasn't going to kill him. He rolled on his stomach and pulled his legs under him. Finally, gathering all of his strength, he pushed up with his arms and legs, slowly regaining his feet. When he made it fully erect, he looked at the group of Indians, who were all now staring at him.

The biggest one said something and, leaving the group, strode over to Floyd. Arriving in front of him, the man said something. Floyd stood facing the Indian. His icy blue eyes were locked on the Indian, and a sardonic grin rested on his face.

The big Indian, his brow wrinkled in a frown, said something to Floyd.

Floyd stood silent, waiting for the blow or shot or arrow that was bound to come.

This time, the Indian almost growled his words at Floyd. When he received no response, the man slapped Floyd across the left side of his face so hard he almost lost his balance, which wasn't surprising, since his legs were still tied together just above his knees. He shuffled to his right, steadied himself, and with a cold, threatening gaze, stared at the man.

One of the men standing over Morg called something and laughed. The others joined in. Above his enemy's vermillion-colored war paint, Floyd could see the brown man flush in anger. This time he slapped Floyd with enough force, with Floyd's legs tied, to knock him to the ground.

Calm yourself, Floyd thought. *Don't let him goad you. That's just what he wants.* He took several deep breaths, then rolled onto his face, pulled his legs up, and stood. His back was straight, and he stood tall. His mind was on Leotie, hoping that Kajika and Shorty would go on with their mission.

The brave in front of him lifted the arrow and shoved the point against Floyd's chest, right at his breastbone. The Indian increased the pressure, probably assuming the mountain man would back up, trip, and fall again. Floyd stood still, even leaning into the arrow slightly to maintain his balance. He felt the point pierce his flesh, and maintained his expression. The Indian increased pressure. Floyd leaned in harder.

Now he had another point of pain to take his mind off his head and legs. This one stung, with an insistent burning, growing worse as it slowly penetrated his flesh, yet he would not move. He locked his eyes on the heartless eyes of the Blackfoot and leaned harder.

The point made its way to the breastbone. If it slipped in either direction, it would find his heart or lungs. Floyd would not give up. He leaned in harder. Then he saw the flicker in the man's eyes. Maybe, just a hint of admiration.

The Indian yanked the arrow from Floyd's chest, wiped the blood on the mountain man's shirt, and gently poked him in the belly. "What name you go by?"

Floyd kept the surprise from his face, at the man speaking English, and said, "The Shoshone call me Igasho, and the Comancia call me Pawnee Killer."

Floyd saw no surprise on the face of the Blackfoot.

"No. What you English name?"

"Floyd."

"Flo-yd." The enemy watched Floyd for a moment longer, said, "Humph," and spun around. He walked back to the other members of the scalping party.

Floyd looked around. It looked like there were no more than six warriors. That meant there had been at least nine at the beginning of the raid, and probably a more accurate number was ten or twelve. He wished he could talk to Morg. He needed to know what had happened to Shorty and Kajika.

The Indians talked for a few more minutes, then the man who had been poking Floyd threw a rope around his neck, and one of the other Indians did likewise with Morg. After releasing the ropes around their thighs, a younger man was given both ropes. He mounted and waited until the others had passed him. Then he kicked his horse into a trot, jerking both Floyd and Morg. They had seen what was coming and were ready. Both began running to keep the slack in the rope. The two men had little chance if they were dragged with the rope around their necks. All it would take was a fall, and they would either die from strangulation or a broken neck.

The Indians seemed to care not at all and kept up the pace for a half mile, twisting around the tall pines and jumping the horses over brush.

Floyd and Morg kept their feet through the worst of the ordeal. Once the Blackfoot slowed, they could keep up with a slow trot. Both young men were in superb physical condition. After another mile, their bodies had settled down from the run. Now only in a walk and occasionally a jog, they were able to talk in low tones.

Floyd asked, "Do you know what happened to Shorty and Kajika? I think I got knocked on the head with something, and the next thing I knew, I woke up tied on a horse."

Morg, keeping his eyes on the ground ahead, said, "They got away, and from the looks of it, took the animals and our supplies with them. I kinda got mixed up in a tussle. Five of 'em piled on me and tied me up."

Every few minutes, the young brave with the ropes would turn around and jerk either one or both. The men had to be ready to maintain slack. If they didn't, they would choke and gag for a few minutes, working diligently to maintain their footing. This treatment continued through most of the day.

Late in the afternoon, they pulled up at a stream to drink. The Indian with the rope kept them away from water until the last minute, allowing them insufficient time to quench their thirst. Moments after their lips touched the water, they were jerked erect with the ropes, and the group continued north.

"Morg," Floyd whispered, "if we let them get us in their village, we're dead men, and it ain't gonna be pleasant."

Morg, continuing to watch the trail, said, "Whatcha got in mind?"

12

"They made a mistake leaving our hands tied in front," Floyd said. "Maybe they didn't think we'd try anything alone in unfamiliar country, but when we get an opening, we yank real hard. It might pull that mean little devil off his horse, but for sure, it'll jerk the ropes out of his hands. When that happens, we get outta here like a rabbit chased by a coyote."

Despite their situation, Morg grinned. "Or a white man chased by a Blackfoot."

Floyd grinned back, his lips cracked and bleeding. "You're right about that. We've already crossed a couple of talus slopes. I figure there'll be more. When we hit the next one, no matter how bad it looks, we yank the rope and head down those rocks as fast as we can go. We might slide off an edge or get crushed to death, but that beats what's about to happen to us."

The young Indian with the rope turned around and glared at them, shouting something. Once satisfied, he turned back to the trail. The big Indian in the lead spoke, and the others laughed. At the laughter, the boy yanked their ropes in hopes of surprising them, but they maintained enough slack to keep from being jerked off their feet.

The sun had disappeared behind the craggy peaks above them when they rode, single file, toward the next talus slope. Shadows stretched down the side of the mountain, and the loose rocks of the scree disappeared into the shadows. Floyd looked at Morg and nodded. Slowly, they both started taking up slack in their rope.

Each of the Indians ahead carefully guided their mounts along the narrow trail through the talus field. At the entrance and exit of the trail through the talus, the mountain fell precipitously into cavernous darkness. Far below could be heard the rushing and crashing of fast water.

None of this is good, Floyd thought, *but it sure beats getting roasted like a pig or skinned alive.*

Finally the boy holding their ropes entered the field. The two mountain men waited until they were about halfway across, hopefully ensuring they would not slide across the talus into the steep slopes on either side. Floyd looked at Morg and nodded. He could see Morg mouth, "Good luck."

With the slack almost completely out of their ropes, they stretched long, powerful arms as far up the ropes as they could, and simultaneously yanked with all of their might. The ropes jerked from the young fellow's hands, but not before he was yanked from his horse. Floyd and Morg leaped straight down the talus slope, running as fast as their legs would carry them. The rocks began moving with them immediately, but their muscular legs drove them down the mountain.

Shouts rose behind them, but the Blackfoot were in a predicament. They couldn't chase them through the talus, or they might slide off the cliff at the end of the slope, killing them and their horses.

Arrows flew past Floyd as Morg, with his long legs, outdistanced him. Two blasts from trade rifles were fired, but by then they were sliding out of sight into the shadows. And they were accelerating. Speed increased with each step among the sliding, rolling rocks. Floyd realized he was totally out of control.

Shortly after starting down the mountain, they had the presence of mind to get the ropes from their necks and hang on to them. The ropes followed each man like a serpent chasing him into the unknown. Floyd realized the drag of the rope against the rocks actually provided him with a bit of additional stability.

He needed it, for it was a constant fight to keep his balance. His body was trying to outdistance his feet, but the rope helped hold him back. As he ran, he began to pull the rope in, carefully looping it in his left hand.

The slope grew steeper, making it impossible to slow, and the loose rocks, which were flying past him, didn't help. In the gray shadows, he tried to divide his attention between Morg, his footing, and recovering the rope. Morg was at least thirty yards in front of him and pulling away. Floyd's foot slipped deeper into the sliding rocks. He snapped his head down to watch his near out-of-control feet. His arms flailed wildly and brought him back to a semblance of balance as he continued to fly downward. Finally tearing his eyes from the ground in front of his racing feet, he looked up for his friend.

Morg was gone.

His heart leaped. *Where's Morg?* The next thought was, *A cliff!*

He had to stop. But he couldn't. Even if he stood still, the rocks beneath him and to his left and right were traveling as fast as he was. With vivid realization, he knew he was about to go over a cliff. It had been a chancy gamble. This still would be better than dying an ignoble death in the Blackfoot village.

The rushing sound of the scree going over the cliff raced toward him. A long wail from Morg falling into the darkness chilled his soul. His left foot drove down—into space. It was like he shot out in a waterfall of rock. Sailing into the darkness, he turned over and over, plummeting to oblivion.

He seemed to fall forever, waiting for that final, crushing blow as he slammed into the rocks below. And then his mind was quiet. *At least I'll die in the land I love.*

Floyd slammed into icy cold water, his left shoulder striking first. The shock caused him to take a breath, and he drew in a mouthful of water before he could stop himself. Choking now, he plunged deeper and deeper. There was no light. Only darkness. No down. No up. Hands still tied, he fought to reach the top, but where was it? Was it below him, or above, or maybe to his left, his right? He needed his hands free, but most of all, he needed air.

There was no sense fighting. He relaxed and went with the flow of the racing water. Moments seemed to take hours to pass. He was trying to hold his breath while simultaneously choking with the water he had swallowed. His brain had his blue eyes wide open, commanding them to see, but there was only blackness. Suddenly, his upper back smashed into a huge boulder, and he felt the pain race to his right hand and fingers. He needed air. *Breathe, breathe,* his mind screamed. He could feel his consciousness fading, and knew the instant he passed out he would inhale.

Suddenly, the roiling ended. He shot out into nothingness, falling again, but he could breathe. He coughed, hacked, and managed to get in one good breath before his body crashed again into the river. But this time was different. He knew what to do, and he had air. For a moment, he felt himself being shoved farther down, and instead of fighting, he went with it, angling to what he hoped was one side of the powerful flow from the waterfall. When he felt himself slip from the power of the rushing water, he stopped fighting. Though he was still racing down the river, he quickly popped to the surface.

There was a faint light from the stars, and he could make out white water and the banks. He started kicking toward the farthest bank, away from the Blackfoot braves, and was amazed. The coiled rope was still in his grip. He flexed his tied wrists, palm against palm, and noticed a little slack in the rope. The water had provided some stretch to the rope. He pushed again while gasping a deep breath, then his head went under. His big hands were helpful in so many ways, but now he would give just about anything to have small hands. Once more he flexed and felt the rope loosen more. Twisting in the current, he managed to get his head above water for another life giving breath, then his head was down again. He worked his wrists, twisting, pulling, and his left slipped out of the grasp of rope. Immediately, he thrust to the surface for another breath.

The sound that had battered his ears from the roar of the waterfall had decreased. His speed took him quickly away until he could hear the roar of water farther downriver. With no knowledge of this river, his only chance was to get to the bank. Swimming with the current, and the use of his hands, he was able to slip past a large boulder and kick toward the bank, when suddenly a long shadow presented itself just in front of him.

He thrust out a hand and grabbed, clamping a short limb extending from a log, half in and half out of the water. The current whipped him around the end of the log, almost jerking his hand free of the limb. Using the coil of rope, he tossed it over a branch while kicking furiously. Straining his shoulder muscles, he pulled himself up the log until he could reach past the rope and grab another limb. He pulled himself along the fallen tree and toward the bank, though the current tried to pull his body beneath the tree. At last, he felt the current weakening, and moments later his feet touched river bottom.

Floyd stood and staggered toward shore. Once there he collapsed. He lay for a moment, his body shaking from exhaustion and his near brush with death. It felt like every muscle was revolting. The convulsing of his body lasted several minutes until, finally, the shaking began to subside, but the cold began creeping in.

It was really cold. *In these high mountains,* he thought, *and this far north, if I don't find shelter soon or get moving, I'll freeze to death.*

He lay there for a moment longer, then drew up his legs and

stood. For the first time since yanking the rope, he was able to celebrate. *I'm free!* He enjoyed the moment. Then he sobered and looked around. Where was Morg? Had he made it out? If he did, did he come out above or below Floyd's location? And on which side of the river?

Those were questions he needed to answer, but the most important was warmth. Fortunately there was little wind. He had to get out of these wet clothes. It was indeed fortunate he had bought several wool shirts and trousers at the rendezvous. The great thing about wool was that even when it was wet, it still kept you warm.

Buckskin kept the wind out, but was hot in the summer and cold in the winter. He stripped his buckskin jacket, leaving his wool shirt and trousers on over his wool long johns. He also was wearing wool socks inside his calf-length moccasins. They too were made with deerskin. As bad as he wanted to leave them on to protect his feet and new socks, he dropped to a log and pulled them off. His only hope of warming quickly was to get moving, but which direction? He was in a deep canyon. The trees and walls of the canyon allowed little view of the sky.

Floyd knew where their camp had been. The Snake River ran in a wide valley running roughly north and south. The question that plagued him was whether or not, while he was out, his Blackfoot captors had crossed the Snake. If they had, then he was in the Teton Range, but he had to be truthful with himself. He had no idea which direction, or how far they had gone while he was out. What about Leotie? Was he closer to her or farther away? Was it possible the trappers who held her might have heard the echo of the gunfire? If so, had they moved on?

Jeb had been all over this country. If he were here...

Floyd lunged behind a tree and faced upstream. He had caught movement. In the dark, it was only a shadow that flitted between trees, but it attracted his eye and created concern. His hand reached for his nonexistent pistol and stopped. *A weapon would really be nice,* he thought, glancing around. Nothing was near on the forest floor, only dried pine needles. *I should have found one when I first came out of the river,* he thought, slowly squatting to scoop a handful of pine needles. If whatever he saw was an enemy, he could at least distract them by throwing the debris in their face.

Nothing moved.

The moon had made it high enough where its faint light reached into the canyon, bringing light on the river and, beneath the tall trees, to parts of the forest floor. His head moved to the side of the tree, just far enough to expose his right eye.

A rock crashed into the pine bark only inches from his face, splinters and dirt flying into his eye. But before it hit, in the moonlight, he saw the owner of the shadow that had attracted his attention. An apparition charged him, and he'd know that height and long-legged run anywhere.

In a low voice, he said, while rubbing his eye to get the debris out, "Morg! What are you trying to do, blind me?"

The tall man slid to a stop by the tree. "I sure didn't want you shootin' me with an arrow afore I got to you if you was an Injun." He chuckled low and said, "I thought it might be you, but couldn't take a chance. If I'd knowed it was an Injun, I'd a beaned him with that rock, not knocked a little dust in his eye."

Still blinking, Floyd looked up at the man, extending his hand. "Rock or no, I'm sure glad to see you. I didn't know if you were dead or injured somewhere above or below me."

Morg grinned at him. "Me too. I'm glad you're here and not Shorty. He'd a got out on the opposite shore just to be ornery."

Floyd chuckled and shook his head. "We'd best get moving fore we freeze to death." His body had begun to shake from the cold.

Morg nodded. "A little food would help."

"What are you planning on killing it with, or skinning it, if you killed something?"

Morg shoved the remaining portion of a skinned and dressed rabbit in his face.

Floyd, surprised, stared at Morg and then looked at the rabbit again. "How'd you kill this?"

"Don't ask questions. Eat it. I already had the other half. As you just seen, I'm danged good with a rock. This little feller was near the water where I come out, and made the mistake of just sittin' instead of running. I eased up a rock and chunked him in the head. Never knew what hit him."

Floyd shook his head, pulled a leg from the carcass, and ripped off a mouthful of raw rabbit. He preferred his meat cooked, but it tasted mighty good. This was the first food he'd gotten since dinner last evening.

He cleaned the meat from the leg bone and, around his chewing, said, "We need to get moving. Distance from those Blackfoot is the only thing that'll save us." He stepped, stopped, and turned to Morg. "Do you know this country? I'm assuming we go downstream."

Morg swung his arm, pointing downstream. "That's the only way to git outta this here canyon unless you follow it up the mountain. I reckon if we do that, we'll be walking right into them heathens." He looked at the rope in Floyd's hand. "You held on to that?"

Floyd almost laughed at the incredulous tone of his friend's question. "Reckon I was too scared to let go."

"Didn't have much problem turnin' mine loose when I went over that ledge. Figgered I had an appointment with Saint Peter, and no amount of rope would help."

Floyd chuckled, and they started downriver, both men shaking until their bodies started warming. Floyd finished the rabbit, chewing every tiny sliver of meat from its body and head. He stopped and, with his heel, began to dig a hole in the soft loam.

"What you doing?"

"I'm burying the carcass. The Indians may find it, but it won't just be lying out for them to easily spot."

Morg stuck out his hand. "Gimme." After he had been given the carcass, he looked around, found a flat rock, and with another rock, cracked the animal's skull. He carefully picked the shattered bones away, put the now open skull to his mouth, and sucked. After chewing, he turned to Floyd. "Brains is good for you. Gives you energy." Then, with a stick, he popped the eyes out, slipping them into his mouth. After he had finished off both, he said, "My aunt always said, 'Waste not, want not.'" He knelt and quickly buried the rabbit's cleaned bones.

The two men started off at a trot. The scattered moonlight on the forest floor gave them just enough light to make their way swiftly and safely.

Once heat began to flow through his body, Floyd stopped, sat, and pulled his moccasins on. He continued to carry his soaked buckskin jacket.

"Morg, we've got to find us some weapons. Something we can make into spears or clubs."

"Been lookin' as best I can. I ain't seen nothin' that would work, but we'd best do our findin' soon, 'cause this canyon's gonna start opening up. If them Blackfoot think we survived, they'll be headin' back down this way to try to ketch us again."

Floyd nodded, and they continued in their distance-eating trot. The weather was cold, and he could feel the stiffness of his face, but he knew that as his and Morg's clothes dried, they would have a better chance of surviving. He thought of his wool coat his ma and sisters had made him. He had nursed that coat for years, trying to make it last forever, but last year he'd retired it, thin and worn. The coat had gotten so thin, it couldn't protect him like his buffalo coat. *I'd like to have either of them right now,* he thought. But there wasn't a chance of that.

They had been running for hours. The pain in Floyd's side, back, and legs had finally subsided, but his head still ached. *If I* keep getting hit in the head, it won't be anything but one big scar. He grinned at the thought.

Since he knew the country, Morg had taken the lead. Floyd, close behind, watched the easy way his friend's long legs ate up the distance and leaped over logs that suddenly appeared in their path. The man's build would fool any man. He looked tall, skinny, and almost fragile. But Floyd knew from experience, his friend was a tough man to beat. Because of his height, his shoulders didn't appear as wide or as strong as they were. Floyd knew the strength that resided in those shoulders, and he'd hate to be slugged with one of those big fists.

Suddenly Morg pulled up. "Let's git a drink."

The two men cautiously examined the riverbank on both sides before slipping to the water's edge. Each man took a turn, kneeling and cupping their hands to drink. When they had both finished, they moved back into the trees, ensuring they left no visible tracks.

Daylight was slowly breaking. Floyd gave a short yank on Morg's sleeve, and the tall man looked where his friend was pointing. At the canyon side, near the wall, was a stand of aspen. The two men trotted to the trees. The aspen wasn't a sturdy tree, but it was straight, and younger ones would be just what they needed to make either a spear or staff. Sure enough, each found a tree that had fallen and fit their needs.

Floyd spotted two boulders that sat close together, but presented room to wedge the tree in between. The downed aspen he had selected had dried and was not yet rotting, as they were prone to do. Leaving what he estimated as seven feet sticking out from the boulders, he stood to one side and leaned into the tree. It bent only slightly before it snapped, causing a low pop.

Morg had found one also.

Floyd turned. "Quick, Morg. Break yours."

The tall man followed Floyd's example and threw his weight

against the wrist-size tree. When it snapped, the report was like a rifle firing, and echoed across the canyon.

Both men were surprised at the volume. Closely watching the river and trees, they took off running. Now was not the time for a trot.

13

After running for another hour, both men were feeling the strain of exertion and harsh pangs of hunger. The canyon had widened, and the thick forest opened. They were running into spots of aspen that were so thick it would be impossible for a horse to get through, but the pines were thinning out. Cautiously the two mountain men ran across several meadows of tall grass. The meadows were beautiful in the bright morning but dangerous if they were spotted.

Suddenly, the canyon ended, running into a wide valley covered with grass, much of it wheatgrass that ran to over three feet tall. Across the grassy expanse was a wide river. Morg pulled up at the edge of the remaining forest. Floyd joined him, both men breathing hard. They scanned the open area, looking for anything out of place.

Grazing contentedly on the other side of the river was a large herd of elk. Floyd watched them, his mouth watering with hunger. A young elk was just what they needed. What little protein the rabbit had provided was now long gone.

The two men had stopped several times upon finding the right rock structure, and had invested time sharpening their spears. They each had a strong, straight spear that was sharp enough at the point to be deadly, and still thick enough, with a good swing, to knock a rider from his horse.

While taking the time to examine the open expanse and tree lines, up and down the river, both men's breathing slowed, almost to normal.

"Whatcha think, Floyd?"

"It looks fine, but I'd sure hate to get caught out there. It'd be a short race."

"How do you feel about making a little crawl?"

Floyd looked at the expanse of grass waving gently in the afternoon breeze. It stood tall, but not thick. The Blackfoot would be mounted, giving them a wider field of view. A man on horseback would have to be within thirty feet to see a man on the ground. With the breeze, the grass tops were already moving, making it more difficult. They had a chance. Of course, they would have to slide into the river and swim or wade across, depending on the river's condition. Floyd didn't like the idea of getting wet again and then turning their clothes into mud sacks. But greater safety was on the other side. Plus they might get close enough to down an elk. He gazed across the river at the tree line slopes.

"Morg, I think that's chancy as all get out, but I like it. Once we get to the other side, what do you think about trying to kill us a young elk?"

"Yore as crazy as Shorty, but an elk tenderloin, raw or cooked, would taste mighty fine. Notice how they're feeding upriver. From here, if we go straight across, by the time we get there, we should be near the back third of the herd, and I figger it should be gettin' mighty late. If we could kill one late and drag him into the timber, we just might eat tonight without anyone noticing."

"Yeah," Floyd said, "if we can figure out how to dress it."

"Look for rocks with an edge on 'em while yore crawling and around the river. Just gettin' one of those fellers opened up will let us at their liver and heart. Then we can worry about the rest later."

Floyd nodded. "You ready?"

Morg answered by taking one last look, dropping to his knees, and starting to crawl. Floyd slipped a hundred yards upriver from Morg and did the same thing. After only a few yards, he started to sweat. *I should have pulled this jacket off before I started,* Floyd thought. *Too late now.*

Crawling, keeping his rear down, was hard work and slow going. He didn't want to kick up any dust, and it was necessary to watch the grass and bump it as little as possible. Grass didn't vibrate from the wind, it leaned and flowed smooth like water. He continued with care.

The first hundred yards had gone well, though his nose, inches from the loose dirt, sucked in a pound of dust with each inhalation. Floyd had never had a problem with dust. He had friends back in Limerick that just a whiff would send them into sneezing or coughing fits. Not him. But even the worst dust he had been in behind two mules plowing a dry field wasn't this bad. He continued to move. Forearm out, opposite leg up, as flat as he could hold it on the ground. Pull with the arm and push with the foot. Change and do it with the opposite forearm, slowly forward.

He had lost count of the number of repetitions he had been through. Down close to the ground, the sun on his back was hot, but now he found himself glad he had left his jacket on. It provided more protection for his forearms against the rocks. Floyd could see the river between shoots of wheatgrass. He was close, no more than twenty-five yards.

At first, it wasn't really a sound, more of a vibration felt through his body. He froze, forcing his now dust-covered body into the ground, willing himself to become one with the earth. For the vibration he first felt had become a sound. The sound of horses' hooves. The sound grew stronger, then stopped. *How close are they? Are they Blackfoot? Where's Morg?*

His heart beat so hard, he was sure whoever the men were could hear it. Then he heard voices. They were farther away than he had thought, too far away to be understood. He lay still, waiting.

After a few moments, he heard English, but stilled himself from standing up. There had been at least one of his captors who spoke English. They could be trying to fool him. Time passed slowly. How long would they sit there? The temptation to look up was strong, but he would be spotted the moment he did.

The dust had become his friend. It covered him, providing a perfect camouflage, as he lay silent in the grass. Finally, the horses trotted off, and by the sound, he could tell they were riding north. Yet he lay motionless. The next concern was had all of them left? What if several remained, waiting? Did they consider the mountain men's plan to crawl across the open valley? Were those Blackfoot that cunning? He waited.

The heat of the sun slowly diminished, yet he remained motionless. What was Morg doing? Had he crawled on? Was he even now reaching the other side, or stalking the elk if they still remained grazing? Was he being stupid for waiting this long?

The sound of two or three horses started from behind him and slowly faded to the north. *They had waited,* Floyd thought. *Those devious devils. What if I'd moved? How did they keep from seeing our trails?* He knew the answer to that. They came from the north and rode back in that direction, for if they had crossed their trails in the loose dirt, the sharp-eyed Blackfoot couldn't have missed them.

This time, he slowly started toward the river. He was starving hungry, but his hunger was competing with his thirst. The crawl and heat had dried him up like one of his ma's dried apples. He immediately wished he hadn't thought of the apples, for his next thought went to the delicious sweet tang of her apple hand pies. Fortunately, he had reached the river. Like a snake, he slithered over the edge, dropping the four feet to the dry bank below.

The rocky surface welcomed him with a thump. Quickly righting himself, he looked first right and then left toward the south where Morg should cross. Even as his head turned in that direction, he saw Morg's lanky length come over the edge. Because of his longer arms, he landed much more gracefully. The two men nodded to each other, still separated by a hundred-yard span, then turned to examine the other side.

With the sun nearing the craggy peaks to his northwest, Floyd figured they were the Grand Tetons he had heard so much about. They had been blocked by lower but closer ridges when they had ridden in last night. They were impressive, but he had more to think about right now than scenery.

The elk were still there. A small yearling stood, ears pricked, staring at Morg. Both men eased themselves as low as possible. Once the opposite bank screened them, the two men started forward, across the dry portion of the riverbed. The river flowed, a narrow channel between the sand and rocks through which it cut, shallow and slightly off color. Color didn't matter to Floyd. When he reached the moving water, he cupped his hand and began to drink. Glancing downriver, he saw his friend doing the same thing.

After satisfying his thirst, he moved forward, careful not to make a splash. Before leaving the other side, he again took several drinks of water. There was little more than twenty feet to the opposite side's cutbank, and he covered it quickly. Dropping to the dry rocks, he leaned back against the bank. In this position he had a clear look at the stretch where they had crawled. The side of the little valley where they had come from had a few deer walking out of the trees for water. That was a good sign. Hopefully, except for the animals, they were once again alone.

He looked down the river at Morg. His friend was also leaning against the bank, resting. Yet Floyd was surprised at what else he saw. The young elk had allowed his curiosity to draw him near the riverbank. Floyd couldn't believe their luck. It looked like the animal, if it kept going, was going to be directly above Morg. He pressed himself against the bank to keep the yearling from seeing him and, using hand signals, communicated with his friend.

Floyd watched the drama play out. The yearling elk would walk a few feet and stamp his foot, as if he was trying to scare whatever was there into the open. He would watch, then put his head down, as if to graze, and quickly jerk it up.

Floyd knew this would be the only chance they would get. With his nervous movement, the yearling had alerted the entire herd, which was probably poised to take off. They wouldn't run far, but certainly a sufficient distance to prevent the two companions from getting a meal with their makeshift spears.

The yearling was almost to the edge. Morg had turned and was holding the spear ready to make a deep thrust. Just stepping into Floyd's view was a big cow elk, and then another. The herd had followed the yearling. All of the elk were tense, ready to leap at the slightest movement.

Here it comes, he thought, his eyes glued to the scene. *Good luck, Morg.*

The yearling took one step closer, almost to the edge of the riverbank, and extended its head over the bank. At that moment, Morg struck upward with the spear, his only target the slim neck of the young animal. The spear drove deep, slicing through tough hide and sinew. In its travel, it ruptured one of the arteries that traveled to the brain.

The animal spun away from Morg, taking the spear with it, and dashed off, following the herd, which was heading for the trees. After the first two leaps, the spear fell to the ground, and the mortally wounded animal raced toward the disappearing herd.

Both men were standing in the river bottom, watching the animal. Nearing the thick timber, it slowed and then stopped. Standing on shaky legs, it went no farther.

The two men watched and waited. They didn't want to dash up to it and have it, with its last burst of energy, race away.

Then it slowly folded its front legs and then its back ones, lowering itself to the ground. It lay in that position for a few moments. Finally it leaned slightly to one side, straightening its slim legs, and rested its head on the ground.

Floyd and Morg waited another five minutes and then started for the elk. Morg stopped only long enough to pick up his spear, wipe it off as best he could on the grass, and move forward. Floyd couldn't believe their good fortune. They hadn't been sighted by the Indians and were steps away from a great meal of red meat.

As they neared the elk, Floyd could see the animal was dead. It was a beautiful tawny color with the longer brown hair around the neck. Growing up in Tennessee, his pa and the Cherokee he associated with had filled him with a love and respect for all animals. Yes, their deaths were necessary, to provide sustenance and warmth, but they were also to be appreciated for their sacrifice.

He was pulled from his reverie when Morg said, "Mighty pretty."

Floyd nodded. "Yes, he is. He probably would've been a big bull one day, but today he's going to provide us with the meat we need to stay alive. Let's get him inside the tree line before those Blackfoot come back."

Morg nodded. "Rightfully so. If they find our trail, they'll be on us like a fox on a chicken."

Floyd moved around to grab a hind leg and stuck his hand out to Morg. "That was a fine shot with that spear. I was sweating it."

"Humph," Morg grunted. "*You* was? I was sweatin' bullets." Then he grinned and said, "Thanks."

The two men dragged the elk into the lodgepole pines far enough into the trees to be completely screened from prying eyes. Once there, Floyd dropped the leg and pulled four rocks from his jacket pockets, laying them on a boulder.

"Ain't that pretty," Floyd said.

Morg walked over and looked at the rocks. "Mighty nice. You good at this?"

"I've been making rock knives since I was a boy."

"Which one you gonna use?"

Floyd hefted the rocks. He picked out the biggest one and laid it back on the boulder. "Think I'll use this chert. I bet it'll flake like crazy."

Morg looked at it, nodded, and stepped back. "Git 'er done."

Floyd positioned the gray rock on the boulder until the angle was just right. "Watch your eyes," he said. He had a heavier rock in his hand, and when he slammed it down against the gray chert, the chert flaked a piece off about four inches long, three inches wide, and no more than a quarter inch thick at the thickest point. But it narrowed on the opposite side to a knife-sharp edge.

"How many of these do you think we need?" Floyd asked.

Morg picked up the thin sheet of chert and felt the edge. "Reckon you weren't kiddin' about makin' a rock knife." He looked down at the remaining rock. "You got enough to make four?"

Floyd nodded and brought the heavier rock down against the chert. He did it three more times, giving them four sharp rock blades.

"With these," Morg said, "we oughta be able to dress this elk out and skin it. Won't be the prettiest skinnin' job, but that'll give us a hide to carry meat in."

"If you can do without your liver and heart, we can get a good load of meat without even opening this fellow up."

"Reckon I want that liver," Morg said.

"Suit yourself, but let's save that to last." With his last word, Floyd went to work.

In no time the two mountain men had one side of the elk skinned and were cutting out the backstrap. While they worked, Floyd questioned Morg about Shorty and Kajika.

"You think they got away?"

"Reckon they might have. Those Injuns were shore working hard to grab you after you killed those two. I figgered you for dead after that big brave hit you in the head with his club. You done collapsed like a rag doll. Then fore I knowed it, the others jumped me. We sure figgered wrong. They wasn't after our horses, they was after us. I think they had some devilish plans for us, should they have made it back to their camp."

Floyd nodded with gusto. "Yessir. I'm thinking all those stories about the Blackfoot not liking whites on their land are true."

"It ain't just whites, Floyd. They'll kill just about anyone who makes a move on what they consider is theirs."

The two men continued to work, now in twilight, the sun gone. They had cut the hide in half along the spine and piled the boned meat from the one side in the hide. Then they flipped the animal over and repeated their efforts with the rock knives. As they worked, each man had been eating the raw backstrap. Though he was tired, Floyd could feel his strength returning. After they had finished, they moved their meat packs well to one side, and Floyd held the front legs while Morg opened up the animal, removing the liver and heart. After the body cavity was empty, and in almost total darkness, he sliced out the tenderloin, handing Floyd a piece.

Then the tall man separated out the liver and heart, slicing a piece of liver and handing it to Floyd. Both men stood for a moment, chewing on the liver.

"Mmm," Morg said. "That there is good stuff."

His mouth full, Floyd nodded.

Each man had a hide pack of close to forty pounds of boneless meat. They pulled the ends together, tied them with the rope, and using Floyd's staff, tied the two elk sacks to the staff. They finished by looping the remainder of the rope over the staff. The two men, in darkness now, ran to the river, washed the blood from their arms, and dashed back to their bounty. Each man lifted an end of the staff and prepared to depart the elk's carcass. Already, coyotes were sitting a short distance away, waiting. Up the river, they could hear the mournful howl of a wolf.

"Them coyotes best get busy," Morg said. "Those wolves'll be here shortly, and that'll be the end of dinner for mister coyote."

The two men started off, Morg in front, Floyd supporting the opposite end of the staff.

"You know where you are, Morg?"

"I should shine. Shorty and I tried our hand trappin' up here a couple of years ago. Did mighty good till the Blackfoot chased us out. It was stay and die, or leave and find safer trapping."

"Where do you think Kajika and Shorty headed?"

"Might've headed on over to where our old camp was. It ain't far, as the crow flies, maybe ten mile. Be longer for us. No chance of makin' it tonight. We need to git far enough away from here so's them Injuns don't find us. Howsomever, we keep goin' all night and we'll end up gettin' a busted leg in blowdowns or gulches, but we can head over that way."

There was a light wind blowing from the northwest, making the chill of the night even worse. The two men slowly made their way by a brightening moon. They climbed and descended, only to do it again. After moving several miles from their elk kill, Floyd could see they were in a shallow draw that ran north and south, in the middle of a patch of aspen.

Morg pulled up. "We'd best call it a night."

"Good idea. I don't want to leap off another cliff unintentionally. I'd say yesterday was more'n enough."

They found a semi-level, thick patch of aspen with a small stream running near.

"We'd best get what we want for a quick meal and then get

this meat hung. I ain't hankering to meet me another grizzly bear," Floyd said.

"Your shore right there," Morg said.

The two men found a tall pine with limbs low and strong enough to hold the two sacks, and hung them together. Once they were finished hanging the meat and eating more of the liver, they settled in for the night.

Floyd took the first watch. He grasped his two weapons, the wooden spear and the sharp rock knife. Neither were much as weapons, but both were more than he had yesterday. He moved away from Morg and found suitable cover with a good view. Easing to the ground, he leaned back against an aspen. In only moments he heard Morg snoring softly, and chuckled to himself. Soft snoring was unusual for Morg. Normally, his snoring could wake the dead.

14

Floyd slept soundly after Morg took over the watch. He awoke without prompting and, before moving, listened closely to the waking of the forest.

The first thing he noticed was the deep bone-chilling cold. He was amazed he had been able to sleep through it, a testament to his exhaustion. He rose, looking around the camp. Morg was close by, still as a statue, watching their back trail.

Floyd gazed in the same direction, listening intently. Nothing.

He stood and stretched, trying to work the cold and stiffness from his joints. Young he might be, and strong, with amazing endurance, but the last two days had taxed his strength and hammered his body.

Morg rose and quietly made his way to Floyd. "Been quiet all night. Darned near froze to death. I'm bettin' there's ice in that stream."

"Yep," Floyd said, "it is mighty cold." He looked at the sky covered with low clouds. "We'd best be on our way. I know it's early, but those clouds sure look like snow."

Morg walked to the tree with the hanging meat, untied the rope, and lowered the eighty pounds of meat like it was ten.

Speaking softly, he said, "I'm hopin' not. We don't need snow to make it easier to spot our trail, much less freeze us to death."

Once the sacks were on the ground, the men untied one and removed the tenderloin. Using their rock knives, they cut off big hunks for each. After retying the bags to the staff, they lifted it to their shoulders and moved to the stream. Sure enough, along the edges of the water, thin ice had formed. *That's the last thing I wanted to see,* thought Floyd. Setting the load on the ground, he and Morg scooped and drank, keeping their eyes moving.

Once satisfied, the two men lifted the load to their shoulders, and with one hand holding the pole and the other the meat, they made their way through the pine and aspen forest, eating breakfast.

Miles slowly dropped away, and their bodies warmed from the exertion. Cold still assailed them, but not the deep, bone-chilling cold that had roused them. They were quiet as they made their way through the forest. *Mighty pretty country,* Floyd thought. *Though I could enjoy it a lot better wearing my buffalo coat astride Rusty or Buck with a rifle in my hand instead of this spear.*

Around noon, they stopped, sat close together, and discussed their situation in low tones.

"Can't say it's warmed up much," Morg said, rubbing his big hands together.

Floyd gave a low laugh. "I'd have to agree with you. At least the snow's held off, and we don't have to worry about the meat spoiling."

"That's for danged sure," Morg said, and spit. "I could sure use a little tobaccy, and this here elk meat is mighty good, but it'd be a danged sight better with a little salt and pepper over a fire."

Floyd nodded. "How much farther to your camp?"

"Couple of hours."

"You think they'll be there?"

"If they survived, I think that's exactly where Shorty would've gone. He'd bet on our escaping. Weren't no sense in them following us. Those redskins woulda spotted 'em no matter how careful they was. Yep, that's what he'd do." Morg nodded his head to support his statement.

"Did you notice the Indians had none of our horses? I was surprised."

"Well," Morg said, "you was out, but Shorty and Kajika put up a heck of a fusillade after they jumped you. I'm thinking them Blackfoot figured there was more trappers than they had spotted, and that's probably what kept them from gettin' the horses. Once they slugged you and took me, they hightailed it out of there."

"It would be real fine if those boys was waiting for us," Floyd replied. "If not, we've a long walk ahead of us."

Both men sat silent, contemplating what would happen without their friends at the camp. They were well aware of the stories of Hugh Glass and John Colter.

Hugh Glass, as the story goes, was mauled by a grizzly. Companions were designated to stay with him. Everyone fully expected him to die, but the tough mountain man kept hanging on. Finally the two men divided up his goods and left him to die. Glass, with a broken leg and horribly mutilated by the bear, crawled and walked over two hundred miles to Fort Kiowa on the Missouri River.

John Colter was another mountain man to be reckoned with. After being captured by the same tribe who had captured Floyd and Morg, the Blackfoot, he escaped, naked. With the braves chasing him, he killed the closest, took his blanket, and eleven days later showed up at a trader's fort.

Brave men, Floyd thought. *Hopefully we won't have similar distances to travel.*

The two men stood and made their way through the waiting forest.

THE CLOUDS HAD GOTTEN HEAVIER, occasionally spitting out small snowflakes, when the two men topped a low rise. Below was a small valley, at the head of which, tendrils of faint smoke made their way from the thick trees into the low clouds. Morg turned around and grinned.

"Looks like someone's there."

"We'd best be careful," Floyd said. "We don't yet know it's them."

Morg nodded. "It's them, but we'll be cautious."

They eased over and started down the ridge, still well hidden in the lodgepole pines. Keeping to the trees, they circled around the ridge until they could make out the structure.

Floyd couldn't keep himself from grinning when he saw the corral. There was Rusty, Buck, and Browny among the other horses. *Finally,* he thought.

Evidently Shorty and Morg had built a small cabin up here. It was a wonder the Blackfoot hadn't burned it to the ground, but here it stood against the elements and the Indians.

They made it to the door, and just as Morg reached for the latch, the door was yanked open, and they were staring down a big .50-caliber muzzle. Behind it stood Shorty. Kajika was off to one side, his bow pulled to full draw.

"Hold up, fellers," Morg said. "We brung dinner."

Shorty's mouth hung open for only a moment. Almost immediately, he said, "I knew it. This was the place to come. I knew you'd escape and come here." He turned to Kajika. "I told you that, didn't I, Kajika?"

The Shoshone nodded, obviously pleased.

Morg frowned at Shorty. "You gonna stand there with that rifle muzzle shoved up my nose, or is it yore plan to let two freezin' men inside so's we can warm up?"

Shorty lowered the rifle, stepped back, and frowned at his partner. "Git on in here, you complainin' old reprobate. I swear you never stop." Then he looked at Floyd and grinned. "Good to see you, Floyd. I was afeared the way that big Blackfoot conked you on the noggin, you was a goner. Reckon yore just as hardheaded as Morg."

Floyd followed Morg into the one-room cabin. The warmth from the fireplace brought a big smile to his face. He looked around. The room wasn't big, but there was space for the supplies to be stacked to one side. The other side of the cabin had a small rough-hewn table with four chairs, still leaving enough space to allow the men to spread their bedding on the floor.

All four men were excited to see each other. Much handshaking and backslapping took place. Shorty filled two cups with steaming hot coffee from the pot that had been sitting in the front corner of the fireplace, and handed one to each of the men.

It was scalding hot, but Floyd drank his first sip, burning his tongue, and savored the biting hot taste. His body was warming, with a little tingling in his feet and hands. It was good to be warm again, and with friends.

"You escape?" Kajika asked of Floyd.

"If you could call it that," Floyd responded. "But before we start telling it, this meat needs to go outside and get hung up."

"We'll take care of it," Shorty said, turning toward Kajika. "That all right with you, Kajika?"

The young Indian nodded.

"First," Shorty said, "I'll take some of what you got there so it can get cookin' when we come back in. You fellers just have a seat and relax yourselves."

Morg pointed at the pack where the liver and heart were. "Untie that one first."

Shorty untied and opened the elk hide to the sight of liver and heart. "Well, I'll be doggies. You're gonna have to tell us how you got this animal with no gun." In addition, he removed the remaining backstrap and tenderloin. Then tying them back up, he and Kajika hefted the pole and headed outside.

As soon as they left, the two remaining men walked over to

the packs and armed themselves. Floyd hated to lose his custom-built Ryland and two caplock pistols, but he was thankful he still had his remaining Ryland Rifle and pistols.

As they were finishing rearming themselves, Shorty and Kajika returned.

Shorty immediately went to the meat and began preparing it. Kajika said, "Now, tell us."

Morg began the tale. Later, Floyd joined in, and the two men told their story.

When they told the part about the talus slope and cliff, even Kajika's eyes were wide, but both of the listeners remained silent, hanging on each word of the story. Shorty got up and turned the meat while still listening.

The aroma of cooking meat filled the interior of the cabin. Floyd could feel his hunger rising. His stomach joined in with a loud growl, which brought an appreciative grin from the other men.

The steak, heart, and liver were finally ready. Floyd was thankful for his plates, as he handed one to Kajika. He cut his steak with his spare knife. It was much like the knife his brother had given him, but didn't hold the sentimentality his brother's did. It still sliced through the steak like butter.

Salt and pepper were in two tins on the table. Floyd added salt to the pepper in his hand and sprinkled the combination over the meat. He lifted the piece of elk steak to his mouth. It was delicious. In little time, both he and Morg had finished their meals. During the eating, there had been no storytelling or talking. After they were done, Morg began again.

When they reached the part where Morg had killed the elk, Floyd took over, regaling the men with Morg's accurate thrust. Shorty was nodding vigorously as the story was told, and he stood, walked over, and pounded his friend on the back. Shortly thereafter they finished, and everyone leaned back and sighed.

"That was a trip I'm sure glad I wasn't on," Shorty said. "You fellers have been through it. Morg, I ain't never gonna argue with you again. Why—"

Morg interrupted his partner. "Shorty, you know there's no way you can keep from arguing. Why, you'd rather lock horns than breathe."

The shorter man looked his partner in the eye. "Morgan James. You cain't leave well enough alone. I was serious, and here you go makin' fun of me. Why, if you wasn't worn out from all that walkin', I'd bust you right in the mouth, but I ain't planning on takin' advantage of a man in yore weakened state." He stomped to the door. "I'm checkin' the horses. They need to be fed, and somebody ought to do it."

Floyd watched the man walk through the door. With the door open, he could see light snow falling in a driving wind. He wanted to check his stock. He stood, walked to the packs, and pulled out his buffalo coat, slipping it on. The weight felt good.

"I'm checking my animals, boys. Be back in a minute." He stepped outside in the biting wind, but the heavy coat blocked it out, and he was warm and comfortable.

He walked around the house to the corral. Shorty was leading the animals into the shed that was attached to the back wall of the house. The trees protected the lean-to from a direct wind. As Floyd walked inside, he could see the two men had built a solid protection for their animals, and space existed for nine, maybe ten horses.

Shorty was giving all of them some oats. He had forked hay into the space so there would be something else for them to eat. Attached to the top of the lean-to was one end of a long tarp that almost touched the ground. Behind this, on the outside, two ropes had been strung across the opening, one at three feet and another at five. The tarp, pulled down inside the ropes, kept the body heat in, and the ropes prevented the animals from straying. Tonight would be no problem. Nothing was going out in this weather if it could keep from it.

Shorty saw Floyd and said, "I don't reckon them Blackfoot will be venturing out in this. We'll be safe for a while."

"Reckon," Floyd said. "Did you two have a chance to ride up the Gros Ventre?"

"Nope. I feel for the girl, but I wanted to wait here just in case you two escaped, and old hardhead in there decided to try for it."

Floyd shook his head. "My mind's been pretty occupied with my own problems for the past couple of days, but come morning I'm headin' out. I've got to find out what's happened to Leotie. I owe her a lot. If it hadn't been for her and Pallaton's wife, Nina, I'd probably be dead." He stopped rubbing Rusty's neck and looked directly at Shorty. "You and Morg don't have to come. This isn't really your fight."

At that Shorty slammed down the bucket he had been feeding the horses from. "Dang it, Floyd. You trying to be as hard to get along with as Morg? I done made a commitment to you, ain't I? I'll be right there till the last bullet's fired. You can put that in yore pipe and smoke it."

Floyd saw the genuine anger in his friend's face at the suggestion he might want to back out. "Sorry, Shorty. I guess I'm feeling guilty about Leotie myself. She's been with those evil men two more days than she should've, and those fellers who were bitten by that wolf could be coming down with the madness." He patted Rusty's neck one last time. "I appreciate your and Morg's help. Now let's get back inside and have another cup of that hot coffee."

Shorty, embarrassed at his explosion, gave a curt nod and marched around the corner of the house to the door. Floyd stepped in close enough behind him to hear him say to Morg and Kajika, "Let's get some sleep. We need to get after that girl in the morning."

Kajika grabbed his blankets and spread them on the floor. Before lying down, he said, "No worry about Blackfoot. They be all in teepees tonight. Storm catch them by surprise."

Floyd was the last to settle down after he finished his coffee.

He doused the two candles, and the only remaining light in the room danced from the flames in the small fireplace. He lay down, and the reflections of the flames across the ceiling tormented his vision as his mind couldn't leave Leotie and Mika. *Hopefully,* he thought, *tomorrow will see us rescuing her from the clutches of McMillan and those other vile trappers he runs with. I owe her my life.* Finally exhaustion overtook him, and he slept, though it was fitfully. Dreams of the worst possibilities beset him, waking him continuously, until he finally rose near morning and stoked the fire.

Once it was going, he slapped his hat on, pulled on his moccasins, and opened the door. A welcome sight greeted him. Dimming though they were, a few stars faintly glimmered and flashed in the clear mountain sky. He took a deep breath, filling his lungs with crisp, fresh air tinted with the scent of pine. A light breeze from the north caressed his cheeks, and, though it was cold, it brought him a feeling of well-being, chasing away the dread he had felt upon waking.

Confident, he was ready to face whatever challenges awaited. Once Leotie was rescued, they would be on their way to find Mika. He and his friends would take them back to the Shoshone, and this bad dream would be forever over. Then he'd search for Jeb. Hopefully his friend had returned from St. Louis with the supplies they would need for the winter and spring.

He walked around the house to the makeshift stable. The horses stood watching him. Browny's long ears were pointed toward him in anticipation of a little ear scratching. He had always liked mules, and Browny was one of the best. He scratched the big mule behind his ears and rubbed his neck, then moved to Buck and then Rusty. "I'm sure glad you boys didn't get captured by those Blackfoot. It woulda been a terrible thing." He moved on to the others and spoke to them.

"Who you talkin' to in there?" Morg said in a low voice as he walked into the stable.

Without looking up, Floyd said, "Just having a friendly conversation with my horses. They're telling me how glad they are the Indians didn't get 'em."

"I'll say. That mule of yours would have been eaten first chance they got. Speaking of eating. Come on back in. Shorty's up and already fixed us some of his biscuits and heated up the elk."

"Good," Floyd said. "I haven't tasted a good biscuit in a coon's age." He slapped Browny on the rump and followed Morg back inside the cabin.

15

The four men, rested, fed, and alert, mounted and rode east. Kajika knew the country far better than either Morg or Shorty, so he took the lead. For many of his growing years, until the hated Blackfoot drove them out, he had lived in this region. Floyd followed Kajika, next Shorty, with Morg bringing up the rear. They rode in silence through the mountains. Tall granite peaks thrust their snow-covered faces to the heavens. The party had to dismount and lead their horses several times, but as the sun reached its zenith, they rode carefully down toward the valley.

The reins in his left hand, Floyd gripped his rifle in his right with the barrel across the pommel of his saddle until he found it necessary to dismount. Then he led the two horses and mule up the steep slopes. His two pistols rested in their holsters, leather thongs released from the hammers. All weapons were ready, no matter what or who they encountered. He knew today was going to be a bloody day. If Leotie had been harmed, there wouldn't be a man of those four escape with his life.

The rescuers did not stop to eat, but they halted occasionally to water and give the horses a break. Jerky from their packs gave them needed nourishment, and water from stream crossings quenched their thirst. They rode through thick timber of lodgepole pine and spruce, with great colonies of aspen. Occasionally they broke into rock- and boulder-studded fields, the space covered with short grass.

But they were entertained by the abundant color breaking through the thin covering of snow and bursting forth upon the mountains, valleys, and streams. Near the beaver ponds, which each of the riders noted, were the brilliant purple of bitterroot and the white of lilies. The meadows, between the stately pines and delicate aspens, were home to the white geraniums and ladies' tresses, the yellow arnica, and sulfur buckwheat. Reds and pinks from prairie smoke and coralroot competed with the blue and purple of lupine, penstemon, and bluebells.

Floyd reveled in the feast for his eyes. This was the country he loved. He knew it, even in Tennessee, as a boy. *No wonder the Blackfoot fight so hard for this country,* he thought. *Were I them, I too would fight for it.*

He marveled at the abundant game present, so much of it almost tame. Like the young elk that had given his life that they might live. Today, in the meadows, they rode past hundreds of elk. The big animals grazed contentedly, stopping only to raise their heads and stare as the horsemen passed.

In the open bottoms, they had seen the big shaggy buffalo, and in the mountains, they saw bighorn sheep standing on cliffsides so steep it was a wonder they could move without falling to their deaths. And of course, the grizzly. It seemed a day didn't pass they didn't see at least one, and sometimes three and four. So far, they had been left alone, but it was abundantly clear the grizzlies felt no fear of them.

Middle afternoon saw Kajika pull up and dismount. Floyd and the others followed suit, moving close to the Shoshone. They had been following a stream that ran south. In one of their earlier stops, Morg explained by following this stream, though it was rugged at times, and difficult, they would arrive at the Gros Ventre River a short distance above Crystal Creek, which was the creek where the trappers they were chasing had their cabin.

Kajika said, "We in open soon. Be ready. We must cross river." He turned to Shorty and Morg. "You take over. I not familiar with cabin."

Shorty nodded his head at Morg, and Morg answered Kajika. "You've done a good job. Thanks." Then he spoke to all three men. Floyd listened intently. "Cabin's up the creek, maybe three miles. We should get there before sundown. Fortunately the wind has died down and won't start until later, so their horses shouldn't smell us." He turned to Floyd. "How do you want to handle it?"

Floyd thought about it, then said, "If Leotie is unharmed, I'm fine with letting them go. But if she's hurt, *in any way,* they're dead men. We give them a chance to send Leotie out. If they refuse, we'll have to take it from there. I don't want any further harm to come to her."

The other men gave sharp nods, and Floyd said, "Let's move."

They checked their weapons again, mounted, and rode down the creek. Soon the trees ahead thinned, and a wide open expanse was visible ahead. The river ran near the tree line. They paused and examined the open area. There was no movement. Cautiously, ready to shoot if necessary, they rode into the open.

Morg led them into the river. It was shallow and easy to cross. The horses attempted to stop, but the men urged them on. This was not the place to be watering horses. They were fully exposed.

Once up the opposite bank and across the river, Morg guided them to the left side of a creek which flowed out of a canyon that loomed ahead. The east side of the canyon had a steep face of over a hundred feet, while the west side sloped.

Across the open bottom area, the men rode. After reentering the trees, Morg pulled up and dismounted. They were on the north side of a point of a ridge that ended abruptly no more than thirty yards ahead.

Morg dismounted and tied his horse. Floyd and the other riders followed suit. Each man checked his weapons and ammunition. Floyd felt for his knife and tomahawk, glad that he had purchased spares under his friend and employer Hugh Brennan's suggestion so many years ago.

Morg said, "Just around that point. The cabin faces the creek. Not a bad place. Whoever picked it out knew what they were doing." Morg looked at Floyd. "Up to you now."

"You know if they have any windows?"

Shorty spoke up. "Nary a one."

Floyd nodded. "I'm sure they have a fireplace."

"Yep," Morg replied.

"Good, let's take a blanket. If they refuse to come out, we'll see if it's possible to get the blanket over the chimney."

Shorty had already gone to the packs and pulled out a blanket.

"Other than that," Floyd said, "you fellers know the plan, rescue Leotie. Let's go."

Floyd had turned to start forward to round the ridge, when the most bloodcurdling scream he had ever heard struck his ears. Without hesitating, he broke into a run. Rounding the ridge, he saw Cleon Harris pulling on a chain fastened around his ankle. The man hadn't seen him, but pulled frantically and finally leaned back and screamed again.

The scream sounded as if it was ripped from his body, high pitched and warbling, ending in giant sobs. Harris stopped pulling and leaped up, circling around the stob that had been driven in the ground to hold him in place.

Morg was passing Floyd so as to move out in front of the cabin. He stopped and leaned close to Floyd and, in a loud whisper, said, "Look out! He's got the hydrophoby."

Harris heard Morg and spun around. He had pulled the chain

to its full length on the opposite side of the stake from Floyd. He stopped for a moment and leaned forward, as if it was hard for him to focus. He stood transfixed for an instant. All at once, his face contorted with an emotion only his tortured mind could know. Harris charged across the stake, reaching the full length of the chain. He was slammed to the ground, but that didn't slow his efforts to reach them. He dug his fingers and toes into the rocky ground, pulling with all of his strength.

It was then Floyd saw his fingernails. All had been torn from his fingertips, the ends covered in brown-red mud from the bleeding ends. Noting the man could not get loose from his chains, Floyd motioned his partners to take up firing positions around the front of the cabin. Through all of the commotion, the door never opened. He moved to the corner of the house, carefully ensuring he was well out of range of Harris.

After first checking with each man and getting their nod, Floyd yelled, "McMillan, this is Floyd Logan. Send out Leotie and you can live a little longer."

Silence covered the canyon, except for the whimpering Harris.

Floyd waited. A minute or two passed with no response. "McMillan, this is your only chance. You, Bell, and Page leave your weapons inside and come out with your hands in the air."

From inside came the voice Floyd knew so well. The voice of the woman who had taken care of him when he was injured, but it was no longer soft and kind. It was hard and brittle and in Shoshone. "Igasho, there are only two, and they—"

Leotie's warning was cut short by a ringing slap that could be heard outside.

Floyd called back in Shoshone, "We are here for you. Hold on for only a little longer." Then he switched to English. "That's gonna cost you, McMillan. Now send Leotie out."

Floyd heard the rough, familiar voice of McMillan. "That weren't me, Logan. That were Page."

Immediately another voice sounded. "That's a lie. I ain't never struck no woman in my whole life, and I ain't startin' now."

"Page," Floyd called, "you send Leotie out to us and come out with your hands up, and we'll let you leave here."

"You funnin' me?" Page responded.

"Nope, do like I said and you can go."

Floyd could hear the argument inside. It was getting heated.

"She ain't comin' out, I tell ya!" McMillan shouted.

Floyd had taken the blanket from Shorty, and he turned to the back of the house. It was time to smoke those two.

The chimney was one of the roughest built he had ever seen, but to Floyd it wasn't surprising. He didn't know who built it, but as sloppy as it was, he figured it must have been McMillan. The rocks stuck out far enough to allow him to get a good toehold with his moccasins. He tossed the blanket over his shoulder and almost raced up the short chimney. Holding to the chimney with one hand, he tossed the folded blanket over the flue while giving the chimney a disgusted look. They hadn't even tried to put a protective cap on to keep the rain and snow out. Once the blanket was in place, he leaped to the ground and picked up his rifle. *It won't be long now,* Floyd thought.

In nothing flat, he heard coughing coming from the cabin. Shortly after the first cough, smoke started issuing from under and around the front door and cracks in the chinking.

A warning yell sounded between coughs. "Logan, if you don't want her dead, you'd better take whatever you have off that chimney. I mean it. I'll kill her."

Floyd's heart skipped. If he guessed wrong, Leotie would die, but he knew McMillan and men like him. They were all blustering bullies. Stand up to them and they would cower like a cur.

"McMillan, the son of Chief Pallaton, chief of the Shoshones, is with me. He and his father are family friends of Leotie. You kill her and I'm turning you over to him to take back to the Shoshones. You'll be taking a long time to die, and they'll be enjoying it. Now send her out and throw your weapons out. When you come out, your hands had best be empty."

Only heavier coughing, from inside the cabin, broke the silence. Then a shout sounded. "We're comin' out. Don't shoot."

Floyd moved up and stood at the side of the door. When it opened, Leotie walked out, tall and proud. He grabbed her by the arm and yanked her clear of the opening, pulling her to the side of the house, where she doubled over coughing.

He laid a hand on her back, her trim body racked with violent coughing. He could hear more coughing at the front of the house, but wasn't worried about either of the two men getting away with his companions out front.

Finally Leotie's coughing began to let up. As she was straightening, Kajika strode up beside Floyd. The two men saw her face at the same time. She was almost unrecognizable, eyes swollen near shut, cheeks and forehead swollen blue from multiple blows. A dried-blood line on the left side of her cheek covered a cut, probably from the sharp blade of a skinning knife.

The two men's faces hardened even more. Floyd said, "They will pay."

"Good!" Leotie responded.

"Did they . . . Have they . . ." Floyd couldn't bring himself to say the words.

Leotie, never flinching, looked him squarely in the face. "All but Page."

"Where is Bell?" Floyd asked.

"Gone. The madness took him at night. He leaped to the door and, without his coat or boots, raced toward the river. That was five days ago. He has not been back."

Floyd nodded, whirled around, and with Kajika and Leotie by his side, stalked to the front of the house. McMillan and Page stood with their hands thrust to the sky. On the way, Leotie said, "The man named Page never touched me. It was the others."

She raised her arm as they rounded the corner of the cabin,

and pointed straight at McMillan's face. "It was mostly him. He likes to beat women."

Kajika pulled his knife and stepped toward McMillan. The brutal man's face no longer showed aggression. Only fear gleamed in his wide eyes.

Floyd laid his hand on Kajika's arm. "Not yet."

The Shoshone stood within inches of McMillan's face. He ran the back of his blade along the man's left cheek, then turned the blade slightly. The sliding blade opened a thin cut two inches long. The man screamed, "Nooo," and fell to his knees. Kajika put his foot in the man's chest and shoved him backwards. In English he said, "He is a coward," and walked away in disgust.

Floyd looked at Leotie. "Anything you need from inside?"

She nodded, eyes locked on those of McMillan, and then turned her dark eyes on Floyd.

Floyd saw the burning question in her eyes and said, "Do what you want."

She walked back into the smoke. Floyd started to worry she might have been overcome by the smoke, but suddenly stepping out of the cabin, she carried a bag, a rifle, a buffalo coat, and had a knife tied around her waist. Dropping the bag, coat, and rifle outside the door, she returned to the interior, to exit quickly holding a burning brand. Going to each corner, she set the dry pine on fire, then threw the torch into the cabin and moved her bounty clear of the burning building

Page said, "Our supplies, our guns, everything we own's inside. We cain't survive without it."

Floyd turned to him. "Do I look like I'm concerned about your survival? Now would be a good time for you to shut up, or you might end up like your friend here."

"He ain't my friend, Mr. Logan. I just joined up with 'em to trap this country. Ain't never been this far north. Planned on trapping a lot of beaver. I didn't plan on nothin' like this."

Shorty spoke up. "A man's known by the company he keeps, mister. That don't say a lot for you."

Page spun to look at Shorty. "I was outnumbered. They would've killed me."

Shorty nodded. "Probably so, but you woulda been able to meet yore maker with a clear conscience. No matter how long you live, you'll never forget what happened here." Shorty turned and spit a long stream of tobacco juice. "If that ain't hell, I don't know what is."

Ignoring Page, Floyd said, "Where's their horses?"

"Other side of the cabin." Morg looked at the burning cabin and the smoke rising to the sky. "Whatever we're gonna do, we'd better do it quick. This'll more'n likely bring us some unwanted guests."

Floyd nodded. "Morg, grab us a horse and a rope."

McMillan had been quiet. At the mention of rope, he looked at the nineteen-year-old mountain man. He saw a hard-bitten man with no pity.

Floyd looked at him, reached down, and pulled the big man to his feet. "You're a mighty lucky man today, McMillan. I was going to give you to Kajika, but I can't do that." Floyd could see relief flood the man's face, and his eyes teared up. "No, I can't turn you over to him no matter how much you deserve it." The hard blue eyes gazed deep into the trapper's eyes. "I'm just wonderin' if there is any sorrow residing in your black heart for what you did."

McMillan gasped out, almost in a sob, "Oh yes, yes. I am truly sorry." He looked over into Leotie's battered face and cold eyes and said again, "I'm sorry." Her expression never changed.

"Well, that's good," Floyd said. "Now you'll be able to meet your maker with those words on your lips. Though, I surely doubt your sincerity."

Shorty handed the rope to Floyd. He made a loop and dropped it over the man's neck.

McMillan's watery eyes were wide open, as if he couldn't

believe what was happening. "No, please, no. Not to me. You can't do this. I won't ever do such a thing again. You've got to believe me. I don't know what happened—"

"Get on the horse," Floyd said.

"No, I mean . . ." In a plaintive wail he cried, "I don't want to die."

Floyd turned to Morg. "Would you put him on this horse?"

The tall, skinny man picked up the blubbering trapper, who outweighed him by at least fifty pounds, and tossed him onto the horse. Floyd led the animal to a lodgepole pine while Shorty tossed the rope over a lower branch.

"Hope that limb don't break," Shorty said. "We got to be makin' tracks. Don't want to have to hang this varmint more'n one time. Besides, that gunpowder in there hasn't gone up yet, and I don't want to be around when it does."

The rope slid over the pine's limb, and Shorty secured it to another lodgepole.

Without another word, Floyd slapped the horse's rump. Its first jump unseated McMillan. He dropped, his weight cinching the noose tight, and swayed back and forth in the air. There had been no knot to break his neck, so he swung and kicked, gasping for nonexistent air. Everyone turned back to the business at hand except Leotie and Kajika.

Kajika slowly unslung his bow, nocked an arrow, and pulled it to full draw. When he released it, the arrow drove into McMillan's belly, the point sticking out past his spine.

Floyd had turned away and, with Morg and Shorty, was getting the horses saddled and ready. At the twang of the bow, he turned, looked for a moment, and went back to work.

Leotie, as if a statue, watched McMillan's final struggles.

When he finished struggling, she walked close, spit on him, and said, "You are lucky Flo-yd has a tender heart. If it had been me, you would have taken much longer to die." Then she turned and walked away.

They worked rapidly preparing the horses. Everyone mounted and, with lead ropes over the others, turned to leave. Page stood looking at Floyd questioningly.

Floyd turned to the others and said, "Let's go."

Speaking up, Page asked, "What's gonna happen to me?"

Floyd looked down on the man. "Page, I don't know, but was I you, I'd take off right now. You can head south. There still might be a few stragglers at rendezvous, but I'd get moving fore them Blackfoot show up. They're probably headed this way right now. You don't want to be around here when they show up."

Page looked over at the chained man, who, possibly lucid for a time, between fits, sat quietly on his heels, watching the proceedings. "What about Harris?"

Floyd shook his head. "Not much anybody can do for him now. He'll die where you chained him unless you turn him loose, and I wouldn't recommend getting that close."

"I need a horse and a rifle. Equipment."

Floyd pulled the knife he had taken from McMillan that now rested behind his gunbelt and threw it to the ground in front of Page. The knife drove almost to the hilt in the soft dirt. "You've got a knife. That's more than John Colter had. Just think of the story you can tell when you get back to St. Louis." He turned to Kajika. "Lead the way."

The four men and one woman galloped out of the canyon. As they turned up the Gros Ventre River, there was an explosion. Over the ridge they saw the roof launched into the sky. Almost as one section, it turned over and over, making a slow whop-whop sound in the air until crashing back to the ground.

With the explosion, black smoke boiled up behind them, dimly visible in the fading light.

They never slowed.

16

The horses picked their way slowly along their forested route, riders giving them plenty of slack. Deep in the forest, faint moonlight filtered sparingly through the tops of the pines. Having much better night vision than their riders, the horses picked their way through the trees.

Leotie had taken the lead from Kajika. She also knew this country and where the Blackfoot were taking her son. The group rode on for another hour, and the woman pulled up at the edge of a small meadow.

"We camp here," she said, climbing down from her mount. She limped slightly, favoring her right side.

The men halted their horses and stepped down, Floyd dropping the reins of Rusty and moving quickly to Leotie's side.

He took her elbow and said in Shoshone, "Come, you're hurt. You sit and we'll make camp."

Leotie looked up into the strong face of the man who trailed them so far to rescue and avenge her. "You are kind, Igasho, but no. I will do better if I move around, and if I am moving, I will be useful."

Floyd had been in this western country for three years, and

he was well aware of the resilience of Indian women. They had a hard life with few material rewards. He had developed great respect for them, especially Leotie. He nodded. "Then we'll get to work, and you do what you can."

"Fix the fire. I will cook."

"Sounds good. The food's in the pack. There's some fine elk cuts still remaining in the sack on Browny. I'll bring both of them over to you after we get the fire going."

She stopped and took his left bicep in a firm grip. "Igasho, I am a woman, not a weakling. Get the fire going, take care of the horses, and leave me to get what I need." She softened her statement with a smile.

A beam of moonlight slipped through the tangle of branches above them and rested softly on her face. Floyd felt a pang of anger. She had been beaten so badly. Her eyes, cheeks, and forehead were swollen. The cut on her cheek pointed toward her jaw.

"It will get better," she said. "Now go to work."

He stood for a moment longer, nodded, and led Rusty to where everyone was unloading and unsaddling.

"Tough woman," Morg said. "I never in all my days have figgered what makes a man do something like that, other than just plain orneriness. I reckon that there McMillan is just where he deserves to be, and a danged sight hotter than we are."

Floyd shook his head. "I had a chance to send him there three years ago, but I let him off. I should've given him both barrels. If I'd known then what I know now, I would've," he said, pulling the second pack from Browny and moving to Rusty.

Shorty stacked his gear next to his saddle and joined in. "Cain't live yore life on what-ifs, Floyd. You did then what you thought wuz right, and today, you danged sure did what was right. Sometimes, life has a way of giving you a chance to correct yore past mistakes. I'd say you done it."

"Yes siree," Morg agreed. "He ain't right often, but Shorty shore hit the nail on the head with that statement." He went on quickly, seeing Shorty swelling and about to jump back at him. "And that Shoshone girl, she's tougher than a buffalo hide. Look at her."

Kajika had been listening, and turned with the three white men to watch Leotie at the fire Morg had built. In English, he said, "She good woman. She Shoshone." Then he looked at Floyd and lowered his voice. "She like you."

Floyd had pulled some wheatgrass and was wiping down Rusty. His head popped up, and in the dark, he stared at Kajika. During his stay at the Shoshone camp, they had become good friends, but he was shocked at what Kajika said. His friend stood there with a grin across his face, along with Shorty and Morg.

"I never heard such," Floyd said.

"You see," Kajika responded, slapping himself on the chest. "Kajika right."

"Humph," Floyd said. "You fellers hurry up. We need to take care of the horses and finish this camp."

Morg chuckled, which brought a glare from Floyd. The tall mountain man held his hands up. "Calm down. I ain't meant nothing."

Floyd finished with Rusty and moved to Browny. It was easy to tell the mule loved a good rubdown and had developed a strong attachment to his owner. Once working on Browny, Floyd quickly pulled himself out of his ill humor at Kajika and the other two. He knew what the Shoshone had said was ridiculous, and anyway he had a lot to do.

By the time the men finished with the horses and mules, had released them on the green meadow, and returned to the fire, Leotie had supper ready.

Even in the dark, she'd found a few green onions she cooked with the elk. After each of them had filled their plate, Floyd sat next to Leotie. He savored each bite, the meat disappearing quickly.

"Mighty fine," he said.

Leotie grimaced involuntarily when she tried to smile through bruised lips. "I am glad you liked it." She looked off into the darkness.

"You're thinking of Mika."

"Yes, he is so young. I know he will be brave, but we must rescue him from the Blackfoot. He must learn the ways of his people."

"You know where he is?" Floyd asked.

At this question, the other men stopped eating and listened. Leotie looked around at them and said, "Yes, the Blackfoot leader, Otaktay, brag much. He said his name means he kills many. He tells me and laughs, saying no one can travel that deep into Blackfoot country and live. He say Mika will grow to become strong Blackfoot in their village. He tell me it is near the Lake of Medicine across the river you trappers call Missouri."

Floyd looked at Morg and Shorty. Morg was shaking his head, and Shorty stared at his plate. "Morg, do you know the place?"

Morg continued to shake his head. "Ain't never been there." He turned to Shorty. "You?"

Shorty shook his head and, unusual for him, said nothing.

Floyd looked at Kajika, receiving the same reply.

Morg cleared his throat and said, "Alls I know is what I heared at rendezvous from some fellers who said they was lucky to get outta there with their hair. Floyd, it's a long ways up north. It gets cold up there early, and it sits out on the plains. The wind, she blows all the time. They said it cuts right through a person."

Floyd glanced at Leotie. If the description concerned her, the determined look on her battered face did not change. "Go ahead," he said to Morg.

"There ain't much more, other than they said you cain't throw a rock, up in that country, without hittin' a Blackfoot. Why it's durned near suicide to head up in that direction. They's bad enough south of the Missouri, but you go north, you can almost bank on losing yore hair."

Morg looked at Leotie apologetically. "I'm mighty sorry, ma'am. That's just what they told me. I'd been doin' myself a sight of drinkin' at that point. I could be mistaken."

Then he looked back at Floyd. "The really bad part is it's nigh on to five hundert miles up there. If we git there, we'll danged near be in Canada. Then you gotta make it back. Figuring where you said the Shoshone village is, we'll be travelin' more'n a thousand miles, and we're almost into August."

Floyd sat silent, thinking. *If we can average forty miles a day, with no problems, it'll take two weeks to get there, riding straight through. We have plenty of horses, and combining supplies, we should be able to do it. Three or four days to look around and rescue the boy, then three weeks back.* He looked at the men. "I figure we can do this in a month, maybe a month and a half. That'll put us back in the middle of September, and we'll still have time to trap."

The fire popped and snapped, throwing shadows across the faces of Morg and Shorty.

They look old, Floyd thought, *and we're all about the same age. Do I look that old? I know we can do it, but am I overlooking the danger to aid Leotie? I sure don't want to get my friends killed.*

Floyd cleared his throat and started. "I don't want you boys to take this the wrong way. I appreciate everything you've done. Why, shoot, if you hadn't come along with me, Morg wouldn't have been caught by the Blackfoot and gone through all of this. Maybe, you should just—"

"Hold on, Floyd." Shorty's voice cut in. "You've already said something like you're a-startin' to say now. Don't you go insultin' me and Morg. We said we wuz with you. We ain't desirin' to have to say it every time things look like they might git a little rough."

Shorty looked at Morg, who gave his partner a sharp nod.

"As I wuz saying, stop it. Now we need to git some shut-eye. Let's git the stuff cleaned and git to sleep."

Floyd looked at the two men and said simply, "Thanks, boys."

Leotie had been looking at her plate. She raised her head,

looking directly at first Morg, then Shorty, and finally Kajika, for everyone knew the young Shoshone was with her until they succeeded or were dead. "Thank you. I will not forget."

Immediately embarrassed, Shorty and Morg were suddenly busy devouring the food from their plates. Each, one after the other, glanced up at her and said, "It's a pleasure, ma'am," and went back to shoveling in the elk meat. After finishing, they started arranging their bedding.

Floyd shook his head, a faint grin on his face. He had made up his mind. No matter how bad it got, he wasn't bringing the subject of them leaving up again. He stood and, finding a soft, level area of pine needles, gathered a few boughs, making a soft bedding, and spread a blanket over it. Then he moved to one of his packs and took out a couple of the woolen trade blankets, laying them out for Leotie, and surveyed his quick work. *Not bad,* he thought.

She was busy at the fire, preparing it for the morning meal. He walked to her side, and she looked up. "We're all tired," he said. "I made you a bed. Why don't you get some sleep. We'll be pulling out early."

She stood from her work, and he found her close next to him. She turned and looked up into his face. The dwindling light of the fire sparkled in her dark eyes. They stood close for a moment, and she said, "Thank you," turned, and moved to the bed.

He watched as she gracefully eased her body down to the bedding of pine boughs, slid her slim legs under the blankets, and pulled them to her chin. Then, embarrassed with himself for watching her, he turned and moved to his saddle and bedding. Only then did he realize how tired he was, and they had failed to assign a watch for the night. Looking around, he caught Kajika's eyes watching him. At once Kajika pointed to himself, then Morg, Shorty, and Floyd. Relieved, he realized that his friends hadn't forgotten.

He lay down with his coat on, pulled a blanket over his feet, took a deep breath, and started to consider the days ahead. As if with a will of their own, his eyes slammed shut, and he was sound asleep.

∽

NEARLY THREE DAYS were behind them. After coming out of the mountains, they crossed the Wind River and found a stark striking land of deep canyons, sagebrush, and ironwood bushes. Rock formations layered in colors from deep orange and red through gray and black. Yesterday, in the evening sun, it was like fire leaping across the red mesas, broken only by the dark green of the juniper trees.

The extra horses had been a handful for a while, but they settled down and were traveling well. Once Kajika learned from Leotie where the Blackfoot were taking Mika, he took over the lead. He was familiar with this country, if not personally then from the many stories told by his father and the older warriors he had listened to at the evening fires. They had been traveling along the Bighorn River. Later that morning, Kajika had turned them almost due north into the Bighorn Mountains.

Leotie was looking better. The swelling in her face was going down. Both of her eyes were opened fully, although there would be discoloration for at least another week. When they took a break for dinner, consisting of jerky and a seal-tight of peaches from his store of supplies, she had told them of her plans.

They were taking a detour. At first, it was hard for Floyd to understand why she would take such a delay, knowing how much she wanted to rescue her son. But she explained about this mystical excursion. Near the top of the mountain they were now slowly climbing, in places so steep they had to ride diagonally across the slope to advance, Leotie said there was a site of great religious significance to the Shoshone.

As they moved up the slope, Kajika and Leotie rode close

together, talking. Shorty followed, with Floyd and Morg bringing up the rear.

Morg began an explanation of what lay ahead. "There's a circle up there, Floyd. It's strange, but when you get there, you'll feel it too. It's like being in a church, but a church from where you can see a hundert miles."

Floyd raised his eyebrows, giving his friend a skeptical look.

"I ain't kiddin', and I ain't crazy. You'll see. It's called the Medicine Wheel, and it's plenty big medicine. The Shoshone claims it was their ancient ones that built it, but the Sioux claim about the same thing. It's a ring of rocks nigh on to eighty feet wide, with a big stack of rocks in the center. I've heard more educated men than me say that it's more'n eight hundert year old. All I know, them rocks is old. From that center stack of rocks, it's got spokes of rocks, twenty-eight of 'em to be exact, same number as the ribs of a buffalo. Them spokes is like a wagon wheel's spokes, laid to the outer ring."

"You say it's over eight hundred years old?"

"No, sir, I'm not sayin' that. I said them other smarter fellers are saying it. I'm just sayin' it's old. Something else that's funny, them tribes don't fight around it, not even the Blackfoot. If members from two different tribes come up to it at they same time, they just do their thing and then leave. They may kill each other later, but not there."

Floyd shook his head. "Well, I imagine this should be interesting."

"I'll tell you something else interesting. You can get only so close, but you ain't suppose to go inside the circle. That there is sacred for the Injuns. Only they can be in that circle."

Morg dropped back, and they continued to ride toward the Medicine Wheel.

Nearing midafternoon, Floyd watched Kajika and Leotie stop their horses and jump down. They tied them to the stunted pines and waited.

Floyd pulled up behind Shorty and stepped to the ground. He tied Buck and then the other horses he was leading, as did Morg, and the three men walked solemnly to the Shoshones.

Not unkindly, Leotie said, "You must not follow us. This is a most sacred place. We will be back soon. You will be able to see it when we leave, for we will ride close on our way north."

Floyd nodded, along with Morg and Shorty. They waited as the Shoshone man and woman walked away. Being close to this sacred place, he had to admit that he felt something. If asked to describe it, he would never have been able to put it into words. But the feeling he had was like a thickness in his chest. It was almost exactly as Morg had described. Like being in a church, but outside. He had felt such moments when the dew kissed the tall grass and sparkled in the early morning sunrise, or when his sister had held a tiny bobwhite chick in her hand and caressed it softly, her eyes brimming with concern and love.

In a short time, they returned. "We can go," Leotie said.

"That's it?" Shorty asked.

Leotie smiled at Shorty. "The Great Spirit does not expect a speech from us. We asked for safety and success."

Shorty spoke up again. "Will we have it?"

Kajika stood silent as Leotie said, "That is only for the Great Spirit to know. We will find out in due time."

Shorty shook his head. "I'll have to say, I woulda liked a little more positive answer."

Floyd thought, *That makes two of us.*

They all mounted and continued up the mildly sloping hillside, past the Medicine Wheel. It was Floyd's turn to finally see the rocks that made up the wheel. It was just as Morg had described. He saw other rocks outside the circle that looked to be placed in strategic positions. He longed to learn more, but today was not the day, for they did not stop, continuing north, into pine forests as they rode down across the slopes and valleys of the Bighorns.

Dusk was approaching as they neared a bench. Floyd rode up next to Kajika, who raised his arm and swept it across the plains several thousand feet below. As he took out and placed his telescope to his eye, the others rode up. Floyd gazed out across the plains below. A sight he was familiar with, but never from such a high vantage point. The impressive vista stretched out below him.

On the plains, as far as he could see with his magnified vision, were thousands, maybe millions of great, brown, shaggy beasts with thick shoulders and massive heads—buffalo.

From north, through east, to south, they packed the plains. He had thought they would all be down around the Arkansas or Brazos by now, but here they were, moving south.

Kajika pointed, across the buffalo, to the northeast. "We go thataway."

Following the pointing finger, Floyd turned the telescope along the same direction and saw nothing but buffalo. In the distance, he could see the Yellowstone River moving north, and it had the thick brown mass extending from both banks. He passed the glass to Kajika, who was now used to the magnification, and closely watched the massive herd. Leotie was next and then the others.

Morg spoke up. "Every time I see a sight like this, I'm amazed. Who would think there could be this many buffalo in one place."

"Moving south," Kajika said. "Big herds drifting away from coming cold."

"Reckon yore right, Kajika," Shorty said. "Would you look at 'em. I reckon if we started shootin' right now and shot every day till I wuz old and gray, we wouldn't put a dent in those numbers."

Kajika nodded. "The buffalo will always be here."

Floyd wasn't so sure. He knew that once the Indians lost control to the white man, there would be farms and cattle. The ranchers and farmers couldn't coexist with the buffalo, and he felt sure he knew who would win out, but hopefully that would be a long time coming. He said nothing.

Morg asked Kajika, "How many more days, you reckon?"

The Shoshone waited while he watched the buffalo, then said, "Maybe ten days, maybe more. Depends on buffalo."

"I reckon so," Shorty responded. "No way I'd want to try to get through that. Why, if they was to stampede, anyone stuck in that mass would be so stomped into the ground, even the coyotes wouldn't be able to smell 'em."

They watched a few minutes longer, and Kajika led out, leaving the shelf, and down the mountain toward the north and Mika.

17

The band of searchers had meandered along the Yellowstone River for three days while the buffalo slowly moved south and east. Leaving the height of the mountains behind, they found the summer heat of the lower elevations welcome. Coats were stowed, giving them more freedom of movement.

The rolling hills and brown grass seemed unending, as did the wind. The second day out from the Medicine Wheel, Shorty said, "I swear, I could never live out here. This danged wind goes on forever, and it blows hard. I've near lost my hat on several occasions."

No one responded.

He looked around at his companions, obviously desiring a comment. When none was forthcoming, he raised the level of his voice and said, "I said—"

Morg quickly cut him off. "We heard you the first time."

"Well," Shorty said testily, "why ain't you answered?"

Morg leaned to the side of his horse and spit, then said, "I ain't heard no question yet."

And so continued the constant needling of Morg and Shorty.

Floyd shook his head, remembering last winter when he'd spent a couple of weeks with his friends in their cabin during a heavy early snowfall. He felt sure an additional day stuck in their cabin would have driven him crazy. He liked and trusted them both. They were dependable and brave, but they could talk, especially Shorty.

Floyd rode next to Leotie. The swelling in her face was almost completely gone. She was looking much more like herself except for her hair. He knew Shoshone women did not cut their hair, and though she said nothing, quite often her hands went to her hair as she felt the short ends around her head.

They had grown closer during this trip. She told him many times how grateful she was for his undertaking this journey to rescue Mika. She spoke often about what a happy and adventurous child he was. One thought kept coming back to him when she was speaking of her son. Women had always amazed him, his ma, sisters, and especially Leotie. *I just hope Mika as resilient as his ma appears to be. I don't know much about women, but after all she went through, it makes it difficult to understand how she can carry on like she does with no complaining. If Mika's anything like his mother, he'll be able to weather this capture.*

Again she reached for her hair, and he glanced her way.

She smiled at him, taking her hand down. "I feel different without it."

Floyd, without thinking, said, "You're a mighty pretty woman, either way."

Her eyes sparkled at his comment. She bowed her head slightly and said, "Thank you, Igasho."

His attention was jerked away as he notice a column of dust, yet distant but moving toward them. He bumped Rusty in the flanks and moved to the front, next to Kajika. Shorty and Morg rode up. Floyd said, "Looks like it's moving toward us." While he was talking, he was pulling out his telescope.

The men and woman had stopped their horses and sat watching the dust.

Shorty said, "We passed that little creek not far back. That'd be a good fightin' hole should we need it."

Floyd said, "Good point, Shorty. Wait till they top that little hill out there. I'll be able to get a good look and see who it is and how many."

Moments passed with only the breathing of the horses and occasional singing lark heard. Abruptly the riders crested the knoll and pulled their horses to a stop. They were still at least a mile away.

Before Floyd could comment, Kajika said, "Sioux," and started stringing his bow.

"He's right," Floyd said as the horsemen dashed from the knoll and disappeared into a draw. The land was made up of rolling hills interspersed with draws and cuts, some deep and wide. It was always difficult to judge the terrain if you had not been over it before.

"Looks like ten or twelve. I didn't see any paint. Probably a buffalo hunting party, but that doesn't mean they won't decide to reward themselves with our horses and supplies, not to mention our scalps."

Shorty said, "Then we'd best head back to that creek. We'd have a better chance there."

"We stay!" Kajika said. "We run now, and Sioux *will* attack. Face them, maybe not."

Shorty gave a quick nod. "Makes sense, but I'm gettin' my firepower ready and recommend everyone else do the same."

Floyd had removed the leather loops holding his two pistols in their respective holsters. In turn he withdrew each one and checked the cap, easing the hammer down and the pistols back in their holsters. He continued to check his rifle and made sure his knife and tomahawk were easy in their scabbards. *Hopefully it won't come to fighting,* he thought. *We don't need anyone killed or injured, but if we must, we'd best be ready.*

Floyd and the others waited. They watched the Sioux top two additional knolls and drop out of sight. When the Sioux dropped into the last draw, Floyd said, "Let's ride to the top of this one, maybe surprise them."

They did as Floyd said, stopping just before they topped out.

The Sioux raced over the top, only to almost run into the armed and waiting group. They frantically turned their horses to the side. Several of their mounts started bucking, throwing two of the braves to the ground. Floyd and his friends remained stoic, neither turning their heads nor laughing.

One of the fallen Indians leaped to the back of his horse and joined the others, but the remaining man watched his animal gallop out of sight, over the rolling hills. Angry, he turned back and jogged to his comrades. One of them, obviously the leader, said something to another brave. The brave he spoke to rode to his grounded companion and extended an arm. Immediately the Indian on the ground grasped the arm and leaped onto the horse behind him. Then the two of them galloped off in pursuit of the missing mount.

That's a good sign, Floyd thought. *If they wanted to kill us, they wouldn't have reduced their number.* With an internal chuckle, known only to him, that thought was followed quickly by another. *Of course, with their two-to-one numbers, they may feel the additional men aren't needed.*

The leader was an impressive man. He rode a big gray on whose back any other man might look small, but this Sioux brave looked as if he was made for the animal. Wearing only leggings and breechcloth, his thick chest and wide shoulders were fully exposed. His hawk nose gave him a regal look that continued with the carry of his chin. Leadership appeared to sit comfortably on him.

Beneath thick brows, coal black eyes took in Kajika and

Leotie, then slid over Shorty and Morg, stopping finally on Floyd. He began to speak in sign language. "Why does the white man bring a Shoshone boy and woman onto Sioux land?"

Out of the corner of his eye, Floyd could see Kajika stiffen at the derogatory comment. "I see no boys," Floyd said. He swept his arm to include the two groups. "We are all warriors here. This Shoshone woman searches for her son, who was taken by the Blackfoot. We are here to help her.

"I am Igasho"—he hit his chest with his fist—"a name given to me by my friend, this brave's father, Chief Pallaton. Who are you?"

At the mention of Pallaton, Floyd thought he saw a response in the eyes of the brave.

"I am Ouray of the great Sioux nation."

Kajika spoke. "You are fearless, and friend of my father. I have heard him speak of you."

"Yes, Chief Pallaton is my friend." Ouray motioned to his eyes, and the tone of his voice changed. "It is good to see the son of my friend. You come with us to our village, and we will celebrate. We chase the buffalo, but must constantly be on the lookout for the Blackfoot and Crow."

Floyd knew time was not on their side. They needed to continue moving north, following the Blackfoot. Any delay could throw their return into winter. He said, "We thank Ouray, but we have many miles to travel to find the son of this woman. We must continue our search. We would ask you, have you seen Blackfoot moving toward the Lake of Medicine?"

Ouray nodded. "Yes, two groups. First, maybe twelve, fifteen days past, we find track moving north. We follow and see Blackfoot with small boy." He held up two hands twice, with fingers extended, and then one hand. "The second group was smaller band. Five, no more. Ride quickly to the north. "We leave Blackfoot alone and continue our hunt," he added, as way of explanation. "It is time for buffalo harvest. This winter will be bad for

Sioux. We must take many buffalo." He looked directly at Leotie. "They have your boy."

She nodded.

Floyd said, "We wish you good hunting. Maybe we'll see you on our return trip."

Ouray gave a single nod. "You will be welcome." With that, he pulled his horse around and, leading his band, loped back the way they had come.

"Who-wee," Shorty said. "I shore figgered we was in deep trouble."

"It could've been," Floyd said. "Good thing Ouray knew Chief Pallaton."

"Yes," Kajika said. "Might be big fight. You see how the others looked at horses?"

"Oh, yeah," Morg said. "They was eyein' these horses. I'm bettin' they was sorely disappointed when Ouray decided to leave."

"Speaking of leave," Floyd said, "I reckon we'd best be on our way." He looked at Leotie. "That's good news Mika is all right."

She gave him a wistful smile. "Very good news."

∽

THEY HAD CONTINUED up the Bighorn River to its confluence with the Yellowstone and followed it north. The journey, so far, had been uneventful since meeting Ouray and the Sioux braves.

Days clicked by. Buffalo were everywhere. The massive herd they had seen was now south of them, but smaller herds, small only when compared with the big one, were still occupying the plains. Several times, the riders had waited. Though anxious to move on, their experience kept them from getting caught among the huge hairy animals, where a horse could get gored, or worse, they could all be trampled should the beasts stampede.

Falling further behind the time allotted, they continued north across the prairie. Floyd had registered the difference in the grasses here and along the plains east of Missouri. The grasses there had been nigh on to a horse's belly. Here, they were still abundant, but shorter, yet covered the plains in a blanket of waving gold. The wind never ceased, which made it more difficult to hear approaching horses. Over the past days, they would occasionally dismount to put their ear to the ground, for eyesight could not solely be depended upon.

After three days of travel along the Yellowstone, they turned north. Kajika assured them this was the best way, and they would strike the river of red water, which would take them to the Missouri. Sure enough, they struck the low-flowing river. Following it until the next morning, they saw the long line of trees continuing both east and west.

Throughout their travel, Floyd had been riding alongside Leotie. Time was divided between silence and talking. The times of silence weren't uncomfortable, they were almost reassuring. He could feel himself growing closer to this woman. Though young, she had been through more than most people suffered in a lifetime. Yet she took it with a confident gracefulness that could not fail to impress anyone who knew her past.

He could tell she liked him and appreciated his attention and concern. With the exception of the one time she had taken his hand, she was not overtly affectionate. Periodically, when they were talking while riding, or at night when they camped, she would touch his arm lightly to make a point. The touches set his heart throbbing.

Marriage had never entered his mind before now. Back home, he had been too interested in hunting, fishing, and trapping to lose his heart to any girl, as his boyhood friend Ezra Mason had done. Why, even though he had been under the spell of the Cheyenne chief's daughter, Dawn Light, when he had first come west with Jeb and Hugh, later, he recognized it for what Jeb called it, puppy love. He had been struck with her beauty. But with

Leotie, this was different. She was pretty, in a strong, calm way that pulled at his heartstrings.

While thus engaged, Floyd had watched the thick tree line running east and west, as it grew in the distance. He rode up alongside Kajika. "The Missouri River?"

"Yes. We will cross above where the river of red water joins the big river."

Shorty had joined them. "They call it the Big Muddy. From the stories I hear, it's a proper name. Always the possibility of quicksand. Kinda like the Red River down in that there Mexican Texas country where they're startin' to have all that uproar. But Kajika here knows the crossing, so it oughta be all right."

Kajika shrugged. "River change often. We see."

Shorty leaned forward to look past Floyd at Kajika. "That ain't very comfortin', Kajika."

The Shoshone brave shrugged again and remained silent.

The Missouri was lined with tall cottonwoods interspersed with burr oak, willows, and chokecherry trees. Beneath the tall cottonwoods, there were dense bushes, some of which were currants and service berries. The service berries were covered with dense, ripe and edible fruit. Much of it had been trampled by massive numbers of buffalo, and those that still stood showed beaten trails passing around and through them.

The riders approached the river, riding abreast.

"Well, bless my tired eyes," Morg said, "if I don't see service berries. Reckon I'll have me a few."

Floyd glanced at Kajika, who made a short, quick shake of his head. "If bottom still good, must cross quickly. Never know when Sioux or Blackfoot come by."

Morg cast longing eyes at the blue-black berries hanging from the service berry bushes. "Reckon I agree, but I ain't happy about it."

The Redwater River drained into the Missouri at the bottom of a big U made by the Missouri. Upriver, only a few yards from where the two rivers joined, the Missouri had narrowed, flowing through a wide section of dry riverbed.

Kajika started to ride forward, and Floyd reached out, touching his friend's arm. "I'll go," he said. "You stay with the others. We don't want anything happening to you. You know where the Blackfoot camp is."

Kajika sat his horse, thinking, then nodded. "You go, but be careful. If still the same, first part deep, may be soft."

Floyd hung his holsters around his neck and, lifting his Ryland Rifle high, nudged the big red roan forward. At the edge of the bank, which rose less than a foot above the water, Rusty hesitated for only a second and leaped into the river. Floyd at first thought the water would reach his pistols, but it was only the splash. The big horse landed easy, water coming up to Floyd's moccasins, and began walking, pushing a wave ahead.

Within seconds, the level of the water began dropping as the bottom sloped up to the bar. Floyd started breathing easier at the feel of his horse climbing out of the water. He registered the solid bottom. *Good,* he thought, *if this remains hard, we can get across quickly.* By the time he had completed his thought, Rusty was on the dry sandbar and moving steadily to the other side, where there was only a trickle of water separating the bar from the bank.

The opposite bank here was only forty yards away. He exhaled a breath of relief and turned to wave to his friends. At that moment, his heart stopped. From the corner of his eye, he saw an Indian rise from behind a chokecherry bush. At the same time, Shorty yelled, "Look out!"

He was spinning around, bringing his rifle to bear on the Indian's chest. Before he could pull the trigger, he heard the twang of the bowstring and caught a glimpse of the arrow headed straight for him. Everything seemed to turn to half-speed. He heard a rifle roar behind him, saw the man fall backward with a red splotch on his chest, and felt the slam of the Indian's arrow into his chest. *Too late!* he thought.

Then five more Indians jumped from behind the thick brush and charged toward him, kicking up spurts as they splashed through the small stream of water. His rifle was aimed at the falling man, and he had not fired. It was simple to move the sights from the dying man to the one leading the charge. He squeezed off a shot. His target clutched at his throat, hands immediately covered with blood, and fell, writhing on the sandbar.

Blackfoot, he thought as he pulled a pistol from the holster around his neck, leveling on the closest man. An arrow from behind Floyd struck that man in the chest. The man kept running toward him, but his steps became less sure. He stumbled and fell onto the sand chest first, breaking the fletched end of the arrow from the shaft.

The remaining two men were almost on him. He jumped Rusty into one of his remaining attackers and fired his pistol into the face of the other. A large black hole appeared at the bridge of the man's nose, and he collapsed like a rag doll. But the remaining attacker was no rag doll.

18

Rusty had hit the brave with a shoulder and sent him flying, but when he hit the ground, he rolled and was up in an instant, again charging Floyd. Floyd dropped his pistol into its holster and tried to pull the other from its scabbard, but it would not move. He had no time to think or fiddle with the weapon. The Indian was almost on top of him. Still holding his rifle by the barrel, Floyd drove the butt into the man's chest, again knocking him to the ground.

This time, he leaped from his saddle, landing on both feet as the Indian charged again. The man carried a massive war club. It was two feet long with a heavy large knob at the end. Protruding from the knob was a deadly spike of at least three inches.

As the brave neared, he swung for Floyd's head. The mountain man, now holding his rifle in both hands, threw it into the face of the Indian. The hammer slammed into the man's cheek, knocking him back and causing the club to whistle past Floyd's face.

The mountain man stumbled back while doing two things. He ripped the holsters from around his neck, for the first time realizing the arrow was stuck in the leather of the right holster, and pulled out his tomahawk.

The Indian recovered quickly and took another swing at Floyd while he was regaining his balance. With his tomahawk, Floyd parried the man's blow, which was delivered with such force his whole hand vibrated. Stepping in closer, with his left fist, he drove a sharp blow to the wound in the man's cheek. The big Indian staggered back, but remained on his feet. Though it was a short jab, Floyd knew the power in his shoulders and was surprised the man did not go down. However, the momentary pause gave Floyd a chance to give the man a quick once-over. *He's for sure Blackfoot*, Floyd thought.

His Blackfoot opponent maintained a guard position with his war club and said something in his language Floyd did not understand. But he had no difficulty hearing the contempt in the Indian's voice. Now more cautious, both men started to circle. Floyd caught the movement from across the river as his friends started across, and he saw in the Blackfoot's eyes he too saw them approaching.

He'll want to finish this and get out of here, Floyd thought.

Sure enough, the Indian feinted to his right, and when it looked like Floyd would move with him, he came back with a low swing to the side. Floyd was expecting it.

Lontac, the Philippine coach who had trained him so well, three years earlier in Santa Fe, was again saving him. He stepped inside the man's swing, grasped the Indian's wrist with his free left hand, raising his arm high, and then he ducked and went under, clamping the man's wrist tight in his big hand. Yanking the arm down and toward him, while at the same time twisting, Floyd leveraged the elbow out of its socket. He heard and felt the elbow pop. He dropped the arm and stepped back.

The Blackfoot's right forearm swung loose from the joint. Though he had dropped his war club, and Floyd had seen the momentary grimace of pain, the Blackfoot brave did not cry out.

He reached back and yanked a long steel-bladed knife from its scabbard. The man's eyes were filled with hate. With no hesitation, he charged Floyd.

Even using his left hand, the Blackfoot was almost successful. Floyd, with all of his training, not only had to fight this man, this brave, this Blackfoot who had learned all of his fighting skills the hard way, but Floyd had to fight overconfidence. When he felt the pop of the man's elbow, he'd relaxed and stepped back, assuming he had won, assuming the Indian was done. He was wrong.

The Blackfoot charged, muscles bunched in his left arm, knife held low with the glistening sharp edge up, the target obviously Floyd's belly. This was the last desperate attempt of a warrior. Barely in time, and reacting more than anything, he dodged right. The point of the knife found only air as it slashed past, and Floyd backhanded his tomahawk into the man's throat.

The razor-sharp blade slashed through skin, arteries, and sinew, finally lodging between vertebrae of the spine. Blood spurted all over the man's chest and Floyd's as the big Blackfoot collapsed to the sand, wrenching Floyd's tomahawk from his hand.

Horses raced to his side. The first to arrive was a pale Leotie. She leaped from her saddle and rushed to Floyd, her eyes filled with fear. She grabbed his biceps and stared at the blood on his chest. After a few moments, and with disbelief, she looked up into his face. "You are not hurt?"

He shook his head, still out of breath, as much from excitement as from exertion. Finally he was able to draw a slow breath and respond.

"No." Then he grinned. "Nary a scratch."

Relief flooded her features as color returned to her cheeks. "But the arrow."

Shorty was walking over, examining the two holsters. He stopped and held them out. "Would ya looky here."

Everyone gathered round to look at the holster. Floyd had

been unable to pull his pistol from the remaining holster because the arrow had cut through the outer leather, gone through the trigger guard, and lodged in the heavy double leather of the holster backing. It still had the pistol locked in the holster.

Morg shook his head. "I swear, Floyd. Don't go a scarin' us like that. We knowed you was a goner. Then we was more amazed when you kept fightin' with that arrow stickin' out of yore chest. I'll tell you this, I ain't never seen nothin' like that. You got to be the luckiest fool on this earth."

Floyd grinned at his friend. "Can't argue with that."

Kajika had moved to the warrior Floyd had just fought. "You want scalp?"

"No, I don't. I don't believe in takin' a man's hair, especially this man. He almost had me. You're free to do what you will with the others, but this one keeps his hair."

Kajika looked at Floyd, then dropped the man to the ground and headed toward the others.

Shorty laid his hand on his tall friend's shoulder. "You was mighty lucky, Floyd. I don't just mean the arrow, or killin' this one. Any one of them Injuns could've stayed behind all that cover"—he pointed at the thick tree line on the destination shore—"and turned you into a pincushion." He shook his head and looked up at the blue sky. "Somebody up there's taken a hankerin' to you, pard."

Leotie had been watching and listening. When the others rode up, she had released his arms and stepped back, but Floyd had seen her lovely dark eyes remained focused on his face the whole time. "Shorty speaks wise words, Igasho," she said. "Great Spirit protects you. You are special man."

Embarrassed now, Floyd looked into those eyes and said, "Leotie, I don't know about that. But if he does, I'm mighty grateful."

Softly, she said, "I am also grateful."

He could see Morg, now uncomfortable, act as if he might be

intruding. He turned to Shorty and said, "Reckon we need to do something with these bodies."

Shorty looked at him, frowned, and said, "What's the rush?"

Floyd caught Morg's quick jerk of his head, and Shorty's recognition. "Oh, yeah, the bodies." Now louder, "Yes siree, we'd best take care of these bodies and right now." He handed Floyd his holsters and joined Morg. The two grabbed the brave Floyd had fought and carried him to the shore.

Leotie stepped forward, reaching out her hand to touch the arrow where it had sliced through the holster. Grasping the pistol with a strong thumb and forefinger, she lifted it toward the outer portion of the holster so that she could see the inside of the holster back. The arrow had penetrated only one thickness of the back.

Floyd watched intently. He could almost see her mind working. He was aware she knew the arrow should have penetrated all three layers and at least wounded him. She looked up, her eyes questioning.

He gave her a sheepish grin. "I made these. I'd seen other holsters that, as they get older, become all twisted out of shape. So I had an idea. I have a friend who made these pistols and my rifle. He's a gunsmith. I went to him and explained my problem. I needed a short, thin piece of steel to be sewn in between the layers to help the holsters keep their shape. He made the sheets for me. It makes the holsters a little heavier, but not much, and helps them retain their shape. That's what stopped the arrow."

Before she and Mika had been kidnapped, she had always had a ready smile. Since the rescue, though she was strong, her smiles were few. It made his heart rejoice as she looked up from the holster and gave him a brilliant smile. "That makes perfect sense, Igasho, but what I said makes more sense. You are under the Great Spirit's protection, which means you are a good man."

That gave him something to think about.

A low yell from the bank pulled him from this wondrous moment.

"We could use some help," Shorty called. Then as an afterthought, "When you can, of course."

Floyd smiled back at Leotie, gripped the arrow, and pulled it from the holster, flinging it to the ground. He swung the holsters around his waist, walked to his rifle still lying in the sand, picked it up, and shoved it in the scabbard. Then he quickly reloaded both pistols, placed firing caps on the nipples, and, after lowering the hammers, dropped them back into their respective holsters. Though he would like to reload his rifle, he would have to do some special cleaning on it before he again poured powder down the barrel. No telling how much sand was packed in the barrel and action.

Leotie had gathered the horses and held Rusty's bridle as Floyd strode to the bank where the others were busy burying the bodies. The other braves had been scalped. Floyd could see the bloody hair and scalps hanging from Kajika's waist. Though he knew that many white men also took scalps, he had always considered it a barbaric ritual, as had his father and grandfather. He understood that most of the Plains Indians believed the taking of scalps gave strength to the scalper and the tribe.

The men worked quickly burying the braves. It was necessary to get them deep enough to ensure animals did not uncover them or expose the bodies until Mika was rescued and they were safely away. As far as they knew, they were still days away from the nearest Blackfoot encampment, and that was the one where Mika was held, so the Blackfoot braves should not be missed for many days.

With the gruesome job done, Floyd's rifle cleaned, the horses watered, and the Blackfoot horses in tow, they started north again. The way Floyd understood their approach, they were still two, maybe three days from the village. According to Morg, they would be following the Poplar River north until, almost a day's ride ahead, it turned west. They would continue north. When they were well north of a line toward the lake of medicine, they would turn east so as to arrive on the northwest side of the village. It sounded like a good plan to Floyd. Anything to do to mask their approach was important. The Indians would not be expecting an attack from the north.

The addition of six more horses would make their hiding more difficult. It was necessary to move slowly to prevent a rising dust cloud that would give away their position. At last, they had a reason to, if not like the wind, to at least appreciate it. For the blowing wind helped dissipate the dust, allowing them to ride faster than had it not been blowing.

One rider and Leotie brought the horses while the other three acted as outriders, sending out a three-prong picket, much like a turkey track. The farthest scout was the man in the center, who rode far enough ahead to spot hostiles before the group was spotted but not so far as to allow those same hostiles to slide in unseen behind him. The other two scouts rode behind the point man and to the sides, everyone taking their time and sweeping the plains with intense eyes.

Before the first day was finished, it became obvious that the two- to three-day estimate was far from accurate. The constant stopping prior to cresting hills, the checking of cuts and canyons, and the constant straining to see threats before being spotted were beginning to tell on them.

In camp, Shorty was growing ill tempered. He was a good man, but with little more than a grain of patience. Their new style of travel was strumming his nerves. Anything Morg said seemed to rankle him, sometimes even Floyd.

So far, they had been very fortunate. On the second day a small dust cloud, to their front, rose, moving west to east. Floyd rode farther out, and after tying Buck, he crawled along the edge of a rocky ridge.

His telescope was hung from his neck for ready use. Reaching a vantage point along the ridge, behind a long growth of rabbit-brush, he eased his head out just enough so he could see the grassy plain. Knowing the sun was well off to one side of him, so there would be no reflection from the telescope, he placed it to his eye. The magnification drew the ten braves almost into his lap.

From the direction they were riding, it appeared obvious their destination was the village where Mika was held. As he lay watching the sight, he couldn't help but marvel. Even in his dreams, as a boy, he had never thought he would ever see such a sight. Blackfoot warriors rode easy on their horses, riding as if part of their steeds. Magnificent cavalry of the plains, who believed this land was theirs to be shared by no man. The background of these northern plains, tan from the grasses turning, cut with dark green lines of cottonwood and dogwood trees outlining the creeks and riverbeds, and dotted with buffalo that had not yet ventured south, caused Floyd to take a deep breath of appreciation. Here was a unique painting, dreamed by many, but seen only by his eyes.

Another deep breath brought him to the reality of his situation. After confirming, one last time, the direction of the braves, and with ever-so-deliberate movement, he dropped below the ridge and quickly surveyed the countryside behind him. This breath he took with relief. All clear. *I'd best not get myself so wrapped up in watching,* he thought. *If I'm not careful, some brave will be brandishing my hair and telling his friends about the stupid white man he slipped up on.*

Careful to dislodge none of the stones along the ridge, Floyd eased down to Buck, stepped in the saddle, and as quietly as possible, made his way along the dry bottom. He guided Buck through the maze of shallow draws until he was well away from the Blackfoot and below a higher hill behind and to his northeast.

Finding a trail cut by deer, he eased Buck up the side of the draw, just until it was possible for him to see over the lip. Clear. He waited for a few more moments. Buck became impatient, nodded a few times, and pawed at the dirt.

"All right, Buck ole boy," Floyd said. He leaned forward and patted the buckskin's neck. He liked riding him on the plains, because the horse's color blended in so well. "You just relax yourself. We'll be on our way shortly."

After finishing his scan, he gave the prairie one last slow examination, then bumped the horse in the flanks. Buck moved up and over the lip, and they were on the rolling plains. Floyd kept the horse to a walk. After a short distance, he looked at his back trail. With each step, the dust rose beneath Buck's feet. But at their slow pace, it rose only four or five inches before the constant wind blew it into oblivion, never reaching a height or thickness to be noticed.

The mountain man took a moment for a closer check of the horse's tracks in the dust. They were there and clear. He could only hope no Blackfoot would cut their trail before accomplishing their mission. He had become to think of it as a mission. He had heard Pa talk about the second war with the British and occasionally mention a mission or two they had been on. Floyd felt like this was much like a military mission. They were riding against unbeatable odds and had to accomplish a feat that seemed almost impossible. Then they must escape unharmed. *Yes,* he thought, *this is definitely a mission.*

After twenty minutes, he topped a rise and saw Shorty and Leotie with their horses. He could see Browny and the mule owned by Shorty and Morg walking along free of their loads. He had thought of that when they had added the horses from McMillan's crew. Why not let some of the horses relieve the mules? The horses had accepted the packs from the mules with no problems. Evidently, they had previously been used as packhorses, maybe switched between riding and packing. Whatever it was, he was sure the mules enjoyed it.

Luckily for the animals, the loads were getting lighter as supplies dwindled. Floyd still hoped he would find Jeb, for his partner would have a full load of supplies for the winter. But he realized, even more than before he started this rescue, the Rocky Mountains were not only high, but wide. *I wonder how Jeb is doing,* he thought. *I'm wishing, for sure, he makes it back all right. We've got a lot of trapping to do during the remainder of this year and next spring, to make up for all the time I'll be losing with this trip.*

A cloud of guilt overshadowed him for a moment. *Reckon I shouldn't be thinkin' about my own self. Leotie's worried sick about Mika. If the truth were told, I been worryin' a sight myself. In the time I was in the Shoshone village, I grew mighty fond of the little tike, mighty fond.*

He pulled Buck up next to Shorty and Leotie. They had lead ropes to all of the horses and mules. It would have been so much easier to release and drive them, but that would mean a lot more dust, and they couldn't afford dust. *Anyway,* he thought, *we might be needin' extra mounts if we've got Blackfoot on our heels.*

"Saw a few Blackfoot 'bout three miles ahead. Reckon there was ten. They were ridin' fast and hard in the direction of their camp."

With a sour note, Shorty snapped, "They ain't seen you, did they?"

Floyd grinned at Shorty. "Well now, I don't think we'd be talkin' all relaxed like if they had."

Shorty just grunted.

Floyd continued. "There's a pond ahead. It ain't much, but I'm thinkin' we ought to make for it and set up a cold camp. No fire."

"That means no coffee, again," Shorty grumbled.

"You're right, Shorty, but I've developed a real liking for this head of hair I've got, and I'd like to hang on to it."

"Humph," Shorty said again.

Floyd pointed to a knoll to their front left. "That's where it is. Circle around the hill at its base so you don't expose yourself. The pond is on the west side of the hill, even has a few willows around it. Don't really expect any company. But we need the water. Looks to be just enough water in it."

When Floyd was explaining to stay well below the hill, Shorty was getting an even more peeved look on his face. Finally, he said, "Floyd Logan, I ain't needin' some young whippersnapper telling me how to stay hid. We'll just mosey over there and do what you was a-sayin' because I know what to do."

Without another word, and before Floyd could reply, Shorty kicked his horse in the flanks, and the animal gave a little jump, then started walking.

Leotie looked at Floyd, a small smile on her face.

Floyd shrugged. He knew Shorty meant nothing with his short temper. He was just Shorty being Shorty. Once the fight started, there wasn't a more dependable friend.

Floyd wasn't concerned with Morg or Kajika. They would be working back soon, would find their tracks, and meet them at the water. The three rode slowly and silently around the low hill and, finding a draw, dropped down into it, continuing to circle the hill as they descended.

Reaching the bottom, a small clear tank, outlined by sparse willows, waited to reward them for their persistence. As they moved closer, the animals pulled at their ropes and reins, straining toward the water.

"Hold them off," Floyd said. He jumped from Buck, untied the water bag, and collected the bags and canteens from the other two. Cautiously he moved to the least steep side of the tank. The opposite side had a bluff bank that rose into the canyon wall, making it unapproachable from the west.

Once the bags and canteens were filled, he hung his back on the saddle and took the others to Leotie and Shorty. Then he moved back to the horses with the packs and removed the last two empty bags from them. During all this time, Buck had been straining at the bit to get to the water. Floyd held him off until the last two bags were filled. Once he had picked up the last two bags, he threw the reins over Buck's head, looped them on the saddle horn, and turned him loose. The buckskin quickly stepped to the water and began drinking. Floyd turned to Shorty and Leotie and said, "You can let those cayuses drink."

Shorty and Leotie released the animals they'd been leading, climbed down from their mounts, and let them go. All of the horses headed for the tank. Floyd strode to the packhorses and, while they were drinking, unfastened the packs. Floyd lifted each pack from the animal's back and carried it near where he figured to place the camp. Soon, all horses had been stripped of tack. Most were gathered at the waterhole, while a few others chose to scratch their backs with a few rolls in the grass.

19

The horses finished drinking about the time Morg rode in. He was followed by Kajika. The Shoshone looked around at the camp and nodded, stepping from his mount. "Good place to rest," the younger man said. "No in open. Blackfoot not find."

"I shore hope not," Morg replied, removing his tack and taking it to the camp. His horse moved quickly to the now murky water. "I'd be plumb mortified if they come ridin' up."

"Onlyest way they'd find us," Shorty said, "was if'n they stumbled on top of us."

Floyd agreed. "I saw this place as I was riding in. Seemed a likely spot to camp. My favorite thing is it's down out of the wind."

"Ain't that the truth," Shorty said. "I swear, there ain't a day passes that this here wind ain't a-blowing. I'm just about tired of it."

Though Floyd joined the others in a chuckle, he agreed with Shorty. There wasn't much in this country he didn't like, even this north country, but the incessant wind, if given enough time, would get on his nerves. Rather than think about it, he dug out the jerky and tossed some to everyone except Leotie, then followed it with an airtight of peaches.

She had laid her saddle and bedding next to his. With a handful of jerky and two cans of peaches, he walked over, sat, and leaned back against his saddle. He handed her half of the jerky and set both cans by his saddle. Leotie took the jerky from him, their fingers momentarily touching. She held her hand against his a moment longer than necessary, then withdrew it full of jerky and began to eat.

All of them bit off hard chunks and began chewing. At first it took some hefty grinding, but finally the jerky became more pliable. Still, there was no talking while they concentrated on the job at hand. The buffalo jerky, though difficult to chew, tasted good and satisfied the appetite. When it was done, Floyd pulled out his knife and started cutting the lid off one airtight. Once he had it cut sufficiently so that he could bend the lid back, he handed it to Leotie. She smiled her thanks, taking the can in her small hand. With her knife, she reached into the can, sliced a peach in half with the sharp blade, and stabbed a portion, lifting it to her mouth. Her eyes lit up with the taste.

Floyd nodded, smiled, and said in Shoshone, "Good, isn't it?"

After she had finished, she responded, "Yes, I don't think I could ever tire of them."

He laughed, nodded again, and replied in English, "I never have. We had peach orchards back home, and my ma used to can them. I loved fresh peaches, but the canned ones were really good on a cold winter night. She'd open several for dessert, and we'd make 'em disappear fast."

The others had little to say as they devoured the peaches. Shorty was finished first. He leaned against his saddle and stared up at the darkening sky. "This is mighty fine country. I'd love to trap it. Why, I think all the beaver in the Rockies decided to go north and make their homes up here. Reckon I ain't seen as many beaver and beaver dams anywhere else as

I've seen up here. They even have 'em out on parts of this prairie land."

Kajika nodded. "Big beaver country. Trap beaver here, lose hair."

Shorty nodded his head fiercely. "Now ain't that the gosh-darned truth. As much as I like it, I like my lovely locks much better." At this statement, he removed his hat and ran his fingers through his thick hair.

Floyd laughed. "Sounds like a smart move, Shorty. I think Kajika hit the target dead-on. I'll reserve my trappin' for farther south."

Morg spoke up. "Speakin' of hair loss, Floyd, you have a plan for getting the boy out of that Blackfoot camp?"

"I do."

"Well, you plannin' on sharing that plan with us fore we get there? It'd shore make me a mite more comfortable."

"I'll do that, Morg. We ride in, take him, and ride out. Short and sweet."

Morg shook his head. "If you don't mind my sayin' so, that don't sound like much of a plan."

Floyd, his face expressionless, said, "It isn't, but I have been thinking on it. Number one, we need to find out where he's being kept. Next, we need a distraction so that Leotie and I can slip in at night and take him. Third, we need to get out of there safely. Does that plan sound better?"

Morg raked his hand down the beard he'd been growing since they'd caught up with McMillan, and spit a long stream of tobacco juice. "Not much."

"That's all I've come up with. I figure we've got to get close enough to look at the camp. We have to spot Mika and identify which teepee he goes into at night. We also need to find out if they're keeping him tied or loose."

Kajika spoke. "Him no tied. Blackfoot . . ." He stopped and switched to Shoshone. "They want him to become a Blackfoot.

He can't if he feels like a captive, so he'll be free. Maybe they'll have someone watching him, maybe not, but he won't be tied."

Shorty and Morg had picked up enough Shoshone to understand the gist of the statement. "Well, if he ain't tied," Shorty said, "that'll shore make it easier."

Floyd went on. "Once we know which teepee he's in, we, Leotie and me, will slip down, cut a slit in the back, take him out, and make a run for it."

"That's a death sentence, if I ever heard one," Morg said. "As soon as that knife slips through the hide of the tent, whoever's inside will hear it, and you'll be dead before you get inside, or worse, they'll capture you. You already came close to a taste of how the Blackfoot treat prisoners. Is finding out so all-fired important to you?"

Floyd's head shaking was difficult to see in the growing darkness. "No, Morg. I'm not anxious to find out. That's why we need a distraction. I haven't yet figured what that should be, but it should draw everyone from the teepees. The tough part is grabbing Mika before he makes it outside."

Leotie spoke quickly to Floyd. "I know how. I used to call Mika using the call of the meadowlark. I will show you." She puckered her full lips and released a whistle that sounded exactly like the high, low, and trill of the meadowlark. She did it again.

A faint smile creased Kajika's face. "It sound like a bird to me. Like what the white man calls a lark. Blackfoot will think it is a bird."

"Good," Floyd said. "The other thing we need to ensure doesn't happen any sooner than it has to is them chasing us. We need to find their horses and drive them off. That may be all the distraction we need. We'll just have to wait and see."

He turned to Kajika. "You have any idea of when we need to make our turn east, and how far to the village?"

"I think we turn now, but I must scout village. It no more than half day's ride, maybe less." Kajika looked around. "This good place to let horses rest. Tomorrow I find village."

"Good," Floyd said, "I'll come with you." He looked into the dark eyes of Leotie. "We will have Mika soon."

She nodded. "Soon."

"Morg, you and Shorty stay here and keep watch. From what Kajika tells us, we should be able to reach the village, scout it, and be back late tomorrow night." He continued to talk to Morg, but glanced at Shorty. "If we don't make it back, continue to *wait* for us here. Don't come looking. It may be farther than we think, or we might get tied up scouting. Fortunately, we have a fairly bright moon, so we should be able to travel at night."

"Humph," Shorty said. "Just make sure if'n you get tied up, it ain't by them Blackfoot. I'm checkin' the horses." With that he stood and stalked off toward the horses.

"He don't like bein' left out of a fight," Morg said.

Floyd nodded. "Morg, I understand, and believe me, before this is over, I'm bettin' we're all gonna have our belly full of fighting."

~

FLOYD AND KAJIKA crawled through a shallow alkaline ravine covered in sagebrush and greasewood. The acrid smell of the greasewood filled the low air they were breathing. They had stopped for a good reason. Ahead, three speckled brown sage-grouse hens and one large rooster, his white breast flashing, topped with a feathered collar of chocolate brown, fussed as they hurried away from the two men. The last thing desired by either man was for the grouse to flush. The large birds didn't fly for fun, but to escape, and even the youngest Blackfoot in the village would immediately be alerted.

At last the grouse turned perpendicular to Floyd and Kajika, and the two men, relieved, continued their crawl. Reaching the crest of the low hill, they moved even more slowly, keeping the gray foliage of the sagebrush between them and the village.

Finding what Floyd considered an excellent vantage point, he pulled out his telescope and began to scan the village. He was surprised to see the number of teepees. There were far fewer than he had expected. He had been led to believe there could be as many as four to five hundred Blackfoot in this village. Counting women and children, it would be hard-pressed to contain a hundred people. He counted only fifteen teepees. Most of the people were either very old or young, less than ten years old. He handed the telescope to Kajika. While the Shoshone slowly examined the village, Floyd looked to their left, right, and rear. He wanted no surprises.

At length Kajika handed the telescope back to him, leaned to his ear, and said, "Look to the north of the weathered, almost gray, teepee. The boy, sitting with the woman next to him."

As soon as his eye adjusted to the focus of the telescope, he saw him, Mika. A thrill coursed through his body. He was overjoyed to see the little boy. He examined him closely. The telescope brought him so close Floyd felt like he could almost reach out and touch him. Mika appeared to be unharmed, though his face showed deep sadness. For some reason, he turned and looked directly at the hillside, and Floyd could see his eyes and the set of his mouth clearly.

It was like he was looking at a man's weary face in a five-year-old. His face was dirty, but there were no tear lines in the dirt. Under his breath, Floyd said, "The boy has grit."

Kajika, having heard, but not understanding, turned his head to Floyd, a questioning look on his face.

Floyd shook his head and continued to watch Mika. Another boy, maybe twice Mika's age, walked up, said something, and when Mika stared straight ahead, kicked him. Floyd felt rage beginning to build, but the woman who had been sitting next to the younger boy reached across him, grabbed the older youth by the arm, and threw him with such force he stumbled and fell to the ground. Immediately an older man who had been watching the altercation stalked to stand in front of the woman. He was obviously angry. He drew his hand back as if to strike her, and quick as a striking snake, she had a knife in her hand. He could see her calmly saying something to the man. He listened, spun around, and grabbed the Blackfoot boy by the hand as he stalked off.

Though without the benefit of the telescope, Kajika had also been watching the altercation. Floyd heard a grunt of satisfaction as he thought, *At least Mika has someone protecting him.*

They continued to survey the village. It was apparent there were no more than thirty braves here. With the older and younger folks here, he figured that most of the tribe, including the braves, was off hunting buffalo. It appeared the Blackfoot felt they had nothing to fear from attack.

Floyd continued to examine the village, the terrain, an escape route, and where the horses were kept. With a plan in mind, he handed the glass back to Kajika. His friend took it and made one last examination before handing it back. The young white man and Shoshone warrior reversed themselves, backing down the hill the way they had come.

Once at the bottom, they eased down the draw until it began to deepen. Shortly they came to their horses. Before leaving, they gave both mounts water, neither man speaking. With the horses watered, they stepped into the saddles and eased themselves along the draw, always keeping the knolls to the east between them and the village.

The two men traveled the rest of the day into evening. The wind had picked up out of the southeast and was blowing tumbleweeds ahead of it. The air was filling with dust, and Floyd had pulled a neckerchief across his nose to keep out some of it.

The moon was well up when they rode into camp. The narrow canyon helped block the wind. It was at least tolerable.

When they rode up, Shorty stepped out from behind a boulder. "Glad to see you made it back. You got a plan?"

"Yep," Floyd said. He unsaddled Rusty and, with some of the grass, wiped the horse down, then allowed the animal to head to the pond. Kajika did the same, and both horses moved rapidly to the water.

Floyd dropped his saddle next to Leotie, pulled some additional jerky from his pocket, and started chewing.

"Well?" Shorty said, not long on patience.

Floyd moved a big hunk of jerky to the corner of his mouth and said, "We saw the village. The good news is there are way fewer braves there than we thought. At the most, maybe twenty or thirty."

He turned to Leotie. "We saw Mika, close, no more than fifty yards. He looks fine, lonely, but fine."

In the moonlight, Floyd watched relief flood her face. Her eyes brightened. "Can you tell me how he is?"

"Like I said, he looks fine. He's in good shape. They seem to have taken good care of him." He then proceeded to tell her about the incident they had seen and how the woman with him had responded.

Her face clouded with concern. "It sounds like this woman has been given my Mika. She may not give him up easily."

"I suspect you're right," Floyd said. "I'm hopin' not to have to harm her, but no matter what happens, tomorrow night he will again be with you."

Leotie's eyes glinted at the thought of her son joining her.

Morg said, "Now you got a plan?"

"I do," Floyd said around the big piece of jerky he was chewing. "Kajika and I worked it out on the way back." He picked up a long stick, took it between his large hands, and broke it in half, throwing part of it away. With the remaining portion, he started drawing the village. Once he had laid it out, his explanation began.

"This has to be coordinated, and that may be tough, with this wind pickin' up. It'll give us cover, but makes it difficult to hear what's goin' on. Now look at this."

Floyd pointed to the teepee on the west side of the camp next to where Mika and the Blackfoot woman had been sitting. "This is where we suspect Mika is kept."

Shorty burst out. "You don't know? You didn't wait until he went in?"

Unabashed, Floyd slowly raised his head and drilled his friend with cold blue eyes. With a soft voice that could barely be heard over the wind, he said, "Shorty, get a rein on your temper. We need to be calm if we're going to pull this off, and your role is important."

Shorty held Floyd's stare for a moment, then dropped his eyes. "Yore right, Floyd. Sorry." He then perked up. "So what's my role?"

"I'll get to it in just a minute. I'll tell you what we first thought about and then discarded. Like I've said, we're gonna need a distraction. We thought about one of us lighting a big pile of creosote brush and dragging it around the village on the opposite side. Now, that idea is useless. The wind's blowing too hard and in the wrong direction. If we drag burning brush around the east side of the village, the wind will blow it back on the village, and with all the kids and old folks, they'll be burned alive. Kajika and I said no to that plan, knowing everyone would agree."

Morg and Shorty both were nodding vigorously. Shorty said, "You got that right for sure, Floyd. We could end up killing that whole passel of Blackfoot. We'd never be able to stand ourselves after that, especially with all those old folks, women, and kids."

Agreeing with his friends, Floyd continued. "So this is what we've decided. Their corrals are just north of the village. This is a job for two men, one of which must be Kajika. Morg, this is where you come in."

Morg stepped forward so he could see the dirt drawing

clearly in the moonlight. "You and Kajika will loose the horses and start raisin' cane. Drive straight through the camp. Shoot, yell, whatever you can do to make noise. The goal is to get those horses out of there, so they can't be used, and to get the Blackfoot folks in the tent with Mika outside."

Morg looked at the Shoshone, and both men nodded. "We can do that."

"Good," Floyd said. He turned and looked at Shorty. "This next part is yours."

20

"Shorty," Floyd said, "take my rifle. That'll give you two. Your job is to take the horses about a mile downstream and tie them tight, but use slipknots. If things work out right, we'll be coming like the devil himself is after us. Hopefully, most, if not all, of their horses will be ahead of us."

Floyd looked up at Shorty, who nodded vigorously. "Have your horse close, and be ready to ride. It'll be your job to pick off any Blackfoot who may have gotten to a horse and is chasing us. We'll go past you like scared jackrabbits, so don't you waste any time. After you shoot, get on your horse and get out of there. We'll pick up our horses and keep riding." He stopped and looked around the group. "Any questions?"

Morg spoke up. "Reckon I do have a question. What's gonna be occupying yore time?"

"Right," Floyd said, and again pointed out the teepee, the creek behind it, and the low knoll across the river. "Leotie and me, we'll be easin' down this hill, across the creek, and into the teepee where Mika is. When the ruckus starts, we'll snatch him out and be on our way."

Morg and Shorty looked at each other. Morg said, "You'll just waltz in, without yore rifle, say howdy, load up the boy, and mosey on out. Just a stroll in the pansies. Am I understandin' you right?"

"That's right."

"You don't see nothin' wrong with that plan?"

"Morg, I said it was simple. I didn't say it would be easy. Every part of this plan depends on everyone else doing their part. Leotie needs to be with me to calm Mika. Kajika needs to go with you to steady those Blackfoot horses before you scare 'em to death, and Shorty needs to give us the cover we need."

Floyd could feel himself getting angry, stopped for a moment, and took a deep breath. This time he spoke to everyone. "Look, if we had an army, we might do this differently, but this is all we have." He waved his arm around to each of them. "We may be a little short of manpower, but we've got good people. We can make this happen. Near this time tomorrow night, we'll have Mika and be headed back south."

Quiet pervaded the camp as each person considered what lay ahead, the possibility of success, and the probability of death. It was almost a sure thing that at least one, and maybe all of this little group would be dead tomorrow night.

Shorty broke the silence. "Morg, you'd best not be hooting like some Blackfoot when you come ridin' at me, or I'm liable to treat you to a lead snack."

Everyone, even Kajika and Leotie, chuckled at Shorty's comment.

"Now." Floyd looked around. "Any more questions?"

Heads shook. They studied the layout of the village a while longer until Floyd said, "We'd better get some rest. We've got a big day and night ahead of us."

"I'll just be glad when we're far enough south of here so I can make me a big pot of coffee," Shorty said as he strode to his bedroll.

Floyd moved to his bedding, noting Leotie had aired it out

and straightened it for him. He sat on it and looked at her, sitting close, little more than a foot or two away. In the moonlight she looked even more youthful than her short stack of years. The soft light of the moon cast a serene ethereal glow over her cheeks and full lips. Occasionally a small cloud would drift in front of the moon, and when it passed, the sudden spotlight on her almost took his breath away. She gazed at him, and his mind wondered, *What is she thinking? Is she worried about tomorrow? She doesn't appear to be. What will tomorrow hold for us?*

"Flo-yd?" she asked, using a name she seldom called him. "What will you do when you return us to our village?"

It seemed there was no doubt in her. No questioning whether or not they would be successful. Her only doubt appeared to be about him.

"Reckon we'd first better get Mika rescued before we start concerning ourselves about what might be happening later."

Another cloud drifted in front of the moon, bringing darkness to her face. The magic moment was gone. He continued to watch her until she spoke again.

"Yes, you are right, but your plan will work. I know it in my heart." Leotie lay back, stretching her slim legs and pulling the two blankets over her. "Good night, Flo-yd."

Floyd, too, lay back against his saddle, considering the question she had asked. What would he do when they were returned to their village? He needed to find Jeb, and with everything that had happened, he had little time for trapping. And what about wanting to see all the fresh land in the mountains and to the west? What about that?

He lay watching the clouds race by overhead, and listened to the wind moan in the rocks above. It would be a cold night.

∼

THEY LEFT for the Blackfoot village later in the day, so it would put their arrival just before sunset. The wind continued to blow, if anything, harder. Dust rode in the sky, blanketing the sun and casting everything in a dirty brown glow.

Arriving where Kajika and Floyd had tied their horses the day before, they stopped, dismounted, tied the animals, and the four of them made their way back to the knoll. Though it was dangerous, and with twice their number the likelihood of discovery much greater, Floyd felt it was worth it. The dust and wind would cover their movement. With everyone getting a good look at their objective, it would hopefully make their tasks easier.

Once everyone had a look at the layout of the village, all but Floyd and Leotie retired back down the hill to their horses, to move into position. After the three men were gone, Floyd watched the village in the fading light. He spotted Mika and handed the telescope to Leotie. It took some adjusting for her to get it focused and then to find her son, but Floyd heard the gasp when she saw her boy.

They lay on the hillside, watching, until the woman took him by his small hand and led him into the teepee. Leotie continued to watch. Floyd figured she was probably hoping Mika would come back out, but the darkness, with the exception of the early, dim moonrise, was taking over from the light of day. It left little to see.

He reached out, gently removed the glass from her eye, closed it, and slid it back inside its case. They would wait here a while longer. They must be at the back of the teepee when the moon hit its zenith, for that was when Morg and Kajika were going to wake the dead. They would drive the horse herd through the village while yelling and firing. Hopefully enough confusion would be created for them to slip into the teepee, rescue Mika, and get away without harm.

Floyd watched the village. Due to the wind, there were no

outside fires. Anyone foolish enough to start a fire, if he could in this wind, would soon have a raging prairie fire that would race across the prairie. He could see glows from the tents, where the Blackfoot women had started fires inside.

The moon rose sluggishly from the horizon. Its brightness seemed reluctant to plow through the dusty night sky, giving only a fraction of the light it would on a clear night.

Floyd watched the slow progress of the moon, and Leotie. She remained calm, unperturbed by the seeming slow passing of time. She noticed him watching and gave him a smile, barely visible in the faint moonlight.

Finally, looking at the moon's position, Floyd figured they had no more than an hour to get into position. He looked north at the horses, but could see nothing indicating his two friends were anywhere around. In the dim light, he could make out several light-colored horses with their heads down, sleeping. He stowed the telescope, touched Leotie on the arm, and the two of them backed off the knoll.

Reaching their two remaining horses, Floyd's mind flew to Shorty. *I sure hope Shorty's in position with the extra horses well tied, 'cause I feel certain we're gonna need 'em."*

They both mounted and moved slowly out of the draw, making their way around the south end of the hill. Once past the base, they entered the trees along Big Muddy Creek, a wide creek bed with a small stream flowing through the middle. Adjacent to the Blackfoot village, the creek flowed from north to south. Here it was not only narrow, but shallow, no more than a foot deep.

He was thankful for the wind. Not only was it keeping everyone inside, but it was covering up whatever noise they might make. They guided the horses into the trees, rode quickly through them on the west side, crossed the water, the splashing even difficult for them to hear, thanks to the wind, and pulled up before entering the trees on the village side.

They dismounted. Floyd checked his handguns to make sure there was no binding in the holsters. He looked down the riverbed. It was clear of rocks and obstructions for at least a hundred yards. They could dash the horses at least that far before coming out of the river and trees to race toward Shorty. Both horses were tied with a slipknot so they could yank the reins and jump on. Floyd patted Rusty, turned to Leotie, and nodded.

The two glided like apparitions into the tree line, eased near the edge, and kneeled, looking at the clear prairie between them and the teepees. No more than thirty yards lay between them and Mika. Only the buffalo hide of the teepee separated the boy and his mother.

The wind continued to blast through the village, driving sand and anything loose before it. Floyd moved his head close to Leotie's. "Whistling isn't going to work in this wind. Hopefully he'll stay in the teepee." She gave a solemn nod of understanding.

Now, all they could do was wait. It was up to Kajika and Morg. If the moon had moved slowly before, it appeared frozen now. Floyd was strung as tight as a bowstring, waiting. No matter how crazy, their plan had to work.

He scanned the village. There was no movement. It would magically transform at the first shot. He waited.

Leotie was close enough for Floyd to feel a quick shudder of pent-up anxiety pass through her body. Without thinking, he put his arm around her shoulders and gave her a quick hug. Immediately, he realized what he'd done and felt a shock of dismay, but she looked up, calming his heart, and smiled in the faint moonlight.

He had no time to think about the moment, for a shot was heard to the north. He leaped to his feet, Leotie with him. The two dashed to the back of the teepee. A high-pitched scream came next, and the thunder of hooves could be heard, through the blowing wind, bearing down on the village.

Though the wind was high, Floyd could hear yelling coming from the other teepees and the one they now knelt against. The horses neared, another scream sounded, and two more shots fired.

Floyd took a deep breath and thrust his knife into the tough hide and ripped a slit long enough to pass through. He was elated when, after moving through the hole, he saw Mika sitting close to the back of the teepee. It was empty except for the boy. Leotie had leaped in behind him. When Mika saw her, he jumped into her arms.

"Quick," Floyd said, "we've got to get outta here."

Holding Mika to her breasts, Leotie spun around and disappeared back into the hole. Floyd could hear the horses racing through the village. There was yelling, and several shots were fired. Following the fast retreating Leotie, Floyd dashed after her, occasionally throwing a glance over his shoulder. *I can't believe it went so smooth,* he thought.

At the horses, they both yanked the reins free from where they were tied. He grabbed Mika, allowing Leotie to mount, and then shoved the boy up to her. Spinning around, he leaped on Rusty from the right side, wheeled the big horse alongside Leotie's, and they charged down the creek, away from the village and toward Shorty.

They slowed, turned the horses into the trees, and before reaching the edge pulled up again, looking north. No riders. Floyd kicked Rusty in the flanks, and they burst from the trees. After running less than a mile, they pulled the horses to a walk and started looking for Shorty. He stepped from a ravine to their left, waving. Turning, Floyd led the way through the cut to where the horses, Kajika, and Morg waited.

"Everybody all right?" Floyd asked as they rode up. Even in the dim light, Floyd could see the grins as the men made out Mika sitting with Leotie.

"Well, now that the boy's here, we sure are. Ain't nobody here hurt. You might need this," Shorty said, and tossed Floyd his rifle.

"Good," Floyd said, sliding the weapon into the scabbard. "Let's divvy up these horses and be on our way. As soon as they figure out what happened, they'll be after us. Good job, all of you."

The lead ropes were separated quickly, and the three men split the remaining horses and mules. Neither of the mules carried a load. Everyone figured they would have an easier time keeping up without their normal loads.

With Kajika leading the way, in the faint moonlight, they galloped south toward the Missouri river, knowing it wouldn't be long before they would have company.

Floyd had a difficult time keeping his eyes off Leotie and Mika. The two, at last, were united after the long and hazardous trip. All they had to do now was make it another four hundred miles.

They pushed the horses hard for two more miles, then slowed to a walk, almost paralleling Big Muddy Creek. It had swung west, while they continued south, but now it was swinging back. As soon as it was near, they rode the horses to water. While the animals drank, and Leotie and Mika talked excitedly, the men changed saddles and gear.

Floyd used his telescope, examining the prairie behind them. In the faint moonlight, it remained—empty. But even if there was pursuit, he wouldn't know. At night and with the wind and dust, it would be almost impossible to see pursuers until they were on top of them. *Finally something good from the wind,* he thought. *We must continue to ride and get as far away from here as possible.*

Constantly, they rode south, pushing the horses and changing frequently. Daylight broke in the east, and day returned. Ahead, in the distance, was the green line of trees that signaled the Missouri.

The horses were tired, especially both mules. Once across,

another day's travel should provide enough room to allow the animals a day of rest. Floyd glanced over at Mika asleep in Leotie's arms. The horses weren't the only ones tired.

Kajika had ridden forward to scout the river. He hadn't been gone long, when he could be seen returning. The group pulled up as he rode in. "All clear."

Everyone nodded and urged their horses forward. Almost in unison, the horses' heads came up. They smelled the water. With renewed enthusiasm, they charged forward.

Floyd couldn't resist turning often to check the horizon behind them. He was astonished that a party of Blackfoot hadn't showed up yet, looking for their scalps.

Riding up to the riverbank, they watched the deep, rushing, dark brown water for a few moments. Then Floyd turned to Kajika. "Is there an easier crossing near?"

Kajika motioned west. "Around bend. Above creek. Ground solid. More shallow than here, but not as where we first crossed." He shook his head. "That is much far. This crossing safe."

Kajika led the group west toward Big Muddy Creek. Once across the creek, they continued for a mile. A trail cut through the steep bank to the river below. Cautiously Kajika led the way across the riverbed toward the wide swath of running water.

Floyd rode next to Leotie, and as they neared the water, he glanced toward her. He had noticed at the previous crossings, each time she had appeared nervous. She never hesitated at the water's edge, but it did not seem she was comfortable with a water crossing.

Nearing the water, she held her son in a viselike grip. That wasn't bad, but her fear for Mika was distracting her attention from her horse and the crossing. Floyd guided Rusty closer to her. When he had her attention, he held out his arms, his expression a question.

Through the night ride the boy, when he wasn't sleeping, had been watching Floyd closely. He felt sure Mika remembered him.

Leotie hesitated a moment, but when Mika extend his little hands toward Floyd, fingers flexing, she relented and passed him across. Floyd grasped Mika and lifted him across the space, pulling him tight against his chest, his strong arm wrapped securely around the tiny lad. The youngster uttered not a sound, only grasped Floyd's buckskin jacket and held on.

Drawing close to take Mika had been necessary, but it had brought Leotie's small bay closer than Floyd would have liked. The shallow water quickly deepened, the current rushing around Rusty's long legs. Floyd glanced at the others, who were suitably spread out, then looked back at Leotie.

As he turned his attention to her, the bay stepped off into deeper water, requiring it to start swimming. Immediately, the horse started pitching, while at the same time, the current pushed it closer to Rusty and Floyd. Floyd wasn't worried about either his horse or himself. The thick chest and shoulders of the big roan would easily fend off the little bay, but Floyd was deeply concerned with Leotie's safety.

She was battling to stay in the saddle and control the pitching horse. "Loosen the reins," Floyd yelled.

Hands still clutching the reins, she turned uncomprehending, terror-stricken eyes toward him. He had never seen her afraid, and this, as much as the rapidly developing dire situation, shocked him. In a flash he could see imminent danger for Leotie. Holding Rusty's reins in his left hand, he grasped Mika and shoved him into the crook of that arm, gripping him tightly. Immediately, he guided Rusty closer to the pitching bay. With a sweep of his right arm, he encircled Leotie's tiny waist and lifted her from her saddle, but she still gripped the bay's reins in her hands, pulling the horse against Rusty, who was now swimming.

"Turn the reins loose!" he shouted again.

Dangling against Floyd's right side, her foot found the stirrup he had vacated for her. She slid a foot into the stirrup and, with sudden recognition of what she was doing, threw the reins at the bay and wrapped her arms around Floyd. Instantly, the horse stopped its pitching, calmed down, and swam toward the shore. Even with the added weight of the two additional riders, Rusty maintained an even stroke. In minutes, his feet touched the bottom, and he started walking his way through the stiff current to the waiting shore.

21

The others had witnessed the near accident, and Kajika was waiting as soon as the horse stepped from the water. He reached for Mika, and the little boy went to him, laughing. He clapped his hands and, in Shoshone, said, "Again, again."

Everyone laughed, relieving the tension. Leotie still stood in the stirrup, her body resting against Floyd. He could feel her trembling and squeezed her close, to reassure her, he told himself. The fear was leaving her eyes, replaced by embarrassment, shame, and something else Floyd found he wanted, something more than gratitude.

She broke the gaze, looked at her foot in his stirrup, then looked back up at him. "Thank you, but I am sorry it was necessary. It is foolish, but water frightens me."

Floyd, his left hand free, swept a stray lock of black hair from her face. "You can't swim?"

"No, it is stupid, but I never learned. My father had to pull me from the river when he was teaching me. When that happened, I swallowed much water and remember staring up at the surface far above me, thinking I would die. After that, I refused to venture into deep water, and every crossing terrifies me. I try to hide it from Mika, for I do not want him to be afraid." She gazed into his eyes. "You have saved me again. I thank you."

He wanted, so badly, to cover her lips with his. It was almost a physical drive that he fought against. She must have felt the urgency, because she smiled, leaned forward, and gave him a soft kiss on his cheek.

The others moved the horses down the river from where they crossed, and were watering them and filling the water flasks. They gave Floyd and Leotie plenty of space. Noticing what was happening, Floyd, while softly easing Leotie to the ground, said, "Guess we'd better get Rusty a drink and get ready to ride."

"Yes," Leotie said. "Flo-yd?"

"Yep?"

"I have a large place for you in my heart."

His heart raced. She felt what he was feeling. "I feel that for you, Leotie."

She smiled up at him, held the gaze for only a moment, and walked toward Mika and the others.

Floyd guided Rusty back to the water and let him drink. While the red roan was drinking, Floyd walked to a spot where he could see between the trees on the north bank. He pulled his telescope from its case, extended it, and put it to his eye.

Kajika was watching him and saw him stiffen.

"Blackfoot?"

"Dust. They're still well behind us. If we keep moving, we can keep some space between us and them, but they're coming."

Shorty had noticed the glass and the earnest discussion between Floyd and Kajika. "See anything?"

At his question, everyone turned to Floyd.

"Dust. Still a ways off. I can barely differentiate from the blowing dust with the glass, but you can see it as heavier. We need to grab something to eat and be on our way."

"Maybe they'll stop at the river," Morg said.

Kajika shook his head. "No stop. Want boy back and our scalps."

Everyone grabbed jerky to chew on as they rode, jumped into their saddles, and were on their way.

Hours passed. They had changed horses once again since crossing the Missouri. It was imperative they maintain their lead. *Tonight is a waning moon,* Floyd thought. *If we can continue riding, they might not be able to follow our tracks, but we'll have to have rest soon. We've all been up over twenty-four hours, and the horses are tiring.*

They stopped once again and switched horses, moving the pack saddles to the mules. Floyd hated to see anything happen to Browny. He had grown as fond of the mule as he was Rusty and Buck. During their stop, Floyd surveyed their back trail with his naked eye. Nothing. But when he put the telescope to his eye, the spot of heavier dust leaped out at him. The Blackfoot hadn't stopped at the Missouri River.

For the first time, Floyd felt a deep fear in his heart, but it wasn't for him. It was for Leotie and Mika. He had to protect them. He couldn't stand to think of them being captured by the Blackfoot. He dwelt on the dark thought no longer and began thinking about what they could do to evade their pursuers.

Daylight was fading. Both parties would have to start slowing soon. It was doubtful the Blackfoot would continue to try to track them in the night, for fear of losing their tracks. But they weren't stupid. There were probably men in this party who had captured both Leotie and Mika. They would know where their prey was headed, and maybe, just maybe, they would continue their pursuit. If Floyd and his party stopped, the Blackfoot could close the distance.

But what about the horses? Their animals were already thin from the long trek north. Now they were being asked to give everything, all of their energy, all of their heart. Even though switching riders and packs gave them a reprieve, they still had to continue moving south with hardly any rest periods, and certainly no time to graze.

When listening to his pa talk about the battle of New Orleans, Floyd had heard him say, many times, "Ole Andy Jackson was caught between a rock and a hard place." Floyd now had a deep understanding of the phrase he had heard so often. If they continued to push the animals like they were doing, it would eventually kill them, but if they stopped to let the horses rest and feed, everyone might be killed. When he thought of that word, *might,* he said a quick prayer of thanks.

They might be killed. He made the decision to stop. They would have to find a defensible place, with water and cover, but the horses needed rest. Besides the horses, everyone needed rest. They had started passing Mika around between the riders. The little boy was exhausted and constantly falling asleep in the saddle.

Currently, they were riding at a lope. Kajika rode ahead, leading the way. Floyd, who was now on a dappled gray that had belonged to the trappers, brought up the rear. The horse was smaller than either Rusty or Buck, but was a real stayer. All of the travel had settled the frisky nature of the animals. There was no bowing or bucking when a blanket or saddle was thrown across a back. These animals weren't docile, but were much more tractable. They were tired.

Floyd rode forward, next to Kajika, and said in Shoshone, "We need to find a place with grass and water that we can defend. These horses need rest, and so do we."

"I know a place," the young Shoshone replied.

"How far is the Yellowstone?"

"It is maybe ten more miles. The place I have in mind is an island in the river. If it isn't low, this will be a perfect place."

Floyd nodded, dropping back to Leotie. "How are you doing?"

In the disappearing light, he could see a tired smile cross her face.

"I am fine." She looked at Morg, who was carrying her son. The tall man cradled him in a long arm, as the pace of the horse provided the boy with a rocking chair.

"Morg and Shorty are good men," she said.

"Yes, good friends."

"We will be stopping in about ten more miles or so. We've got to give these animals a chance to feed and rest. If we don't, we'll kill them and, in turn, ourselves."

She nodded. "Yes, and we also need rest."

He gave a short nod and dropped back to the rear. He was behind Shorty, and every once in a while his friend would start leaning and then suddenly jerk erect. *I'm mighty tired myself,* Floyd thought.

The time seemed to stagger by, but finally they reached the river, and Floyd's heart leaped. The Yellowstone River was running steady. Kajika turned them upriver to parallel it, and they continued to ride. There was no use trying to hide their tracks. There were just too many.

They had slowed. Kajika was looking for a specific spot in the river. When they reached it, he turned them toward the Yellowstone.

Floyd eased the gray next to Leotie. "It'll be all right. We're just riding out to the island."

She threw him a small strained smile.

"Relax your grip on the reins. He'll feel your tension."

This time she was concentrating on her horse. He could see her will her hands to relax, but even in the moonlight, he could see the tension in her neck and shoulders.

They entered the water. Thankfully, it wasn't as fast as the Missouri had been, nor was it as deep. *I would've liked it a lot deeper,* he thought, *but at least it gives us some space. And it announces their arrival. It's too shallow to swim.*

The island rested in the middle of the river, each side at least thirty feet from the respective shore. It sloped up slightly from the water, with scattered trees on each edge, and grass in the middle. It was perfect, even the thick brush on the upriver end. It would be almost impossible for their attackers to get to them without making a lot of noise. Since they had time, they let the horses stop and drink where they stood.

Floyd could see this decision did nothing to calm Leotie's nerves. Softly, he said, "Relax the reins. Let the horse drink. We won't be here long, and the water is pretty shallow."

She turned a hard eye toward him. "It may look shallow to you, but it certainly doesn't to me." But she relaxed her grip on the reins, allowing her horse to drink.

At the curt reply, Floyd sat back and remained silent. After a few minutes, the horses had their fill, and the procession continued forward to the island.

Once through the trees and into the glade, everyone dismounted and stripped the tack from the animals and released them. Floyd felt sure they would stay on the island unless chased off, which he was sure the Blackfoot would try to do. However, even if their pursuers had continued riding into the night, it would take them until well past morning to arrive.

"Might as well make a fire," Shorty said, gathering tinder and small sticks. "They're gonna find us anyway. We oughta be comfortable until they do."

"Danged right," Morg joined in. "These cold old bones will welcome a little heat."

After stripping the gear from the gray and unloading packs from Browny, Floyd pulled some grass and wiped both animals down. Browny sniffed at his pockets, looking for an apple, but there was none to be had. Floyd scratched behind the big ears, then shoved him away. "Go stuff your belly with some grass."

The mule looked at him for a moment, then his stomach won out, and he wandered to the other horses, found Rusty and Buck, and started eating.

Floyd watched the mule walk away. "Wish I'd brought more oats."

Shorty heard him and said, as he sat back to view his successful efforts at building a fire, "Aw, Floyd, it wouldn't done no good. We'd used it all up on this trip, just like what you had."

"You're right, Shorty. It'd still be nice to have something special for these fellers. They've sure worked for us."

"That they have, Floyd," Morg joined in. "Look at 'em. Ribs are showing on ever' last one of 'em."

Floyd nodded. "This'll help 'em. I wish we could spend two or three days here. They sure need it."

Following his last comments, Floyd walked to one of his packs and pulled out a shovel. "We need to build this embankment up to provide more protection." He turned to Kajika. "Where do you think they'll come from?"

The Shoshone pointed back where they had crossed, and said, speaking in English, "First attack there. Then probably try slipping in from behind, maybe upriver through brush."

Floyd nodded as he drove the shovel into the ground. "Good, that's what I was thinking." He turned to Morg. "You have a shovel?"

Morg had already started for their packs. "That we do. It won't take the two of us long to build us up a little more protection. I'm thinkin' we'll enjoy it come daylight."

Morg pulled out his shovel and joined Floyd. While they worked, Leotie dug a big pot from one of Shorty's packs. She walked to the river, dipped water, and set the pot on the edge of the fire. Once she had it positioned, she went back to the pack and pulled out a large coffee pot, with which she did the same thing. Then she again moved to the edge of the water and pulled several plants from the water. When she returned, she laid it all down, looked for and found a flat rock, took out her knife, and started cleaning and cutting.

Shorty had spelled Morg, but handed the shovel back to him

and walked over to the boiling coffee pot. "If'n you don't mind, ma'am," Shorty said, "I'll take care of the coffee."

She glanced up at him, nodded, and went back to work.

Morg stopped for a moment, looked up at Floyd, and said, "Shorty is mighty picky about his coffee."

Floyd watched the smaller man at the fire. "So I see. But I've tasted his coffee, and it rates about the highest of any I've tasted." When he finished talking, he drove the shovel back into the ground, lifting a huge amount of dirt out.

"Yep, it's mighty good." Morg followed suit, and the men continued to work.

Kajika had slipped off to examine the island, and Mika slept soundly.

Leotie tossed in a double handful of jerky, and having located Floyd's salt, she added some generously to the pot.

Shorty had just tossed a small handful of cold water into the coffee when Leotie said, "It is ready."

All four men grabbed a plate and stepped up to the pot. Floyd was thinking, *It doesn't matter how bad this is, at least it's food. It'll be good for all of us.* He took his first bite. *It's delicious. Maybe because none of us have had anything fresh cooked for the last several days, but it tastes great.* He looked up at Leotie to find her watching him. He licked his lips and said, "That is mighty good."

She smiled back at him and lowered her head to Mika. She had awakened him and held him in her lap. He sat half-asleep, but when she placed a spoonful of the stew in his mouth, his eyes lit up, and the little Shoshone boy said, "More."

There was enough for everyone to have seconds, which they did with steaming coffee. The wind off the river was cold, and each person wrapped up as best they could. Leotie wrapped an extra blanket around her son and laid him back down. Within moments, Mika was again sound asleep.

Eyelids drooped around the camp. Leotie quickly cleaned the pot and placed it back in the pack. Once loaded, she settled next to her son and pulled the extra blanket up and over the two of them. The fire and then the coals, once it burned down, would provide heat through most of the night.

Kajika had searched around the island and found several fairly straight pieces of driftwood. They were waterlogged and heavy. Using his tomahawk, he cut and sharpened six spears and laid one alongside each adult, leaving him two. He dropped them by the spot he had chosen for himself. Floyd watched him moving around. Shorty and Morg had just finished improving their fighting spots, almost holes. They had dug until they reached the water level and stopped.

"We need to stand watch," Floyd said.

Shorty spoke up. "I got quite a bit of sleep on the back of my horse. Why don't I take the first watch, then Morg, and Kajika, and then Floyd."

"If that's all right with all of you, then it's fine with me," Floyd said. The other two nodded their agreement. Each had their weapons arranged the way they wanted them. Floyd was satisfied they were as prepared as possible. He stretched out and was asleep immediately.

He awoke to a bump on his foot. His eyes flew open to see Kajika poking his foot with one end of his bow.

"All quiet," the Shoshone warrior said before returning to his bed.

The fire had given off heat all night. Floyd took the coffee pot to the creek, rinsed it out, and refilled it. After taking it back, he set it well off to one side. Shorty would want to make it when he awoke. Then he moved carefully around the island. Starting at the water's edge by their camp, moving downstream to the end of the island, upstream to the end near where they had entered, and to the spot he would use as his stand.

He moved around, looking for a well-hidden spot that would be sufficiently comfortable so that he would not have to move once positioned. Finally finding it, he eased himself down, stretched out his long legs, and relaxed. The hot food and sleep had done wonders for him. He was yet tired, but not the exhaustion he had felt yesterday and last night. They would be ready.

He had no idea how many Blackfoot were on their trail. Hopefully, the main body that made up the hunting party had not joined them. They would have to leave men behind to protect those families remaining in the village. With that, he hoped it wouldn't be over fifteen. Fifteen was too many, but it would be much better than three or four hundred. With fifteen, they'd have a chance. *I sure wish I hadn't lost my other rifle and pistols to the Blackfoot. I could sure use them now.* At the thought, he rubbed the seasoned wood of the forearm on his rifle and reassuringly touched both pistols. A fight was coming, and it would be chasing the sun.

22

Floyd watched the sun rise dull and red. Though the wind had dropped, dust lingered in the sky, taking the brightness from the morning sun and rendering it a drab, depressing orb. Its color brought no warmth nor cheer, only foreboding.

Fortunately, from his position on the island, Floyd was well above the north bank. He could see no dust in the distance. Maybe they did stop. He began considering their options.

They could load up now and be on their way, and it would keep them ahead of their pursuers, for a while. Though the rest would give their mounts renewed energy, it wouldn't last long, and they'd be right back in the same spot.

Or they could wait a while and see if their pursuers had given up with darkness. Maybe they had turned around and headed back toward the Missouri River. As much as he liked this option, he knew it wasn't true. Once their stalkers crossed the river, it was a foregone conclusion. The Blackfoot were in it to the end.

That left the third and final option. Stay and fight. They could die, here, today, with that dreadful-looking sun staring down upon their mutilated bodies. He wholeheartedly believed that would not happen. They would fight. He wasn't brought into this world to turn tail and run. Not only would they fight, but they would win. Those Blackfoot had not had the time to go after the hunting party to bring more men. Fifteen, that would be the maximum number.

He gazed along the prairie path they had traveled yesterday. Nothing, no movement and no sign of dust. He could hear people up in camp. That meant that Shorty would be making coffee. There was a slight breeze from the southwest, and he picked up the smell of—it couldn't be. He smelled frying venison. His mind must be playing a trick on him. Floyd held his head up toward the camp. He could smell the woodsmoke, the coffee, and *venison*.

There had been no shot, so that meant Kajika had silently killed a deer this morning. His stomach growled and his mouth watered. *One last look before I go back,* he thought. Again, there was no dust. He placed the glass to his eye. The one thing he had hoped not to see, dust. Removing the glass, he looked again. With his naked eyes, he saw nothing, but when he checked again, the dust was unmistakable.

He stood and stretched long arms reaching out like the spread of an eagle's wings. Then he moved silently back to the fire. There, hanging from a limb in a cottonwood, was the skinned carcass of a deer, missing the tenderloin, backstrap, and one ham. The meat was sizzling in the skillet.

Leotie looked up, a smile on her lips that quickly disappeared at Floyd's expression.

"They're on their way," Floyd said.

"How far?" Morg asked.

"At least forty miles. We have a decision to make. We can saddle up and run, or we can stand and fight. Personally, I'm tired of running. If it was up to me, I'd say fight, but there's more to be considered than my desire to end this." He turned to Leotie. "You've got more to lose than any of us. What do you say?"

Mika was sitting next to her, chewing on a fresh-cooked piece of venison. She placed her arm around her son, her back straightening and her chin raised high. "I agree with you, Igasho. It is time to stop running. The Great Spirit said we would be safe, and we will. I say fight!"

Kajika let out a long Shoshone yell that made Floyd's skin tingle. No need to ask him. He turned to Shorty and Morg.

Morg's head was nodding, and Shorty, after looking at his friend and partner, said, "We fight."

"Good," Floyd said. "Now I need some of that venison and a cup of coffee."

Leotie forked three big pieces onto his plate, along with some cooked wild onions, while Shorty poured him a cup of hot coffee. He took the cup from Shorty, still keeping his eyes on the woman. *The red scar from McMillan's knife is fading,* Floyd thought, *but even if it wasn't, your about the most beautiful woman I know.* Finally, he admitted it to himself. *I love you.*

He could also see his feelings reflected in her eyes. *Leotie,* he thought, *if we survive this battle, I'm finding a preacher, and we're getting married, legal like.* He looked around at his friends. They were all grinning and staring at him, even Kajika. "What?" Before anyone could answer, another thought came to his mind and he spoke it. "Did you just hear what I thought I thought?"

Leotie stood and walked over to him. "Yes, Igasho. You did not think anything, but said it out loud."

Floyd looked around again and said, "Dang." Since his hands were full, he set down his coffee cup and plate. Then he reached out to the slim Shoshone woman, grasping her around her upper arms. "Well, is that all right with you?"

She smiled up at him again and said, "Yes, that is very all right with me." Then she leaned forward and kissed him full on the lips, and he kissed her back.

He could hear little hands clapping behind Leotie. He pulled his head away from those intoxicating lips and said above her shoulder in Shoshone, "Mika, can I be your pa?"

The little boy laughed and clapped his hands, then reached up to Floyd. The mountain man stepped past Leotie and swooped his new son up in his arms, tossing him high into the air. The river's rushing sounds, the calls of meadowlarks and mockingbirds, were mingled with the happy, tinkling laughter of a five-year-old enjoying life.

Pride and happiness showed in the eyes of the Shoshone woman who had been so bruised, beaten, and harshly treated, but the fire of an unquenchable spirit also burned in those beautiful dark eyes. Floyd had seen it when he first opened his eyes from the bear attack, and when he had rescued her from McMillan and the others. Now he saw it again. And the thought blazed through his mind, *We will survive.*

With the thought, reality settled back in. He stepped forward, gave her a crushing hug, set Mika back on the ground to finish eating, and turned to his friends. "If you can think of anything else we can do to strengthen our position, now's the time to speak up."

"I reckon we're ready," Shorty said.

Floyd looked at Kajika. The Shoshone nodded. "Ready."

Morg shrugged. "We're as ready as we're gonna get, but if I'm gonna have to fight Blackfoot, I reckon I need some backstrap."

"Good," Floyd said. He moved over next to Mika and started wolfing down his venison. It was good. Maybe the best he'd ever tasted. He glanced up at Kajika, and it was as if the young brave read his mind.

"Young buck came to drink. Easy shot from here." He held up the bloody arrow.

"You sure made my day," Floyd said as he tore a chunk off his last piece of venison and handed it to Mika. The boy took it and shoved it all into his mouth. He grinned back at Floyd and said, in English, "Good, Flo-yd."

Floyd laughed and tousled the youngster's hair.

The group continued to eat venison until both hams were

gone along with the backstrap and tenderloin. Then Floyd let out a long belch. "If I eat any more, the only way I'll be able to fight is for you boys to load me up with powder and fire me at the Blackfoot."

Everyone chuckled as Floyd stood and looked out across the prairie, serious now. He could see the horsemen coming hard. "Guess we'd better get into position. I'm thinkin' we should hold our fire until they're in the water, then let 'em have it."

"Sounds good to me," Shorty said. He stood and moved to his position, where he had both of his rifles laid out, along with two pistols.

Morg joined him and stretched out in the grass. The men had tied the horses to keep them from running when the shooting started. Everyone was ready.

Floyd pulled his pistols from his holsters and handed them both to Leotie. "Use 'em as you need 'em."

She laid her hand on his before taking them. "You must hear this from me, Igasho. You are in my heart and have been there since we first met. I will always love you." She then took the two weapons.

"I love you too, Leotie. We'll come through this, because we have a good life ahead of us. You take care of yourself and Mika. We might get a little busy."

He could make out the individual Blackfoot braves riding their tired horses. Paint covered not only the braves, but also their horses. As they drew near, they started screeching and yelling. Upon reaching the bank, they rode headlong into the river. Water flew in all directions from the horses' hooves. They were halfway across when the first volley fired. Four men rolled out of their saddles, one with an arrow driven almost completely through his chest.

Shorty picked up his second rifle and blew another brave from the saddle. Now he dropped it and grabbed both pistols.

Floyd immediately started reloading after he fired. He had

made sure the spear Kajika had fashioned was close at hand. He also laid out his shovel and tomahawk. His knife still rested on his belt. Seeing he would not have time to finish reloading his rifle, he bent and picked up the spear.

The Blackfoot had made it to the island and were racing up the slope. Floyd glanced over at Leotie. She waited, outwardly calm, in the middle of the camp with Mika. Seeing she was safe, for now, he turned back to the charging braves. One, on a black with his face painted white except for red around his eyes, was almost upon him. The Indian's face was contorted with the lust of battle as he charged straight toward Floyd. In his hand he swung a wicked-looking tomahawk.

The Blackfoot leaped his horse at Floyd. As he was moving, Floyd saw that the horse was extremely well trained. It was trying to turn to run over Floyd. But the mountain man was too fast for him. He jumped aside and ducked. The tomahawk sailed by his head, missing so closely he could feel his hair move, and then Floyd struck as the brave was passing. He drove the spear in under the man's right shoulder blade. Much of the spear pierced through and out of his body, traveling straight through his heart.

The man's chilling war cry was cut short. He slumped against the spear, driven so deep it was jerked from Floyd's hands, and fell from the saddle. The black horse continued through the camp, the water on the other side, and up the bank behind them.

While Floyd's battle was going on, he heard Shorty's pistols go off one after another, and heard a blast from one of his. Anger and concern filled his soul as he spun to see Leotie standing with a smoking pistol and a dead Blackfoot at her feet. He looked around. The charge had broken. Their pursuers were scrambling to get back across the river. Floyd grabbed his rifle, finished reloading before they could clear the bank, and shot a Blackfoot brave in the head. The man collapsed from his mount, and it was over.

Floyd looked again at Leotie and Mika to make sure they were all right, and, along with Shorty and Morg, began reloading his rifle. Once finished, he moved over to Leotie and took the fired pistol. He quickly reloaded it and handed it back to her. Finally it was time to survey the damage.

He could see blood on Morg's sleeve. Shorty was fine. He looked around. "Where's Kajika?"

As he spoke, the Shoshone brave stepped from the brush on the downstream end of the river, carrying several scalps. He held them up and let out a bloodcurdling yell. A challenge that was immediately answered by yells from beyond the bank.

Blood covered Kajika. Floyd couldn't tell if his friend was injured or not. "Are you hurt?"

"No hurt." He threw the scalps to the ground and walked to the opposite side of the island, where he waded into the water, washing himself.

Floyd watched Kajika stalk to the water, then turned back. "It looked like to me, before they hit us, there was only fifteen or so. Does that sound about right?"

Shorty's head bobbed up and down. "Yes siree. I counted fourteen of them devils, but there ain't near as many now as they was. I saw you get two. I got two and winged one." Shorty turned to Morg.

"I got one. Wished they hadn't got my other rifle, but I reckon you're in the same shape, Floyd."

"Yep. Leotie killed one, and..."

Kajika came stalking back. "I kill three. They no have the men they had."

Floyd figured rapidly, then said, "The way I figure it, they've got six or less. We're in a lot better shape than when this started." He turned to Kajika. "Do you think the last ones will fight or leave?"

"They leave. Boy no worth this many braves unless man who stole him for wife is still alive. He might rather face death than wife if he returns with no boy."

Floyd looked around at his friends, all in good shape except Morg, whose arm needed attention. It was as if Leotie read his mind. She moved briskly across the knoll to Morg's side and grasped his arm.

He almost jerked it back. "I'm all right, Leotie. You needn't worry about me."

She smiled up at the man towering above her and said, "I'm not worried, but I can fix you."

Then she gently rolled up his sleeve, exposing the wound. A passing arrow had sliced the side of his bicep, leaving it open and bleeding. "Come," she said, retaining her grip on his arm and marching him to the river on the opposite side from the attack.

As she started cleaning, Floyd moved over to Mika. The boy's eyes were still big. Floyd reached down and picked him up. Chubby arms encircled the big man's neck, and he felt a tightness in his chest. Even in all this death, there was life and happiness, and a future. *A future,* he thought, *I never much thought about the future, just the here and now.* Mika squeezed his neck. *I reckon I could enjoy planning on a future with this little fellow.*

"You all right?" Floyd asked in Shoshone.

"Me fine. I want to be strong like Flo-yd."

Floyd leaned Mika out so that he could see the little face. "Your mama is strong, too."

Big dark eyes stared back at him. "She is big strong."

Morg and Leotie were on the way back. She heard her son and laughed happily. She stood on her tiptoe and kissed Mika on the cheek and said, "When I have to be."

Floyd handed Mika to Leotie and turned to the men. "We need to get the remaining bodies out of here and prepare for another attack. I'm hoping there won't be one, but we need to be ready." He followed his words up with action, walking to the side of the brave he had killed with Kajika's spear. He moved the man to where he could get a solid grip on the spear and pulled. It came out slowly with a sucking noise. He wiped the blood from the spear, laid it by his rifle, and dragged the man to the water's edge. Once there, he rolled the body into the current, watched it float downstream for a moment, and turned back to see everyone preparing their positions.

Morg had the shovel, and he was widening his depression. Shorty had reloaded all of his weapons. He had picked up a rifle to double-check it, laid it down, and picked up the other one. With a deadpan expression he said, "Morg, it would shore have help if you and Floyd ain't gived yore rifles to them Blackfoot. I ain't never heard of such a thing."

Floyd grinned and shook his head as he watched Morg jerk his head up to stare at his friend.

Finally the tall mountain man growled, "You ain't careful, I'll be givin' you to 'em next," and they were off.

Ignoring their back-and-forth, Floyd checked the horses. They needed water, but other than that, they were fine. He took Rusty, Buck, and Browny to water. While they drank, he saw Kajika untie three more. The Shoshone brought them to water close enough for him to converse quietly with Floyd.

Floyd felt the younger man had something to say, so he kept his questions to himself. Finally, Kajika turned to him and spoke in Shoshone. "We must be prepared. The Blackfoot are very difficult to predict. As I said, if the man who adopted Mika is dead, I feel they have probably left. If he isn't, they may still leave, but maybe not. Either way, there will be no more attacks as we just had. Look for them to slip in with the current. It will be difficult for them with the shallow water, but they may try. We must remain alert."

Floyd agreed. "It looks as if we have enough grass to last another day, maybe two. This is good for the horses. We can't wait long, or we could get caught in an early winter storm, but another day will do us all good."

"Yes, you are right."

The horses had finished drinking, and the two men led them

back, tied them to a new spot where they could graze, and took more horses down. Once all the horses were watered, the five of them relaxed as best they could. The day had warmed, and the afternoon was pleasant.

They had a lunch of venison and vegetables and took naps in turn. No attack came.

23

The remainder of the day was pleasant. The warm sun shone down through the big cottonwoods. The wind, which blew constantly on the prairie, died with the setting sun. Floyd sat by Leotie, enjoying the closeness of her and Mika. *Life can be really good,* he thought. *I miss my folks some, but I reckon that's natural. I'd like to see them and the rest of the family. Funny how Martha always depended on me. Wonder if her or Jenny's married yet. I'd better be getting back there before too long. It's already going on four years.*

He turned to Leotie, who was watching him. Mika was asleep with his head in his mother's lap.

"You were in deep thought," she said.

"I was thinkin' about my family back in Tennessee. Before too long, I need to go back to see them. It's been almost four years, and my folks aren't getting any younger."

Leotie laid a hand on his. "It is good to go home. I know they miss you. Do you send them . . ." She stopped, searching for the word.

"Mail?"

"Yes, mail. I have heard white men talk about sending let-ters to their family. Is that right?"

"Yep, letters, and I have sent them a couple. Don't know if they made it all the way to Tennessee, but at least I sent 'em."

They continued to talk into the evening, until Leotie jumped up and started cutting the last of the venison. She broke several of the larger bones and dropped them into the pot, along with the venison and the vegetables she had earlier picked. Everyone ate, enjoying the meal and the relaxed peace they were enjoying. Vigilance was still maintained, but it had now been accepted by everyone that the remaining Blackfoot had headed home.

Floyd took the first watch that night, checking Leotie and Mika often. The incessant wind had picked up again, moaning through the trees and across the open plains. Shorty took over the next watch, while Floyd covered his two charges with his buffalo coat and pulled his worn wool coat on. He fingered the thin fabric for a moment, thinking again of his family, lay down and pulled a couple of blankets up to his neck.

He lay there for a while, watching the clear sky and twinkling stars. Tonight the moon had an open sky to illuminate the prairie. Its reflection glinted off the flowing waters of the Yellowstone River. His last thought as he drifted off was how thankful he was he had followed his dream and come west.

He was awakened by a hard grip on his shoulder. Daylight was showing through the trees. It looked like another beautiful day.

"Floyd!" Morg said, his voice tight with foreboding. "Get up. You've got to see."

The tone of Morg's voice propelled sleep from his mind. Grabbing his rifle, he leaped to his feet, the blankets falling to the ground in a heap. He didn't have to turn to know what was on the north bank, because the south bank was lined with mounted Blackfoot. He stared, despair setting in, and then he turned. The north bank, the direction of the Missouri River, was a copy of the south. A copy, except for the chiefs who sat resplendent in their long, flowing war bonnets, staring at the little group on the island.

"Reckon we're done for," Morg said.

"Not yet," Floyd responded. He snapped a look at his friends, at Leotie and Mika. His mind was racing. *What can I do to resolve this? Is it even possible?* Then a wild thought came to his mind. "Maybe, just maybe," he said softly to himself. He turned to the others. "Put your weapons down."

All of them looked at him like he was crazy. "If they attack, you can pick them up, but look around you. There must be three hundred or more Blackfoot. Is there one of you who thinks he can win this fight?" Floyd waited as the seconds ticked by. "Then put your weapons down."

Floyd turned to Morg. "Morg, would you saddle Rusty for me. I need to face these chiefs."

"Shore, what do you have in mind?"

"Something so crazy, it just might work. I've heard the Blackfoot nation holds great pride in the prowess of their warriors. We're going to find out." He remained facing the chief who appeared to be the leader, his face as inscrutable as the Blackfoot.

Morg saddled Rusty and led him to Floyd. "I hope you know what you're doing. They have almighty fun torturing folks."

Floyd didn't take his eyes from the chief. "Thanks, Morg." With a somber voice, Floyd said, "Y'all take care of Leotie and Mika."

Equally somber, all three men nodded to Floyd. They knew what must be done, as did she. Leotie, like all of them, could not be taken alive. What had happened to her at the hands of the trappers was nothing compared to what the Blackfoot would do.

Floyd could not take his eyes from the chief, but in his peripheral vision he saw Leotie walk toward him. She reached for him, and he extended his hand. Grasping it, she turned it so his palm was toward her. Leaning forward, she kissed the palm of his hand and rolled his fingers closed. "I love you, Igasho. May the Great Spirit ride with you, as my heart will."

"I love you, too."

She dropped his hand, and he swung into the saddle, guiding Rusty into the current of the Yellowstone. He could smell the faint odor of the cottonwoods, along with the pungent smell of sagebrush. A flight of little green-wing teal flashed by in front of him, the green strip on their cinnamon heads vivid in the early morning sun. Floyd took a deep breath. It felt like all of his senses were tuned to these great outdoors. *I may die in moments,* he thought, *but I have lived. I'd love to have more, but no man has lived the life that has been mine.*

He cleared his mind, riding straight to the chief. Once there, he stopped, the water coursing around Rusty's legs. The bank was about the height of Rusty's head, and the Indians' horses were lined above him and along the edge of the bank. Stationary, he stared at the chief. Finally, the man turned and said something. The braves blocking the trail leading up the bank moved back, giving Floyd space to guide Rusty up and onto the prairie. Once out of the river, he turned his horse to the chief and advanced. Floyd stopped when he sat facing the imposing man. From his position, he could have easily touched him. He sat motionless, holding the gaze of the chief. Many of the other braves began to push their horses in against Rusty, but the big roan, nostrils flared at the Indian smell, held his ground.

Knowing he would have to break the silence, Floyd spoke in a hard, firm voice in English but using the Indian hand signs known by most tribes. "I am Floyd Horatio Logan.

"I am known to the Comanche by the name they gave me, Pawnee Killer.

"My Shoshone brothers named me Igasho, or Man Who Wanders.

"What is the name of the great Blackfoot Chief I see?"

While Floyd had been speaking, a brave sitting next to the

chief had been translating the man's spoken words into the chief's ear.

The chief sat staring at Floyd. Minutes passed. Then his hands began to move as he spoke. Also the brave next to him spoke in English. "I am known to my people as Gray Wolf. Why do you steal children from my people and kill my braves?"

Though the words were sharp, Floyd never flinched. He maintained a steely gaze at Gray Wolf, knowing that any sign of fear would be his and his companions' death warrant. "I did not come to your land to steal or to kill. I came to take back what is rightfully my own."

At this, the braves nearest Floyd, though they did not understand his words, understood the sign language, and they let out spine-tingling cries of anger.

The chief held up his hand and spoke harshly to those around him, then turned back to Floyd. "What do you mean, your own. You are not Shoshone."

"Is it not so with your tribe?" Floyd said. "Did your braves not act cowardly in their theft of a young Shoshone boy? And wasn't he adopted into your tribe?"

Again, cries burst out, and braves pushed in against him.

The chief raised his voice in what sounded to Floyd like a threat, and the men shut up.

The chief motioned for him to go on.

"I have taken this boy's mother as my wife, and the boy has become my son. I love him, and it is my duty to protect him. We followed your braves all the way from near the head of the Powder River to your village. We intended no harm. Were any of your braves killed at your village? Was anyone shot or hurt?" Before the chief could answer, Floyd said forcefully, "No!"

He looked around at the braves, showing contempt for them. "Without the great chief, there were nothing but old ones, babies, and *women* in your village."

This time the braves could barely be restrained from killing him, but the chief shouted them down. Again, he motioned for Floyd to continue.

"We ran your horses as a distraction, and your *braves* fell for it. It was easy for us to slip into the boy's teepee and rescue him, for he was not guarded. We rode quickly away without bringing harm to anyone."

Floyd turned to the island and his friends and swept his arm toward them. "Upon seeing that we were followed, my wife and son and my friends chose this spot to defend ourselves. We would not have fought if your braves had not attacked us. Those who died brought it upon themselves, as will anyone who falls upon us."

He only hoped he wasn't taking it too far, with the bragging, desperate statement. He knew this people admired courage, but he didn't want them so mad, they would kill them all.

The chief sat watching Floyd as he spoke. When he was finished, the chief said, "You are young, but have scars."

"I have fought and survived."

The chief waved his arm, encompassing all of his men. "You will not survive this."

Floyd looked slowly around and nodded. "Great Chief Gray Wolf is right. But I and my wife and my friends will die knowing we took many Blackfoot with us. But I have knowledge of a way that can prevent more crying and wailing in the Blackfoot teepees." Floyd stopped to let his statement sink in.

Finally, his face breaking into a sardonic smile, the chief said, "What is your idea to save our women sadness?"

"Chief Gray Wolf, I understand in the great Blackfoot Confederacy it is allowed when a man is terribly wronged by another, he can challenge the evildoer. This is what I do. I challenge the coward who came into the Shoshone camp to steal infants. Let this be between him and me. Let it be settled by blood."

The chief leaned to one of his subchiefs, and the two of them spoke back and forth for several minutes. Then the subchief spoke to a brave sitting next to him. The man pulled his horse out of the group, turned, and rode off. He returned quickly with another man. Floyd waited, keeping his eyes on the chief.

The chief spoke again. "We are many. We could kill you easily."

"You are partially right. You could kill us, but even with your numbers, it would not be easy. Many of your braves would die."

The chief shrugged. "But I could kill you. In fact, I could kill you right now."

Floyd held his eyes on the chief and waited for a moment. Then he calmly said, "Yes, that is in your power. It is also in your power to honor my challenge and, when I win, let me, with my son and wife and friends, return to my village."

The chief watched Floyd. He saw a deep-chested, wide-shouldered mountain man, who, even though outnumbered in the extreme, faced death with a calm and confident air.

At last, he waved his arm and said, "So will it be."

The horsemen moved out onto the prairie and, with their horses, formed a circle of about fifty feet. The horses faced inward with the warriors leg against leg, a ring of horseflesh. Floyd dismounted and handed the reins to the brave next to him, who took it, giving Floyd a look of contempt. Then he slowly drew his finger across his throat. The Blackfoot braves broke out in laughter.

Floyd walked into the ring with his knife and tomahawk in his belt. He turned to face the chief.

Gray Wolf waved into the crowd, and the biggest Indian Floyd had ever seen walked into the ring. Floyd was a big man for that day and time, when the average height of a white man was barely seven inches over five feet. He stood slightly over six feet tall. But this Blackfoot dwarfed him. The man had to be at least three or more inches above Floyd's height, and he was big. The Indian's biceps were half again as big as Floyd's, and his long arms gave him a greater reach of at least four inches.

His face must have communicated his astonishment and awe, for again the Indians burst out in laughter, but the big Indian wasn't laughing. He stood holding a long knife in one hand and a war club in the other. The war club was a fearsome instrument. With one swing from those huge biceps, it could crush Floyd's skull.

Floyd turned to the chief. "This is the man who stole my son?"

Floyd could see the laughter around the edge of the chief's lips and eyes when, as solemnly as he could, he said, "Yes."

Again, the roar of laughter arose.

Floyd thought, *Lord, I remember my ma's story about David and Goliath. I'd be real appreciative if I could get your help with this big fellow.* He reached back and pulled his knife from his belt, leaving the tomahawk for later, if he needed it, and nodded to the chief. The chief said something to Floyd's opponent and jerked his lance down.

The big Indian went into a crouch and started circling to his right. Floyd, across from the man, moved to his right and watched the man's movements. They stood almost twenty feet apart. Floyd's mind raced over what his Filipino instructor, Lontac, had taught him. He kept remembering, relax and watch. Stay relaxed. Surprisingly, he realized, the size of his opponent was intimidating him. He was tense. He took a deep breath and charged.

The charge surprised the big man, who obviously expected this white man to be cowering in his moccasins. He straightened slightly in surprise, and Floyd recklessly dove between the man's widespread legs, leaving a deep slash on the man's inside upper thigh.

Blood flowed immediately, but Floyd was disappointed. The cut wasn't deep enough to reach the artery. He comforted himself with the knowledge that any cut helped. The more he could make, the faster this man would bleed out. No matter what his size, if he lost enough blood, he would grow weak.

Startled by Floyd's charge though he was, the Blackfoot whipped around, and as Floyd rolled to his feet, the sting of a blade across his right shoulder let him know he was too slow. A great shout went up from the observers. *Not deep,* he thought, *but I too can suffer from the loss of blood.*

Both men, having had their blood drawn, now circled warily, searching for a weakness in their opponent's defense.

Floyd feinted a charge again, and his opponent stood rocking on the balls of his feet, ready.

He's done this before, Floyd thought. *I'd best be careful of those huge hands. If I let him get me in the grip of one of them, I'm done for.*

The Indian feinted with the war club, bringing it up toward Floyd's head. The mountain man stepped back. Too close to the ring of mounted warriors, Floyd felt a foot slam him in the middle of his back, driving him forward and to the ground. The Indian charged him. He rolled completely over twice, keeping his eyes on the huge brave, who was almost on him. The man leaped, attempting to land on Floyd's chest with his knees, to crush it, and bash his head in with the war club. Floyd continued to roll. The big Blackfoot missed and was again on his feet, charging.

The brave had started a swing, when Floyd, still on the ground, drove both feet into the side of his opponent's knee, fully expecting to hear the crack of a breaking knee. The man was knocked from his feet, giving Floyd an opportunity to at last leap up, but he was only slightly ahead of the Blackfoot. The man came up, his legs working as if nothing had happened. *Any other man would have a shattered knee,* Floyd thought, circling to stay out of range of the waving club.

Both men circled cautiously, feeling out the reflexes of the other by feints and jabs with their knives. It was all Floyd could do to stay away from the deadly club, which had whizzed too close to his skull several times, threatening to smash his brain with one blow. Again the Indian saw an opening and swung the club at Floyd's head. This time Floyd had miscalculated the man's reach and had to wrench his body violently to prevent the heavy club from colliding with his head. He felt the wind of the club as it passed his temple, and breathed a short sigh of relief. In dodging the club, his left side came in range of the Blackfoot's knife, and he plunged forward.

Floyd, still perilously off balance, managed to parry the thrust, but again felt the blade bite as it slid past his back. Balance regained, he leaped away and, finding his balance, went into a fighting crouch.

Once again, at the sight of more blood, the braves let out another roar.

The fight continued with Floyd feeling like he was constantly on the defensive. Twenty minutes into the battle, he remembered Lontac saying, "If you are having difficulty with an opponent, reevaluate. No matter how good you are, you will meet someone better. Then you must outsmart them."

Floyd, as he circled, was shocked with the thought, *Is this huge Indian better than me?* He watched the man closely and came to a logical decision. His skills were better than the Blackfoot's, but up to now, he had let the man's size intimidate him. Finally, he was starting to feel the rhythm of the fight. It began to pulse within his body. The previous tension in his body started relaxing. It was time to take the fight to the Blackfoot.

He charged. The Blackfoot leaned forward and came up on the balls of his feet, just as he had done before. The club was in the man's right hand and the knife in his left. Having watched his opponent, he knew, from the position of the club, the man would have to draw it back to make a strike. In fact, where he held the club, other than using it in a backhand fashion, which he was big enough to do, it was almost useless.

Floyd feinted to the man's left, then slipped behind the right swing and brought his knife blade, in a slashing motion, across the top and side of his opponent's right bicep. He kept moving. The man tried to swing a back-slash at Floyd, but it was awkward and he was off balance. Floyd let the swing go by and leaped in the air. He kicked out with both feet, striking his opponent full in the chest. The blow knocked the man to the ground and dislodged the club from his hand, which was now covered in blood from the deep gash in his bicep. He tried to push himself up from the ground on his right arm, but it gave way.

The watching warriors were now silent, disbelieving the sudden turn of the match.

Floyd was on him like a mountain cat. He kicked the wrist holding the knife and saw it fly away. The man was game. Though his weapons were gone, he pushed from the ground with his left hand, only to find his neck locked in the grip of Floyd's muscular forearm. The big Indian continued to struggle until Floyd bent his head back and slid the edge of the bowie's blade against his throat. With that threat, the man ceased to struggle and relaxed.

Floyd held his position as he looked around the circle of braves. Each face showed shock. When he reached the chief, he released his hold and stepped out of range of the big man's reach. Holding the gaze of the chief, he said, "Is it done?"

The chief, looking older and more tired than he had before, nodded. "It is done. You, your family, and friends may leave in safety." He looked around at his braves. "No Blackfoot warrior will bring harm to your party." Then his voice strengthened. "But never set foot on Blackfoot land again. We will not be so generous if there is a next time."

Floyd said nothing. He kept his eye on his bleeding opponent, who never looked at him, but staggered slowly from the circle, until several of the braves dropped to the ground and helped him to his horse. The Indian who had been holding Rusty rode to Floyd and handed him the reins, respect in his eyes. In broken English he said, "You good fighter," then rode off.

He was about to step into the saddle when he saw another brave riding toward him with a rifle in his hands. *Oh no,* he thought, *not now*. But the man didn't shoot. He rode up to Floyd and held the rifle out to him. It was his Ryland. Floyd looked closely and recognized the Indian. He was the son of a gun who had captured him and Morg. When Floyd had taken the rifle, the man pulled the Ryland pistols from his breechcloth and handed them over, followed by the knife from his brother. Floyd took them, and the two enemies gazed at each other for a moment, mutual respect showing in their eyes. The brave gave a sharp nod of his head and trotted his horse toward the departing Blackfoot.

Floyd stood, watching the Blackfoot depart until he heard splashing in the river. He led Rusty to the edge of the bank and stood transfixed. There was Leotie, rushing through the calf-deep water. Stumbling, falling, rising and splashing forward, she continued against the current, tears coursing down her cheeks. She scrambled up the embankment and leaped into his arms.

She was covered with mud from climbing the steep embankment.

He was covered with blood, but neither minded.

They melted into each other's arms, their lips crushed together. Floyd felt his heart soar. The mountains were where he belonged, in the arms of this Shoshone girl. He would love and take care of her and Mika forever.

They pulled back, and Floyd gazed into her deep brown eyes. His whole being was flooded with happiness. A smile broke across his face at this Indian girl who was a perfect example of strength and beauty.

With his thumbs, he gently wiped the tears from her cheeks, then held her head in his big hands. Smiling softly down at her, he said, "Let's go home."

EPILOGUE

August 12, 1840, Valley between Sangre de Cristo and Greenhorn Mountains

Floyd, with Jeb alongside, pulled Rusty to a stop and gazed across the valley where the Shoshone had chosen to camp. The two of them were returning from the rendezvous on Horseshoe Creek, a few miles west of the Big Horn River.

Their pelts had sold for only four dollars a pound. If they had needed supplies, it would've taken almost all their year's earnings. However, they had a plan. They would stop and see their families, for Jeb, the eternal bachelor, had also married a Shoshone girl, who was expecting their first child. After a few days, they'd ride over to Bent's Fort, no more than a three-day ride each way.

Leotie filled Floyd's thoughts, though he'd had bad news at the rendezvous, the nearer he rode to Leotie and Mika, the less importance the news held. His heart was nearly singing when they rode into the valley and viewed the camp.

"Mighty pretty valley," Jeb said. "You ever been over here?"

Floyd's hair, long and brown except for the gray streak where the bear bit him, glided left and right as his head shook. "Nope.

Been north and south and west, but I never crossed the Sangre de Cristos except when I headed out to find you in '31. Why, tucked down between the Greenhorns and the Sangre de Cristos, I reckon this is about the prettiest valley I've seen is this country. Why, if I had the money, and know'd who owned it, I'd buy it right now."

"Too late," Jeb said. "One of them wealthy Mexicans from Spain owns this valley. He's got him a Spanish land grant. I heard from Hugh, he don't come up here often. Fears gettin' scalped by them Utes."

Floyd turned in the saddle and grinned at Jeb. "Reckon he's a smarter man than we are."

"Yep, I guess he is. I swear, I feel like I've been chased so many times by them Utes, I'd be better off if'n I just scalped myself and give 'em my hair."

Floyd nodded solemnly. "Now that's some smart thinking." But Floyd had only one thought, and it wasn't about Jeb's hair. "Jeb Campbell, reckon I like the looks of this here valley, but I've admired it about as much as I'm going to. There's a fine woman down there, and I know she's tired of waitin' for me."

With his last words, Floyd bumped Rusty in the flanks and galloped toward the camp, Buck and Browny in tow. Browny tossed his head a couple of times, in revolt against the yank of the rope, to let Floyd know he didn't like his abrupt start.

Nearing camp, Floyd let out a loud whoop, followed by a similar one from Jeb. Dashing from around one of the teepees, Mika raced toward them, Leotie close behind. A big smile split his bearded face, his eyes filled with the two people he loved most in the world.

Mika didn't slow his run. Floyd eased Rusty into a lope and watched his adopted son race toward him. At the last moment, the boy leaped for Floyd. The big mountain man dropped Rusty's reins and wrapped his powerful arm around his son.

Mika, twelve years old now, pressed his face against Floyd's cheek and yelled into his ear, "Why'd you take so long?"

Floyd picked up Rusty's reins with his right hand and slowed the big red horse.

The boy had shoved a foot into the stirrup and was watching his ma approach. He watched Floyd slow the roan to a fast walk approaching Leotie. Knowing what his pa was going to do, his face was wreathed in a big grin.

Leotie stood in the tall grass, hands resting on slim hips, and happiness glinting in her eyes.

Floyd guided Rusty slightly left, reached down, and swept her into his right arm, lifting her high enough for her left foot to find the stirrup. She laid her hand on his cheek and turned his face toward her, meeting his lips with hers. They held the kiss for a long moment. Then Floyd broke free to guide Rusty to their teepee.

Before turning in front of the teepees, Floyd pulled the roan to a halt and looked back. They had passed a lovely young, very pregnant Shoshone woman, with her eyes locked on Jeb.

Smiling, Floyd and Leotie watched their friend leap from his saddle and sweep the girl into his arms. Floyd laughed with joy, clucked at Rusty, and walked the horse out of view of the embracing couple.

"Pa, I asked you why you took so long."

Floyd turned back to Mika and hefted him with his left arm, frowning. "How'd you get so big? You're way big for a twelve-year-old. Has your ma been letting you get into the pemmican?" With the question, he turned a frown on the grinning face of Leotie. Her scar, which he never noticed, was slightly redder than the surrounding skin due to her flushed face.

"No, Pa!" Mika said. "I'm so much bigger because you've been gone so long."

With Mika's statement, Floyd laughed again, letting his son down in front of their home. Then, seriously, he said, "It's been too long for me too, son. Now would you go bring in Buck and Browny?"

"Sure, Pa," Mika responded and, with his friends, dashed out past the teepees to take care of the other animals.

Floyd feasted on the face of his lovely wife, softly lifting her out of the stirrup and lowering her to the ground.

Most of the tribe surrounded him for news, but opened as Jeb and his bride rode up. There was much chattering and mirth. Floyd swung to the ground to greet his good friends, Chief Pallaton, Nina, and Kajika. It was good to be home.

Jeb strode up, his arm around his wife, Aiyana. She gazed up at the mountain man with tender, caring eyes.

Pallaton looked at Aiyana and said to Jeb, "It is good you are here. Nina says, in not too many days, you will have a warrior son."

Jeb beamed down at his wife, happiness in his eyes. "I'm shore glad we made it back in time."

Mika came back with not only Buck and Browny, but also Jeb's animals. Respectfully, he stepped to Floyd's side, waiting until Jeb quit speaking. "Pa, we"—he motioned to the other boys with him—"can take Rusty and Browny and Uncle Jeb's horse. We'll rub 'em down, and take care of all of them."

"Thanks, son," Floyd said. "I'd appreciate that. If you'd put the gear in its proper place when you unsaddle the horses, that'd be fine."

Jeb was in arm's reach of Mika. He reached out, enclosing the boy in a big bear hug, which sent the other boys into paroxysms of laughter. "Ain't you gonna give yore pore ole uncle a hug?"

Mika was growing strong. His wirelike muscles responded in a playful attempt to throw his uncle, with no success.

At last, Jeb released the boy, but not before tousling his hair.

"Whew," Jeb said, in Shoshone, and mostly for Mika's peers, "yore gettin' mighty strong in them muscles."

Mika jerked away, but the look of pride on his face from Jeb's comment was obvious. He grabbed the reins of Jeb's horse and, with the other boys, led the animals off.

"We must talk," Floyd said to Pallaton. "Let me and Jeb get cleaned up, and we'll tell you everything this evening."

"Good," Pallaton said, "we will celebrate the return of our white brothers."

At the mention of a celebration, there were many whoops and cries. Everyone was interested in the news Floyd and Jeb carried.

The two men split up, going to their respective teepees with their wives.

Leotie went in first, followed by Floyd, who dropped the flap behind him. When he straightened, she was smiling. He took her in his arms and crushed her body to him. He was always astounded as his arms encircled her. They had been married for seven years, and each embrace was like the first.

Passionately their lips connected in a long kiss. Then her hands rose to his shoulders and pushed him gently away.

Puzzled, Floyd looked down into Leotie's face. He read sorrow. "What's wrong?"

Leotie released a long sigh. "Aiyana is about to have a child, and she is strong. She will have many more."

She paused, her head down. "I am sorry, Igasho."

"For what?"

"I know you wanted children of your own, and since the trappers, I have been unable to make a child. I am so sorry."

Floyd gazed into her sad and tender face. Anger stirred his heart at the acts of McMillan and his bunch, which brought sadness to this woman he loved. He raised a calloused hand to her face and stroked it gently. "You ain't got nothing to be sorry about, Leotie. You and Mika have brought happiness I had never known into my life. I love you both."

Sadness was replaced with joy. "Yes," she said. "I know how much you love Mika, and he feels the same about you, as do I."

She rose again on tiptoes and pressed her warm lips to her husband's.

∼

THE CELEBRATION LASTED FOR HOURS, but had finally begun to die. Floyd and Jeb sat to Pallaton's left and Kajika, to his right. The women and children, including Mika, though he did not want to leave his father's side, had retired to their quarters. Only the warriors of the tribe circled the fire. There was a constant hum of conversation until Pallaton held up his hand. Immediately silence fell on the gathering.

He turned to Floyd and Jeb. "It is good you have returned safely. Now it is time for us to hear the news of which you spoke."

Jeb looked at his friend and nodded. Floyd rose to his feet, and though his message was primarily addressed to the chief, he walked within the circle and spoke sufficiently loud for all to hear, even those in their teepees.

Fluent in Shoshone, Floyd addressed them in their language. "First, Jeb and I have news from the north, of the Blackfoot."

There were murmurs around the gathering, for the Blackfoot remained dangerous enemies of the Shoshone.

Floyd began. "The Great Chief Pallaton has again made a wise decision in moving us farther south. The Blackfoot of the far north country, along the Missouri River, have been attacked severely by the great sickness. Many have died. This sickness you know as smallpox."

At the mention of the dread disease, which killed young and old, strong or weak, there was a distinct gasp heard from the teepees of the village. The disease was brought by the white man, and the Indian nations had no immunity. No reason could be applied to why one person died and another didn't.

Floyd continued, "It is believed that a traveler brought the disease. He has long since died. But so far, the disease has stayed north of the Yellowstone."

There were several positive grunts from the circle, acknowledging the good news.

Chief Pallaton spoke. "It is bad news you bring us, Igasho, but it is good that you bring it. It is in my thinking that we stay in this valley until the return of the geese. Only then will we think of moving back north, along with the buffalo."

Again agreement sounded from the circle.

Floyd hoped that one winter would be enough for the disease to complete its cycle.

The chief watched him and then said, "There is more."

"Yes, oh great Chief. It is both good and bad. Many of the white men you have known, Bridger, Meek, Doc Newell, we have met and talked with at the Horse Creek rendezvous. They have told the great brother of the Shoshone, Jeb Campbell, and myself there will be no more rendezvous. This year, eighteen forty, as the whites figure, is the last rendezvous. It is the last time any will come west to trade for the beaver pelt.

"Far away, over the great water, those who used the pelts to make hats no longer need them. They are using something called silk. Also, the great numbers of beaver we have known are gone, and most of the trappers will soon follow."

Silence followed Floyd's statement. All that could be heard was the crackling and fluttering of the fire, and the forlorn moan of the wind in the valley.

After many moments, Pallaton spoke. "Does this mean the white man will no longer invade our country?"

Floyd shook his head. "Sadly, no. There will be more coming. It may take many seasons, but they will come."

He looked around at the Shoshone warriors in the circle. These were his friends. They had saved his life and welcomed him into their tribe. He knew them, and now he read the sadness on many, and the anger of some, especially the young braves, at the thought of more white men.

"Will you leave, Igasho?" He turned and looked at Jeb. "Will our brother Jeb Campbell leave us?"

Floyd glanced at Jeb, who gave a short shake of his head. Then he turned back to the chief. "The Shoshone are our people. Our families are here. There are many more animals we can trap that the white man values. There is the mink, ermine, raccoon, and beaver, the white men will buy, though the beaver will bring much less. But even if there was nothing we could sell to the white man, we would stay. As long as we are welcome by our Shoshone brothers."

Pallaton nodded solemnly and swung his arm, including both Jeb and Floyd. "You are truly our brothers. You have helped us in hard times as we have you. You will always be welcome with the Shoshone."

Floyd turned so all in the circle and in the teepees were included. "We thank you, and look forward to many fruitful years." He returned to his place, sat, and leaned to Pallaton. "We will go to our teepees now."

The chief grinned at Floyd and Jeb. "Yes, you have wasted much time at this council."

The chief's words were heard by the braves in the circle, and there were several whoops and yelps in response to Floyd and Jeb leaving.

The two men nodded good night to each other and hastily strode to their separate teepees. Upon entering, Floyd felt the slight warmth of the fire, which had burned low to only a few flames and embers. As always, there was a thin, almost imperceptible veil of smoke. He had grown accustomed to it, hardly noticing.

Mika was sound asleep, his regular breathing a comforting sound. Leotie was in their bed. "Come," she said, lifting the corner of the buffalo rug, exposing her still slim arm and delicate hand.

Quickly he undressed, laying his weapons close, and slipped beneath the cover. The warmth and the weight of the cover felt good on his body.

He stretched his long legs to their full length. His tired muscles began relaxing. Floyd started to roll over to face his wife.

"We need to talk," she said.

"Now?"

He felt a silent laugh from her before she went on.

"Yes, now. Remember what you have told me, 'All good things come to those who wait.'"

He let a grimace cloud his face. "I said that?"

"Yes, my husband, those are your words." She turned toward him, rising slightly and resting on her forearm. "Igasho, it is time."

"Time for what?"

"Time for you to go home."

Puzzled now, he said, "Leotie, I am home."

"Yes, you are," she said, placing a loving hand on his chest. "But I do not mean our home."

"You mean I should go back to see my folks?"

"Yes, they grow old, and I promise you, they need to see their youngest son before they cross over."

"When do you want to go?"

She held her breath for a moment. "Mika and I will not go. We must stay here. Nina needs help with those who will have babies. I have become almost as good as her. I am needed here, and it is approaching the time for Mika to go on the search for his spirit guide. This he must do."

Floyd lay silent, his mind working. *I know I need to go back, but not now. Life is too good. What if something happens while I'm gone? I want to be here to protect them.* But another thought pushed its way into

Floyd's internal conversation. A reminder of what Salty, an old friend, had said to Floyd on his original trip west. *Salty told me to go home in five, at the most ten years. He didn't, and his folks had died by the time he went back.* Then he realized how long it had been since he left Limerick. *It's been almost ten years. It's gone by so fast. Is it possible they may have died while I've been in the mountains?* He lay quiet, thinking.

"Igasho," Leotie said, as if reading his mind, "we will be protected. The tribe is here, Chief Pallaton, Kajika. I will not be alone, and Jeb will also protect me." She waited for an answer.

His mind raced. *She is right. With the tribe and Jeb here, I needn't worry. She and Mika will be safe. Now is a good time. Yes.*

She extended one shapely finger and pushed his head gently. "Are you asleep?"

He rolled over and looked up at his wife. Her eyes sparkled and her skin glowed golden in the faint firelight. "How could I be so lucky to marry such a smart wife?"

She giggled and said, "You almost got eaten by a bear."

"Yes, the grizzly. The scariest and luckiest day in my life. You are right, Leotie. I need to go back home to Limerick and see my folks."

She gave one firm nod. "Good."

"Now are we through talking?"

A modest smile played across her full lips. "Yes, my husband."

AUTHOR'S NOTE

Thank you for reading *Trials of a Mountain Man,* the second book in the Logan Mountain Man Series.

If you have any comments, what you like or what you don't, please let me know. You can email me at: Don@DonaldLRobertson.com, or you can use the contact form on my website.

www.DonaldLRobertson.com

I'll be looking forward to hearing from you.

BOOKS
Logan Mountain Man Series
(Prequel to Logan Family Series)

SOUL OF A MOUNTAIN MAN
TRIALS OF A MOUNTAIN MAN

Logan Family Series

LOGAN'S WORD
THE SAVAGE VALLEY
CALLUM'S MISSION
FORGOTTEN SEASON

Clay Barlow Texas Ranger - Justice Series

FORTY-FOUR CALIBER JUSTICE
LAW AND JUSTICE
LONESOME JUSTICE

NOVELLAS AND SHORT STORIES

RUSTLERS IN THE SAGE
BECAUSE OF A DOG
THE OLD RANGER

Printed in Great Britain
by Amazon